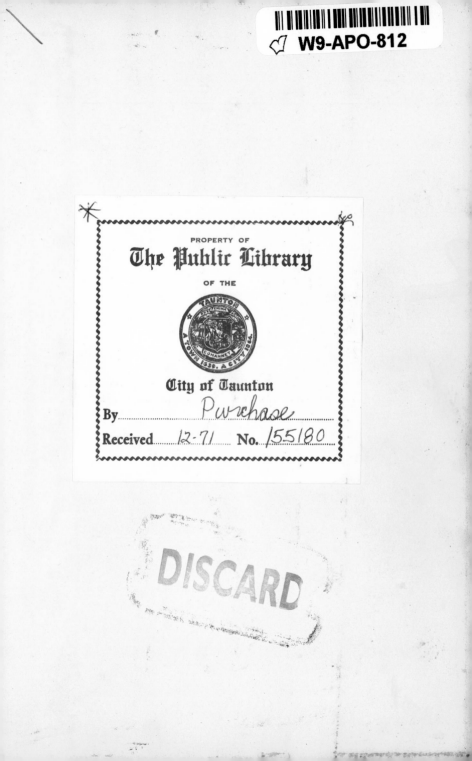

THE DOCTOR'S SECOND LOVE

## OTHER BOOKS BY ELIZABETH SEIFERT

# THE
# DOCTOR'S
# SECOND
# LOVE

Elizabeth Seifert

DODD, MEAD & COMPANY

NEW YORK

copy 2

155180

ISBN: 0-396-06388-8
Library of Congress Catalog Card Number: 72-163074

Printed in the United States of America
by Vail-Ballou Press, Inc., Binghamton, N.Y.

THE DOCTOR'S SECOND LOVE

CHAPTER 1

DURING AN INTERVIEW of this sort, Tom told himself, is no
time to judge anybody or anything. We are all on our best
behavior; we have been careful about our clothes—I spent
five minutes this morning selecting my tie. We are also on
the defensive, to a degree. They want me, or someone, for
their job, but they are afraid to make concessions for fear I
shall take advantage later. I want the job, but I won't be
slavish in *my* concessions.

I have presented my credentials. Other interviews have
been conducted. All but one of these men have seen me before; they know I am as thin as a rail, that my hair gets a
bit thicker and longer than it should, perhaps—that I speak
forthrightly.

And I know pretty damn well that the job is mine, if I
want it. I shall be hired to work for the Sociomedical department of the Research Institute of this huge hospital complex. That distinguished, gray-haired gentleman, Dr. Bonley,
will be my Chief. He can't be more than five years older
than I am. Dr. Lewis, who would be sixty, is the Director of
the Research Institute. If I've pleased those two, why do all

the others matter, and what could they have to say to me?

Thinking these things, Dr. Kelsey sat back in his chair, crossed his knees and waited for the questions to come. He knew that he was being watched, observed, judged; he showed no sign that this scrutiny disturbed him—as it did, a little.

But in the investigations which he also had been making, he had decided that he wanted this job, and would, if necessary, make something of a fight to get it. Research in how to bring medicine to those who needed it and would not get it otherwise would be exactly his sort of project. Health for the poor, the ignorant. That was what it amounted to. He nodded his head at his own thoughts.

"Then I take it, Dr. Kelsey," said the man named Lenox—everyone called him Jack—"that all aspects of the salary offer will be satisfactory?"

Tom smiled a little. They would be—better than he really had expected. He decided not to worry about his dilatory ways with barbers. This Lenox's hair was not only long, it was not kept brushed, as Tom did brush his.

Tom straightened in his chair. He really should listen. Lenox was still talking. "The benefits are attractive, wouldn't you say?" he asked.

"Very attractive, Doctor," said Tom.

"I am not a doctor," said Lenox stiffly.

Tom ran his finger down his cheek. "I'm sorry," he murmured.

"You surely have offended no one," drawled Dr. Lewis.

Tom shot him a glance, then looked quickly back to Lenox. How would *Jack* field that one?

Pretty well, Tom thought. He was most courteously explaining to Dr. Kelsey that he was in the administrative department of the complex. He managed to make the business office sound like the choice spot. "Our office maintains the financial control of the Research Institute," he continued. "In brief, we pay the bills and distribute the pay checks."

"That's control, all right," Tom conceded.

There were smiles on the faces of the other men seated around the room, but Lenox did not smile. "It is my opinion," he said stiffly, "an opinion well known, that the Institute and its work should be entirely under the direction of the hospital group."

"Why?" asked Tom bluntly.

This created a stir. Jack Lenox gathered his papers into his folder and rapped the edge of it smartly on the desk. Dr. Bonley exchanged amused glances with Dr. Lewis. The other men in the room, introduced to Tom as heads of various departments of the Institute, nodded to each other. Tom would not be a head.

Lenox was earnestly explaining to this new man that the Complex was a big organization. Tom knew that. Eleven tall buildings, besides the handsome concrete, glass and steel Institute, were arranged like dominoes stood on end. These were the University Hospitals; there were nine clinics, all for the application of medicine. The whole concept was huge, and spoke of riches, of thousands of workers, of good administration, of much good accomplished.

Tom's own building—three days before he had taken possession of the Institute—stood handsomely surrounded by well-tended lawns, trees, shrubbery, and flower beds. There was a fountain. The office where they now sat was the penthouse of the building. In the twelve floors below, there were hundreds of rooms, dozens of laboratories, offices, wards, miles of corridors, people—doctors, technicians, and patients.

To Dr. Kelsey's way of thinking, here was the beginning and the end of all medicine and its practice. Research was the i.v. bottle, the slap on the buttocks of a newborn idea, the testing of that vitalized idea, the development of it, and finally its use, after which it was handed over to the doctors for the comfort and cure of their patients.

To have all this research housed in one large, handsome building, to have each floor, or section, devoted to such magnificent projects as the way to cure and revitalize failing kidneys, or how to restore a brain injured at birth, by illness or accident, by stroke . . .

Aware of his excitement, Tom shook his shoulders and rubbed the palm of his hand down along his slim trouser leg. If others guessed . . .

He looked up into the eyes of Dr. Lewis. He had detected Tom's reaction.

Smiling a little, the Director took off his glasses and polished them. "Thank you, Jack," he said. "Tom will get into the vast complexities of the hospitals, I am sure. For now, his familiarization with the Institute will do, and specifically the Sociomedical unit. I am sure he is aware of the sort of thing we do here, but perhaps it will be valuable if Dr. Bonley, Chief of that particular service, will summarize it for him, and for the rest of us."

For Lenox, specifically, thought Tom.

He looked expectantly at Dr. Bonley, a handsome man, slender yet muscular, who carried his head high on broad shoulders beautifully draped in brown cashmere. The man's fine eyes were also brown, and his silvery hair was surely premature.

He disclaimed any wish to make a speech. But he would point out to Dr. Kelsey what was new, what was being researched in his department of the Institute in the way of medical care for the poor.

"Medical care for the urban poor is no new concept," he

conceded. "Ever since it began, the University Hospitals have afforded such care. But we have been developing some new approaches, Dr. Kelsey. Instead of confining that care to clinics situated for the convenience of the doctors, we are taking medical care to the people who need it and who cannot, who will not, who do not get on a bus or walk painful blocks to those clinics. Rather than make those journeys, a mother will try to care for her sick baby, an old man will wrap his rheumatic bones in such quilts as are at hand, a young woman will seek to ignore a pain, a cough, a headache.

"We have, with the generous gift of the Clausen family and the largesse of the Federal Government, established a clinic close to these people. It is close at hand, the sick can come to it for diagnosis and treatment, it is not a part of a huge, frightening mass of buildings, corridors, offices, and waiting rooms. It is a building of their own; they can get to it readily, they are attended to promptly, they come to us as families and give us a chance to raise the medical level of their community, which in turn betters the medical picture of the city and of the whole country."

"Do you have . . . ?" Tom asked, leaning forward.

"Centers in all parts of the city? No, we do not, Doctor. Not yet. We hope to. But we do have the Clausen Center in the heart of a district which concentrates poverty, crime, disease. We have another clinic building, and a third in the planning stage."

"What would I . . . ?" Tom asked.

"The people come to the clinic, they are interviewed, their immediate needs attended to; we explain our ideal of family care. They are hospitalized if necessary. If the situation so indicates, we bring them here, not too far away, for histories, specific examinations, tests. Sometimes for bed care, even surgery. This is the 'Big Clinic,' in their parlance. Clausen, to them, is simply the clinic. It does not frighten or bewilder them. The personnel become their friends; they can be persuaded to make the trip to us here so that we can get family records on our books, where, even in a year, we have begun to chart graphs by neighborhood, by family origin—oh, all sorts of exciting things. We learn about their diseases, their problems; they come to realize that they are helping us, and we get some pretty good results."

"Cockroach research," said someone.

Tom's head went up, and Dr. Bonley's. "You think that's not important?" Both men spoke at once, in chorus, then laughed and looked at each other.

"You've got him, Bonley!" cried the smiling, smooth-faced man whom Tom knew to be in cancer research.

And Dick Scott was going to be proved right. In that instant, as Tom was aware, there was to begin the rapport which was to mark the work which Tom and Jim Bonley would do together.

As the meeting broke up—Tom was to have lunch with the Personnel Director—Dr. Bonley gave him a brief idea of what his place at the Institute would be. "To begin, you'd deal with the family service aspect of our works, Kelsey. I'll want you to get to know, cockroaches and all"—he smiled warmly—"every family in the near north side. Keep the records, correlate the activities and the ailments of the family members, from great-grandma to the baby still unborn. This can be an involved thing, you know, what with illegitimacy, promiscuity, crowding, desertion of the family by a father . . ."

"Or the mother," said Tom.

Bonley pressed his arm. "I hope Personnel doesn't take you to our cafeteria," he said, leaving.

6

Personnel did not. He, a pleasant man named Kenneth Franzel, with close-cropped hair and a way of insisting on saying what he had in his mind to say, whether it was a mildly funny story or ordering their lunch, took Tom across the Center's grounds to the Boulevard and down that street for a block or two to a good hotel where they had a table in a sheltered corner of the big room. The high back of the pale green banquette isolated them from the rest of the room. The service was good, and unobtrusive. People moved about them, but neither to disturb nor distract. Tom had a casserole of veal and mushrooms, a glass of good wine, and he listened to Franzel talk about what he called the "skeleton" in the closet of the business complex of the Hospital Center.

"I thought Lenox was going to discuss this at the meeting," he told Tom.

"Didn't he?"

"No. But it is something Dr. Lewis would agree should be explained to you. With all the people we employ, the variety of those people and their jobs, this skeleton rattles its bones quite often, and loudly, too, on occasion."

"Mr. Franzel, could I finish my meat before you scare me to death?"

Franzel laughed. "I'm a fair judge of men," he began.

"My hair," said Tom, "is in its present state because I hate to go to the barber."

"Oh, it's not bad. Thick, maybe, but not bad."

Tom brushed his thick, dark hair back from his forehead. "I'll have it cut before Monday morning," he promised.

"All right. That takes care of the hair."

"But not the skeleton?"

"No. That's—" the Personnel Director touched his napkin to his lips—"that has to do with what we comprehensively call 'love in the office.' Office being an euphemism for every inch of the hospital complex."

Tom frowned. He set his cup down and leaned forward. "Did you say . . . ? Oh, come now, you can't be interested in my romances."

Franzel shook his head. "Not unless they are conducted within the hospital confines and during business hours."

Tom leaned back against the damask cushion. The table-cloth was pink linen, his water glass was dark, rich green. He frowned at the cup which his fingers turned around and around on its saucer. "Does this have anything at all to do with sociomedicine?" he asked.

"It can have a great deal," said Kenneth Franzel.

Now Tom looked at him, a frown between his eyes, a crease in one cheek showing deeply. "You're serious?"

"I told you it was a skeleton."

"Hospitals take skeletons in stride. Usually."

"My metaphor was poor. Bogeyman might be better. Though the Personnel office does not want to become famil-iar with this skeleton."

"Love in the office," Tom repeated softly. "No bussing a nurse on a stair landing, no pinching the girl from the steno pool."

"We even tolerate a single lipstick smudge on your coat above the name plate." But Kenneth Franzel was not joking about his skeleton.

Tom drank his coffee. "What happens," he asked, speaking slowly, "if a man—not me, but any man—does stir up one of your romances, Mr. Franzel?"

"Within the structure of the organization," Franzel spec-ified.

"That's what I meant." Tom's eyes were steady on Per-sonnel's face. Those eyes were blue, the iris rimmed in black. They could look very probingly at one.

8

"The procedure," said Franzel, calm under Tom's gaze, "is for the supervisor—in your case, the Chief of your service—to talk to you."

"Pointing out the lipstick, and so forth."

"Pointing out whatever evidence he has. And he would make a full report to the Personnel Director's office."

Tom could not imagine Bonley doing any such thing. To an orderly, perhaps, not to or about a member of his staff. "Ridiculous!" he said aloud.

"Not ridiculous at all," said Franzel. "We have cause to take these things seriously."

"All right. Now say I've had three dates with the redhead in the office. My chief has talked to me about it warningly. Then what?"

"If the affair continues . . ."

"Affair?" cried Tom, so loudly that the bus boy looked at him.

Mr. Franzel turned a little pink. "By then it would be an affair," he said. "And your conduct would be discussed with you by the Personnel Director."

"But that's you! Can't we discuss it now and be ahead of the game?"

"Please, Dr. Kelsey. This is serious business."

"It is to you. I can tell."

"I wish I could persuade you that it is important."

"Well, for the sake of this exposition, I'll agree to its importance. I believe my private life was being discussed by the Personnel Director. What sort of fellow is he, by the way?"

"Dr. Kelsey . . ."

"All right, all right. What does the man say to me?"

"Our procedure is to question the person involved."

Tom groaned.

"I would," Mr. Franzel continued with dignity, "inquire about your family life."

"I don't have any family."

"We were not discussing you personally."

"I was. I am."

"This matter may come up for you to handle for some person working under you, Dr. Kelsey."

Tom considered that. An orderly, an aide, a nurse . . . "I wouldn't touch it with a ten-foot pole," he declared.

"But, Dr. Kelsey, in accepting a position with University Hospitals, you assume certain responsibilities."

"Yes. I suppose I do. All right. You were talking to me about my family."

"About your family life."

"That's different, isn't it?"

"It can be very different. And then, if the situation so indicates, we would perhaps suggest that you have professional help. Counseling."

Tom laughed. "Not over a water-cooler affair, Mr. Franzel."

"No," said Mr. Franzel stiffly.

Probably the man did have troubles. If Tom would give the matter some thought—a doctor romancing one of the nurses, a man with his family to be considered— "Why do you suggest that I would be a possibility for one of your situations, sir? Because I am a bachelor?"

"Oh, no." Mr. Franzel spoke so readily that Tom had to believe him. "Our experience is that men are vulnerable; they do these things."

"And women, too?"

"By preference, we deal with the man involved."

"I suppose you have to choose some approach. Now, what finally happens if I do get involved in such a deplorable situation? I mean, after the discussion of me and my family."

"My first advice would be to avoid the situation if you can."

"I came here to work," Tom pointed out.

"Good! That's what we want, and need."

"It's what I need, too," said Tom earnestly.

During the remaining days of that week, Tom had his hair cut, and found a place to live. Inquiry told him that most of the hospital people lived fairly close to the Complex. In tall homes along two or three well-cared-for private streets, in apartments or row houses. Some lived in hotels close by, some had bought or rented old homes. . . . He found a row house and saw his mother's furniture moved into it. He would find someone to clean for him. On his second night in residence, he was adopted by a black cat with three white feet and a white nose. "Now I have Franzel's family," said Tom, feeding the animal. He began calling it Cleopatra because of its seductive ways, but the next morning he changed that to Caesar. "And you'd better watch your step!" he admonished his new friend.

On Monday morning he began to work in the office which he had already inspected. His personal effects were in his desk, his name had been stenciled on the door, he found his own white coat hanging on the rack, with the name plate pinned in place.

And he met Dr. Sahrman, who was to be his co-worker. Steven Sahrman was a refugee doctor, Tom was immediately told. He had been educated in one of the satellite countries, and then had sought asylum and freedom in America, where a license for him to practice medicine was difficult to obtain. He must undergo further training, pass various examinations, repeat work he thought he already knew, and which he did know.

Tom's sympathy immediately went out to this man. He was about Tom's age, and Dr. Kelsey spent some time trying to place himself in a similar situation. "I couldn't take it," he decided. But then he could not have taken living in Sahrman's native land either. "Be glad you're a cat, Caesar," he said aloud. Caesar opened one eye and closed it again.

Dr. Sahrman was tall, and a very handsome man—dark-haired, with short sideburns which curled against his swarthy cheeks. His eyelashes and brows were heavy and dark, his nose aquiline, his mouth sensitive, his cheekbones high. He was a volatile man, gay one minute, moody the next. He was willing to work hard, and appeared to be a perfectionist. He demanded rigid adherence to aseptic techniques; he would not tolerate clutter. If a test tray were brought in and used, it must be immediately removed. Reports must be made completely, quickly, and filed. He could not tolerate loose ends.

"I can get that for you in a minute, Doctor," some hapless technician might say to him.

"If you can get it in a minute, get it *now!*" Sahrman would shout.

When Tom ventured to protest this shouting, he found that Sahrman could speak eloquently and idealistically about the work which the clinic did. The poor, the sick, the old, were Sahrman's brothers, he declared. They were Steven Sahrman himself, to be cared for, protected, and defended.

But still, Tom quickly decided, the man had essentially no talent with people. He himself was the victim of mistreatment and outrage, yet he had a vile temper which he could turn upon anyone who crossed his path. In that first week, Dr. Bonley ordered a wide screen testing for lead poisoning. He wanted every possible small child from the Clausen district brought to the Institute for blood tests. He emphasized that histories were desirable, records of places the child lived or frequented, previous places . . .

The children came to Clausen and were bussed to the Institute. The Sociomedical department was on the first floor and the halls of it quickly became noisy with wailing children and frightened parents. Was something wrong with the kids? What were the doctors doing? Would the child be sick? Die?

"Just do what we tell you and answer the questions," Sahrman told them. "Then go home. You will know if the child gets sick! If he does, come back. Now, let's get this tube around his arm. Hold him still, for crying out loud!"

He spoke English fluently, but with a thick accent. He was doing, basically, a kind thing for these people. But the round-eyed baby and the anxious mother failed to detect the kindness. The baby was frightened of the syringe, the mother heard the doctor's strident voice; she had to be coaxed to talk to the volunteer at the desk and answer her questions. "Nobody's got no right to yell at me!" she declared.

No one had that right.

Tom, reluctant because he was new in his own job, undertook to protest with Sahrman. "Look," he said. "Don't run these people away from us. It's just fine that the Government and the Clausen family built the Health Center to give us material for our research work, but that same center, *and* our work, has to gain acceptance from the neighborhood, or where would our guinea pigs come from?"

He had to explain the guinea pig bit to Dr. Sahrman. Patiently he explained that their research in lead poisoning among the children of the poor could be conducted only if the doctors—himself and Steven—had little arms from which to take blood. "Lots of little arms," he concluded.

Sahrman retorted profanely.

"You'd better be gentle with the mothers," Tom told him. "In this particular investigation, their morals are not your concern. Just do your work, and don't yell. We want them to come back, you see, for this and other reasons."

It helped. Sahrman did not yell any more. He became all doctor, letting the aide cajole the child, letting the record-taking volunteer explain the dangers of lead poisoning and the advantages of being tested for it.

"In spite of being a refugee," Tom told Dr. Bonley, puzzled about Sahrman, "he has no sympathy with the people. He admires our Institute, he admires Clausen and the work we are doing. But the people—they mean no more to him than the forceps in his hand or his stethoscope. I can't figure out why . . ."

"Tom," said Dr. Bonley, "wherever you went to school—grade, or even secondary—did you know a bully?"

"Not well," said Tom. His alert way of entering into a discussion was Dr. Bonley's delight. "I stayed away from all bullies."

"A child genius."

Tom grinned.

"But you did know that bullies were around. Did you ever witness the bullied bully chain reaction? A boy who had suffered at the hands of older, bigger bully boys, and then, when he became the older, bigger one, turning himself to knocking the little fellows around?"

Tom thought that over. "Sahrman?" he asked.

"Sahrman. In his own country, he was one of the oppressed. He escaped. And he would, if permitted, oppress in his turn."

"Is it my place to permit him to do anything, or not do anything?"

"Do as you started. Explain the situation, and make friends

with the man.

"If I can."

"Yes. If you can. In the ways he will be open to friend-ship."

So Tom tried—with only partial success. After a few days of offering his friendship and being rebuffed, he protested with the man. "I am only trying to make friends with you. Because we work together. If we like each other, our work will go better."

Dr. Sahrman said nothing.

"I know this can happen," Tom persisted. "I feel sure I can work better for Dr. Bonley because I like him."

"You have to like Dr. Bonley."

"I do not have to like him!"

Sahrman shrugged and walked away.

Within that first week, Tom had familiarized himself with Clausen, where the people of the surrounding depressed areas came for emergency clinic care, examination, and treatment. The place was clean, with wide halls and pleasant waiting rooms. Tom himself had to learn how to use some of the sophisticated equipment, the eye-testing machine particularly, afforded by an ample Federal grant.

Certainly here was a new approach to medical care for the poor, who too often had to depend upon crowded clinics, understaffed and poorly equipped, or who went to no clinic at all, got no medical service. Tom was enthusiastic about the work he could do at Clausen and at the Institute.

That building, too, fascinated him. He wanted to explore it; he could do it in his spare time, his off hours. He thought it would be all right. He asked Lonnie, the orderly who worked in his own wards. Lonnie was strong and willing, though not too bright. Some kink in his brain made him re-peat the final words of almost every sentence he said. It took patience to get an answer from Lonnie, or even to greet him each morning.

"How are you, Lonnie? Beautiful weather we're having."

"Yes, it is, Doctor. If it doesn't rain, doesn't rain."

"I wonder," said Dr. Kelsey one morning, "if before I go home some evening, or maybe at my noon break—would it be all right if I looked at some of the other departments? Would I be welcome?"

"You're a doctor, just like them," said Lonnie. "Just like them."

"Well—yes. And they would be welcome down here."

"You go right along, Dr. Kelsey. Tell them I said you could. They all know Lonnie, know Lonnie."

"Well, if you say so, I guess it would be acceptable," Tom agreed.

Lonnie came to the side of his desk. "Now, Dr. Kelsey," he said kindly, "you can go anywhere you want in this building. Because you're a boss. You're a boss."

Tom looked up into the man's solicitous eyes. He had only wanted to know if the other research men visited about. "What makes a boss, Lonnie?" he asked.

"Men," Lonnie answered unexpectedly. "Men doin' things, and other men helpin' them to do them. To do them."

"Yes." Tom accepted the definition. "That should cover it."

So Tom explored the burn unit, the pathology research floor, the orthopedic—and he went to see the surgical research work being done up on Seven. Heart work was done on Three, but other surgery, mainly internal, and mainly for cancer, was done here. In charge of this research was Dr. Richard Scott, called Dick by everyone. He was a friendly fellow, and seemed anxious to talk to Tom about his work. "You send us up some good cases, and I'll buy you a beer," he promised.

"Look, my aim is preventive . . ."

"So is mine. Have you heard about our nucosa detection?"

"No . . ."

"Then come right along with me."

Tom went right along, he listened to Dick, he looked at X-ray plates, he read pages of statistics.

"My work is being duplicated by a man in Japan," Dick told him.

"That's one of the gambles of research."

"It's to be expected. We reach a certain plateau, then there are logical steps to be taken. When we began to examine the stomach and intestines with the aid of barium, it was only natural to seek ways to refine that examination. To make it more precise. I mixed air with the barium, this chap did the same. We compared notes at a convocation last summer. His statistics added to mine make an impressive showing."

Dr. Scott was genuinely pleased to have his work confirmed by that other doctor. If cancer could be detected early, the chances for cure were raised. Barium used as a contrast medium in the examination of the stomach had allowed only limited areas to be seen by X-ray. By adding air, photographs could be obtained of the nucosa, the lining of the stomach, and small cancers could be detected before they could spread and invade the entire gastric system. Dick's results had been good. Of sixty-three patients studied, he told Tom, fifty-six were still living after the cancer-bearing nucosa had been detected and removed. Three of the other six had died of causes other than cancer.

"But that's wonderful!" cried Tom.

"It is satisfying. Now if we can eliminate car wrecks, and find a way to prevent the cancer cells from forming at all . . ."

"You are a dreamer."

Dick looked at his watch. "I'm operating on my sixty-fourth case in thirty minutes," he said. "Would you care to observe?"

"You couldn't get me off this floor with a gun!" Tom assured him.

"All right. Before I scrub, I'll show you the X-ray plates I have."

They started down the hall. This research department was a busy place. There were more rooms for patients than Tom had on One. Not so much foot travel, but much more in the way of carts, wheelchairs, nurses, orderlies, and doctors. Notably Dr. Daives, a staff neurologist, who was approaching at a fast pace.

"Oh, oh," said Dick Scott below his breath.

Daives was waving his clip board at him, the papers on it fluttering. "Just a minute, Scott," he called.

"Watch this," said Dr. Scott to Tom, speaking softly.

Daives came up to them, and Dick introduced Tom. "Oh, yes, I've heard about Kelsey," said Harold Daives. He was dark, tautly built, his brown skin smooth, his black hair close-cropped, his eyes deeply set. Tom wondered what he could have heard.

But Daives was rushing on, talking as rapidly as he had walked. He understood that Scott was about to operate . . .

Dr. Scott agreed that he was.

"Without a consultation again, Doctor?"

"I have a competent staff. We work, and consult, together."

"But you also have at your disposal the whole gastric surgical department over at University, sir!"

"I know they are there. I used to work there. I was chosen to head this research work, Daives, by that department."

"You are supposed to consult!"

"Who supposes that?" asked Dick, his face and manner pleasant, his words as rude as he could make them and stay within ethical bounds.

"A good representation of the Center's staff, Doctor!" cried. Daives. "We are unalterably opposed to your doing experimental surgery!"

"The way to tell me that is not by a single, unauthorized emissary, but through channels, Dr. Daives. Excuse me, please?" He touched Tom's arm, he went around Daives, and pushed through the door to scrub. "You can wait here until the coast is clear," he told Tom. "The entrance to the observers' deck is three doors down, but don't expose yourself to that jackdaw again."

"Does he have any right . . . ?"

Dr. Scott was preparing to change his clothes. He talked to Tom over the swinging door of the dressing cubicle. "What I am about to do," he said, "is experimental surgery. At regular intervals, I have to plead my case because of complaints made by Daives and his friends. They have no faith in research, and certainly not that done by men they know so intimately. My Japanese opposite number could come in here, remove a nucosa, and be lauded, wined and dined, invited to lecture and to demonstrate. But I came up through ranks at University. Student, intern, resident—and finally I was assigned to our Institute here to do exactly what I am about to do this evening—use a technique which we have recently developed, hoping that each time we use it we move closer to an established and routine bit of surgical procedure.

"This patient wouldn't have much of a chance without the surgery I plan to do. Stomach surgery doesn't offer much of a field in which to save him. If, by operating—experimentally —I can avoid the spread of his cancer, he and I both are ready to take a chance." He came out, clothed in his shape-less green scrub suit, and went to the basin. Two other men had come in and were changing.

"I think it's safe for you to go into the hall now," Dick told Tom. "And don't let yourself even think 'To hell with Daives.' He's a man to watch."

Tom was troubled, as Scott did not seem to be, as Tom would have been after such an encounter. Attack. It really had been one.

On a house phone, he located himself to his department, and found the door to the observation area. This was a matter of three benches at one end of o.r. Before surgery began, these benches were full, with two students leaning against the wall.

"Scott is good," his neighbor told Tom.

"I believe you're right."

"Are you on his team?"

"No, I work down in Sociomedical."

The man nodded. "That's good work."

Tom felt that it was, but he wondered about his own behavior should Daives, or someone like him . . . ?

As he watched Scott work, his respect mounted by the minute. The man was a skilled surgeon and a good teacher. As he went along, he explained what he was doing, particu-larly to the intern who worked at the table, but the benches were benefited, and Tom Kelsey. There was no trace in the surgeon's eyes or voice and hands of any disturbance because of Daives.

He declared that this was still experimental surgery. He pointed out the chance offered their patient, a man of fifty-seven. "A man that age has a lot of life to live. He was ready to take the chance that we have found a way to stop the cancer he knows he has—knows through his symptoms, and through faith in our diagnosis."

The surgery proceeded, the first incision, the second, the retractors, the sponges, the whole bit. And the stomach lining was exposed; it showed what Tom would have called certain evidence of cancerous cells. Dick Scott excised a specimen, and another, and sent the material to pathology. Meanwhile they would wait a little, he said, watching the way the nurse spread her towels.

The time was only "a little." The circulating answered the telephone, and even as she listened, she nodded to Dr. Scott. The towels were whisked away. Dick held his hand out for the next instrument—and the lights went out. The room was black.

Tom gasped.

"Oh, not that again!" cried the surgeon, loudly protesting.

The circulating had not left the phone; she could pick up the receiver . . .

An operating room in velvety darkness was an eerie place. There was no hiss from the autoclave, no beep or sign from the anesthetist's equipment. He would, by manual effort, continue to assist the patient, but . . .

Someone knocked a pan, clanging, to the floor, and Tom Kelsey wiped his sweaty palms down the sides of his white coat.

The lights came on, flickering, then, strongly. The surgeon bent again to his task, his hands moving, Tom thought, even more swiftly and more surely.

What had happened? A power failure? A fuse failure?

When Dick Scott, by prearrangement, joined him in the lounge afterward and asked Tom what he thought, Tom's reply had to do with the power failure.

Dick shook his head.

"I would have screeched aloud!" Tom assured him.

"The first time, maybe."

"Then you really meant that *again* business?"

Dick looked at him inquiringly.

"Yes. You said, 'Oh, not that again!' "

Dick drained his coffee cup. "It happens all the time over here at Research."

"What happens?" Tom asked, an edge to his voice.

Dick stood up and put his cup in the bin. "You're not talking about the lighting failure, are you?"

Tom ran his hand through his thick black hair. "I guess I don't know what I'm talking about," he admitted. "But specifically, no. I didn't mean the failure. Though God knows that was big enough. If you hadn't had a perfectly disciplined crew . . ."

"Sometimes someone does screech," Dick told him, smiling a little.

"Look," said Tom earnestly. "If there was sabotage—if there possibly could have been . . ."

"Sometimes I do wonder," Dick agreed. "When little things happen."

"But this was a big thing!"

"Yes, it was. But of sabotage or bad management—both could have been the cause—which is worse? I train against such developments."

"And thank God for an auxiliary power system."

Dick laughed, but as Tom went back to his own office, he was remembering that the man's eyes had been dead-serious.

On Tom's next sortie—he made it the next day at his noon break, counting on getting a sandwich to bring back to his desk in the way of lunch—he went to the pediatrics floor. Here there was a psychiatric ward, an orthopedic-congenital department, a speech and palate section. And a leukemia wing, where he met Carter Bass.

He had been hearing of her. "Have you met Carter Bass?" he was frequently asked.

He had seen her at a staff meeting; Bonley had pointed her out across the heads and shoulders of other staff men and women. But this day—Tom spied her as he started down that hall. A fairly tall woman she was, with the sunlight from a window making a halo about her dark blonde hair. As he passed them, he glanced in through the room windows. Children in bed, children at play, and finally children having lessons. Leukemia-afflicted children, gathered about a round table and attending, with varying degrees of concentration to what was being said to them.

He stood in the hall and watched.

"We used to think having them taught was futile, a time-passer," said Dr. Bass, coming toward him. "But now things are more hopeful. You're Dr. Kelsey." She held out her hand.

Tom extended his own. "I'm Kelsey," he agreed. "Snooping and gawking."

"And interested."

He was certainly interested in this young woman. Hen-medics could put him off, but not this erect, handsome girl. She had the most beautiful eyes! Gray-blue, and clear . . . Her voice was low, just a thread husky.

"I'm interested," Tom agreed.

"Come in and meet the kids," said Dr. Bass. "Since we have your department, a lot of them are coming to us from poor families."

Tom looked at her sharply. "And they didn't before?"

"Not often. A child developing leukemia became ill slowly; he was treated at home or given superficial medication by uninformed private doctors. Even the busy clinics, should the 'sickly' child reach one, didn't make the specific diagnosis, or there was no follow-up. And then, too, there was that futile aspect. Leukemia was incurable; we must spend our time and money on more hopeful things."

"Clausen has helped?"

"Clausen, and Dr. Bonley's work. Yours now. He praises you."

Tom felt his face warm, and he mumbled something about hoping he deserved praise.

"You do, or you will." The lesson period was over, and they went into the classroom. The children were free to clamor for their doctor's attention and to meet Dr. Kelsey. He was shown drawings, he listened to a child read. He threw and caught a ball for a thin little boy of eight, and submitted to the doctoring of a curly-headed four-year-old with a nurse's kit.

"Lessons for *her?*" he asked Dr. Bass.

"Her sister . . ." she indicated an older girl in a plaid robe.

"Both of them?" asked Tom, shocked.

"Both of them. They won't willingly be separated."

So Tom was administered "shots"; he ate pills, but looked dubiously at the bottle of red medicine. "I think that should be analyzed," he told the four-year-old.

She loved the big word, and agreed. "I don't like medicine neither," she confided.

After ten minutes of this, Carter led him down the hall to her office, a pleasant place. There was a busy-looking desk, file cabinets, a couch in green corduroy, and three chairs. At the big corner window there were draperies in brown, chartreuse yellow, and dark blue. Coffee on a hot plate, and dark blue mugs that matched the carpet.

He settled luxuriously into his chair. "I must do something about my office," he said. "First, I'll get rid of the paper cups."

"These taste better, but they have to be washed."

"Maybe I can persuade Lonnie."

"He'll do it, he'll do it," Dr. Bass said, smiling.

"Don't tell me he mops up here!"

"Oh, no. His visits up here are social."

"Lonnie is smarter than he sometimes seems. I'm all for his social visiting program. Though," he glanced, bright-eyed, at Dr. Bass, "he may never have been warned about the dire consequences of office romance."

Her head tilted to one side. Her hair was loosely gathered and tied at the back of her neck with a blue scarf, the color of her dress. "Warned?" she repeated.

"You wouldn't know. Franzel said that his office chose to deal with the male side of such involvements."

"Doctor, are you feeling all right?"

The crease was deep in his right cheek. "I'm feeling just fine," he said, "and inclined to tell Mr. Franzel to bring on his procedures."

"All this because of a ceramic coffee mug?"

"It's the little things that count, Doctor."

She shook her head. "I've heard about you, but not that you were crazy," she told him.

"I am not crazy. Franzel maybe, but not me. Never me."

"Would you want to tell me about Franzel? Isn't he the Personnel Director?"

"Yes, and you will remember that I am a recent victim of interviews and appraisals. I have the needle marks, fresh and aching." He went on to tell her, swiftly and exactly. He set his coffee mug down and gestured with his strong-looking hands. He was still talking when a nurse came in with papers for Dr. Bass to sign. Finished, she looked up at her visitor.

"The inference behind what you have been telling me is shocking," she assured him.

"It is shocking," Tom agreed.

"I can see you didn't enjoy the experience. Has anything else bothered you? Or happened?"

He frowned. Were things supposed to "happen" in Research? He recalled Dick's seeming acceptance of incidents of sabotage or mismanagement. Should he question this friendly young woman on that subject?

Before he could decide, a man passed the open door, stopped, came back, and entered the office. It was Lenox, the business office executive who had been present at Tom's final interview with the staff. He greeted Tom warmly, and Carter. No, he didn't have time for coffee, he said, but he was glad to see them both. "How are you getting along, Tom?" he asked. "It is Tom, I believe."

"Yes," Tom agreed. "And I think I am getting along all right, Mr. Lenox. In odd hours, I have been getting acquainted with the rest of the building."

"Good idea. Of course you have joint staff meetings. How do you like the way we run this particular zoo?"

Tom buttoned his lab coat. "Well," he said slowly, "of course I am new here. But if there are things I find I don't like, Mr. Lenox, I'll see what can be done to change them."

Mr. Lenox's eyes were keen behind the glasses he wore. "Good!" he said heartily. And he was off down the hall again.

Carter refilled their coffee cups. She was studying Tom's face. "Did you mean that?" she asked.

"Did I mean what?"

"That you would change things."

"Oh," said Tom, "that was a thing to say. I probably did mean it, though I doubt if I'll change much of anything very soon. For one thing, I'm no expert in management. I find that I'm not even expert in my own job. I am working into it, I believe. I know the policy of single-standard medical care is our goal. I have been told to be alert that such care be afforded the poor with whom we work. So far everything seems to be going along those guidelines. The poor come to Clausen, and those who seem to offer themselves to our research of family disease and medicine come to my notice. Sometimes the work is frustrating."

"All research is."

"Yes, of course. I hope things can continue to seem fine. About the only thing, really, that has gone against my liking was the romance interdiction. It does seem to be shocking interference with an individual's privilege to conduct his life as he pleases. Man meets girl is a basic part of American life."

He stood up, and Carter looked up at him. "Are you a Lothario, Dr. Kelsey?" she asked.

He laughed and shook his hair back from his face. "I just may become one to prove my point," he said.

She laughed at this, freely and gaily. "I don't believe I'd worry too much," she advised. "Probably a management firm set this office-romance thing up as a way to improve efficiency, control costs, or even maintain a good moral atmosphere."

"You're making it sound worse and worse."

She opened a desk drawer, rummaged among papers and folders, and finally produced a half-sheet. "Here it is," she said. "I quote: Guidelines on how to handle professional gossip . . ." Her eyes lifted to his face. "As well as the office Romeo," she added.

Now the crease in Tom's cheek was very deep, his eyes were shining. "How does your guideline suggest you proceed?" he asked gravely.

She turned the paper over. "In the final hint," she said, "it says to fire all such."

Tom laughed, and she joined him. She put the paper back

into the drawer and stood up, then walked with him to the door and out into the corridor. They both spoke to a child in a wheelchair. "Thank you for coming, Tom," she said to her visitor. "Do it again. I do think I might say, and seriously, that this whole building, this whole research setup, is a sensitive, controversial operation. Within, and without. Enough things can happen . . ."

Tom nodded. "I'm beginning to get that message," he said. "Things like that lighting failure in the midst of Scott's suture yesterday afternoon."

Carter stopped dead where she was. Her head went up, the smile drained from her face, leaving it grave and, Tom thought, a little pale. "That didn't happen *again!*" she cried.

He looked at her. Yes, she had paled. And that word *again* . . . "Is something going on?" he asked, really puzzled.

"Always," she answered. "Always. For instance, in tonight's newspaper, count the lines in the account."

"Oh," Tom protested, "it wasn't important enough for a news report. The auxiliary went quickly into operation."

"I think you will find that the failure was important to someone. You'll read about it. *Doctor doing experimental abdominal surgery . . .*"

Tom could not believe it, would not. He opened the door to the stairwell and turned to thank Dr. Bass again. "I've ruined your lunch hour," he apologized.

"Come again; it will be good for my figure. Good luck, Dr. Kelsey. By the way, don't you have that refugee doctor, Sahrman, working in your department?"

"Oh, yes."

"How do you like him?"

Tom made some reply, too puzzled to remember what it was he said. And he forgot to eat any lunch.

CHAPTER 2

For six months, from June until December, Tom worked at the Research Institute, and liked the work he did. He liked to see an old man patiently sitting in the waiting room be approached by a receptionist in a crisp white uniform.

"Mr. Schenker," she said, "you are waiting to see Dr. Scott. Right?"

The grizzled head lifted. "That's right," the patient said. "I come here—my daughter brought me. She said I should see the doctor."

"That's right," agreed the woman in white. "But Dr. Scott just called and said he would be thirty minutes late. An emergency has come up. He said he would see you at two-thirty, if that will be all right?"

"It's all right," said Mr. Schenker, not at all annoyed. He settled down again to waiting.

A thing he was used to doing, he told Dr. Kelsey, who spoke to him. "I'm used to it"—waiting to receive public medical attention, the old man meant. Here at Research, referred here from Clausen, it still was public medicine. "But it's different here," he told the tall doctor. "Here somebody seems to care that I am waiting."

Tom treasured that small episode. He remembered it and told about it, he wrote a paragraph about it for the records which he kept. It was the sort of thing he could feel good about.

He felt good, as well, about the people of the street, the poor, the "hippies" who came into the Clinic and whom he often put to work. These people would come in, sometimes accompanying an old person, a sick one. Girls with long hair, draggled skirts, and wise, yet anxious, eyes. Boys, young men, a swaggering black in a sleeveless shirt, a flat hat cocked down over one eye, a chap in a sheepskin jacket and ragged jeans—barefooted—even a man with carefully combed, rippling hair, a carefully nurtured beard, and sharp clothes. . . .

Sometimes they had business at the Institute; they were parts of families or neighborhoods being investigated. Sometimes they came in from curiosity, or even perhaps to make trouble, which they sometimes did. Who else wrote such graffiti on the restroom walls?

But Tom had formed a custom of putting some of these people to work. "Give me a hand here, will you?" he would ask one of the girls when he had several young children to corral and handle. "Just hold the kid for me."

"Hold this," he might say to the youth in the sleeveless shirt. And he would hand him his clip board while he examined a man who had chosen the corridor to have an epileptic seizure. The hippie, or fat cat, or whatever his classification, held the clip board and watched fascinated as Tom pried open the jaws and fished the tongue from the man's throat.

"What's wrong with him?" asked the awed young man.

Tom explained about epilepsy. How it happened, what happened, the chance for control, if not cure.

"That's sure interesting," said the youth. "If I don't get me a job, maybe I can help you again. How about that, Doc?"

"Be fine," said Tom readily. "We need all the help we can get."

"I'll come round." He rubbed his bare arms. "I ain't no junkie," he offered.

"I can see that," said the doctor. "But maybe when you come around you could scrub up a little? We all have to around here."

"Yeah. Sure, Doc. I notice."

The boy—he was twenty and rejoiced in the name of Scooter—did come back, and often Tom would make use of him. There were those who did not approve. Scooter carried a switchblade, Sahrman informed Tom.

"I've never seen it."

Scooter now always came in as clean as could be, and he even was willing to hang his hat on a hook in the doctor's office. He did the things Tom found for him to do. He toned down his language at Tom's request. "We've got some fussy people around here."

Tom found ways of paying him a little. And he paid him good wages when he cleaned the snow from the walk and steps of his own home, or helped move a couch from the living room down to the basement family room.

"You live here alone, man?" Scooter asked.

"Why not?"

"You should get yourself a chick."

"I'll think about that."

"What's to think? You got all kinds of chicks over at the Clinic."

"All kinds," Tom agreed.

It was through Scooter that he found his cleaning woman. This deal also brought an interesting family to the Institute and their records into the files. But it was through Scooter—

"Look, I need a woman, not a chick, to clean my house for me. Change the bed, clean up a bit—dust—"

"You sure like to be clean, man."

"I sure do."

"I could clean for you and sleep in the basement."

Tom shook his head. "I want a woman who knows how to do the women things of housekeeping. Not a young woman, probably. And somebody honest. I'd have to give her a key."

"If I find one, she'll be straight."

Scooter did find him a cleaning woman. She was German born, not young. In fact, because of her age, she had just been released from the bakery where she had worked. She walked with a slight limp which she pointed out to Dr. Kelsey. It had, she told him, been caused by a suture. This intrigued him, and his intrigue led to the discovery of a whole family suffering from a bone disease. Mattie was supporting and caring for her son and his children. The son's bone trouble was much graver than Mattie's. Except for that hitch in her gait, she seemed not to be troubled. But she had to supplement her small social security benefit; the doctor's housecleaning, and what he paid her for it, would be exactly what she needed.

"And you are exactly what I need," Tom told her.

Scooter had found her for Tom because he was going to replace her at the bakery. "I'll snitch you a Danish sometimes, Doc," he promised.

"No snitched Danish!" Tom told him sternly. "They give me a bellyache."

He told that story to Dr. Bonley, adding that he would miss Scooter.

"There are plenty of hippies for you to work on," the Chief assured him.

It was through Mattie Miller, that compactly sturdy little woman, because he insisted that everyone in her family come to the Institute for examination and possible treatment, that Tom got a break he was always to value.

This came through Roxie Turner, a niece of Mattie's. She too, was a wheelchair patient. Mattie's son Jesse had refused all offers of treatment and corrective measures. At forty-six, he said he was too old. But Roxie . . .

She came with the others for the family evaluation. These people were poor but respectable. They lived in Clausen's general neighborhood; they were the sort who did without medical care rather than seem to ask for charity. And without charity they could not afford medical care.

But Tom was able to sell his research project to them. He needed families, he said, and family examinations, to pursue his work. He was not happy to get a young girl like Roxie in the turnout, but he always said, as he told Roxie, that she had done more for him than he did for her.

This was true. A doctor entering a new field of his profession can, with his first important case, win or lose his future. The results of his handling of that case can establish him or mean immediate failure. Roxie was such a case. She was as crippled as was Jesse, but she was nineteen, with a cheerful outlook on life. Tom thought there was a chance she could be helped. He could put the decision up to Roxie's family, none of them with medical training or understanding. Or he himself could take on the burden of experimentation; Roxie would do what he recommended. So the chance really was Tom's for the taking. Thinking about it, he recalled what Dick Scott had said to him: "We have to try these things. It is what we are here for."

Without surgery, Roxie was unable to bear her weight on her right leg; she would never walk. With it—

He designed a regimen of diet, exercise, and therapy for Mattie's grandchildren, a preventive rather than a curative measure—and for Roxie Turner, he recommended the transplant of several tendons. He had an orthopedist examine the girl; her X-rays were exhaustively studied. But Tom was the one to talk to Roxie and to her family. He would say only that he felt such surgery was well worth the try. Mattie was afraid. "I won't take no stand," she said.

It was Jesse who came to Roxie's, and Tom's, aid. "If I was her age, and know what I know," he declared, "I'd let 'em saw my legs into inch-wide pieces."

So it was decided. Roxie entered the orthopedic-surgical ward of University Hospital. After more tests and X-rays, the surgery was planned and scheduled. The orthopedist, recognizing Tom's study of the case, asked Dr. Kelsey to be on his surgical team.

Tom approached the experience with mixed emotions of fear and excitement. Scrubbed and at the table, he accepted the tasks which the surgeon assigned to him. He held retractors, he lifted the tendon, he sutured . . .

"You're a pretty fair country surgeon," he was told. "You could have done the job yourself, Kelsey."

Tom knew better. But he had made the diagnosis.

"You got the girl here!" Bonley told him.

"Well, there was Mattie, and Jesse—yes, and even Scooter."

The hospital, the Institute, and Roxie, knew who had made it possible for the girl to be able, by December, to walk with a brace and a cane. In another six months . . . Best of all, Tom thought, the word went around the Clausen neighborhood. Those docs really took care of folks.

Tom felt that he knew where his success lay. With Roxie, certainly, but his department at the Institute was laboring to find all ways, new ways, to bring medical care to the poor.

These people had not been receiving health services except on a crisis basis, and then usually too little and too late. Tom Kelsey, by patient persistence, was demonstrating that their future health could be bettered. Roxie had come to the clinic, she had consented to all the tests and planning, and finally to the operation. She had gone into surgery as a "healthy" young woman, able to care for herself. Like Jesse, she could have got along.

But now . . .

"You were lucky," Sahrman told Tom. "If the surgery had not worked, your big case would have dropped you into a big black hole."

Tom agreed with him. "I was lucky," he said.

He talked to Carter Bass about the luck element.

"I am proud of the whole thing," she told him.

"You haven't answered me."

Carter looked up at him. She most certainly did have beautiful eyes! "The only luck," she said, "lay in the fact that you got this case. And we doctors need a lot of luck in our work."

Tom nodded. Yes, they did.

"For instance," said Carter, "you might not have seen this girl at all."

"Yes," Tom agreed. "Yes."

"You sound like Lonnie."

Tom laughed. He did like Carter, and was as interested in her work as she seemed to be in his. Of the many friends he made those first six months, Carter was special with him.

She appeared to be as pleased to have met up with Tom Kelsey. She told him that, along with Roxie, Tom had established himself professionally by her Girl Scout Troop. She said this at an Institute staff meeting. Heads turned her way. Tom, who sat over against the wall, was grinning.

It was simply great, Dr. Bass insisted. "My girls—I am getting them older now, you know, with the success of regression methods for leukemia—my girls decided that they wanted a scout troop. Actually it was a mixture of Brownies and scouts, but it seemed like a good idea. We had manuals and neckerchiefs, but the girls wanted uniforms. This presented a problem, but Dr. Kelsey knew what to do. He scrounged, he purloined, perhaps seduced some of the women in linen supply—" Her eyes sparkled. "But we had uniforms. Originally they were surgical robes, but they have been dyed a good scout green . . ."

"By Dr. Kelsey?" asked one of the men.

"You know?" said Carter "I don't examine his devious ways too closely. I just know that we have the uniforms, and morale has risen one hundred percent in the leukemia ward."

"How about your boys?"

"Haven't you noticed, Doctor," asked Carter blandly, "that when the girls are happy, the boys seem to be?"

Tom took a lot of ribbing about that circumstance, but he didn't mind. He seemed to be well liked by his colleagues. People had been cordial to him. The staff doctors, and other doctors in the city; he had been offered memberships, courtesy club cards—all of which was pleasant and flattering.

Of the Institute doctors, he had seen most of, and become closest friends with, Dick Scott.

He had also seen a good bit of Lenox from the business office, Dr. Daives, the neurologist, and Dr. Rosenthal, a biochemist. Each frequently dropped into his office; he would run into them over at the hospitals, see them in the bar of the hotel where he sometimes stopped if he walked from the Institute to his home. Twice he had encountered two of them when he was playing tennis at a club he liked, and where his name was up for membership.

He mentioned this one evening when he was invited to Dick's home for dinner. Judith, Dick's wife, and the two teen-agers, Linda and Tim, got along very well with Tom. They would talk to him; he was taken to see the progress Tim was making with the apartment he was fixing for himself over the garage.

"I'd call it the carriage house," Tom told the boy. He never, Tim pointed out to his parents, had asked why a boy of fifteen should need an apartment.

Linda talked to Tom, too. About skirt lengths. It was terrible, she assured this other doctor, to have a father who had studied anatomy. "Shorts have to be short, or you should call them something else!"

The Scotts lived in a huge house, one of the old grand houses of what had used to be the grandest part of the city. Some streets of these big houses still hung on; privacy was maintained and policed by the owners. Some had slipped toward decay and then had been rescued by younger people who reveled in high ceilings, big rooms, a stair rail down which the children could slide.

"Big houses with fuel bills to match," Dick Scott would say wryly.

These large and aging homes, once part of the city's fashionable district, as witness the carriage houses and the porte-cochères—which the kids called carports—the wrought iron and the marble, the servants' quarters now converted into apartments or shut off to conserve the expensive heat, now were occupied by university professors and young professionals who had bought the homes cheap and, in many cases, had remodeled them .

Dick Scott's red brick home was charming, its white-columned entry gracious, its twelve-paned windows sparkled with hospitality. The rooms were large, comfortable, and were ideal for a family to live in together, for the children to grow.

The Scott living room was blue in every shade from that of the Gulf Stream to a brilliant turquoise. The floor had been color-stained, a handsome secretary had been antiqued. Everywhere blue in woven and striped and plain fabrics. An emotional color kept from being moody by a disciplined use of white. The room soothed one by its single color, balanced by a dark blue hassock, brightly flowered curtains at the French doors, and the wide white mats of the prints and water colors hung on every wall.

Tonight, which had turned cold and biting with a wind from the north, a small fire burned on the hearth, and the perfume of a ham in the oven drifted through the rooms.

Tom sniffed appreciatively.

"No exhaust fans for you, eh?" laughed Dick, taking his topcoat.

"If you could bottle that smell, you'd make a fortune," Tom assured him, bending to kiss Judith's cheek, and going on to the fire. His foot gently nudged the family dog, a red cocker named Crackers.

"Do you want a drink now?" Dick asked him. "Or can you wait for the other guest?"

Tom turned to look at him, and Judith chuckled. "Not a perfectly lovely girl," she told him.

Tom dropped into his favorite corner of the blue and white plaid couch. "Then I'll wait," he decided.

"Our guest," said Dick, "is—I think I should brief you about him—is Dr. James Hubbell." Dick and Judith each looked keenly at Tom.

"Should I recognize the name?" he asked.

"You might," said Dick, sitting down on the hassock. "He was a successful physician, specializing in diabetes."

"Was?" Tom repeated.

"Yes, was. Six years ago, he was accused and convicted of manslaughter because he used sulfanilamide elixir, and the patient died."

"Oh, but—" Tom protested.

Dick's uplifted hand silenced him. "We know all the buts, Tom. He was convicted, and he has served five years of a prison term. Now he has been released on parole. His wife has divorced him, and has his two children. The Medical Board has revoked his license. He has come back here to dispose of his property, which consists solely, I think, of this house."

Tom looked again around the blue room in which he sat; he thought of the house's dignity as one approached it from the street.

Dick was watching him. "He bought it the year before all his troubles began. It meant a great deal to Jim."

"He's black," said Judith softly.

Tom drew a deep breath.

"I took over the house," said Dick, "partly in protest at what had happened to a good, and even honored, doctor. He was one. This whole affair has been shocking. No one ever thought Jim Hubbell had murdered anybody. He was on the Hospital's staff, he taught in the medical school, he did notable research before the Institute was established. He—"

The doorbell interrupted. Linda answered it, and Dick went to greet their guest in the hall. Judith and Linda went to get dinner on the table, and Dick brought Dr. Hubbell in to meet Tom. To have a drink.

Jim Hubbell proved to be a quiet, reserved man—a tall man with broad shoulders. He was a light-colored Negro, with an ascetically handsome face, deep-set, glowing eyes. His black hair was thick and straight. He shook hands with Tom, accepted his drink, and listened rather than talked.

When dinner was served, he enjoyed the food and the talk as well. He was keenly interested in the work which Tom was doing for the poor, with them.

When Tom confessed that he often forgot that only on his first floor could the patients be expected to be poor—"You should have heard me condescend to one of Dick's millionaires!"—Dr. Hubbell laughed with the others, and with Tom.

"I suspect that you do not condescend to your poor patients," he told Tom earnestly

"Well, now," said Tom, "these hippie types, these soul brothers and their sisters are not easy subjects for condescension, Doctor. As for the older ones, the women have been trained in ways of demonstrating for better housing, more and larger welfare checks—you don't condescend to them, either."

Dr. Hubbell asked keen questions about Tom's work. He obviously was a doctor to his bones, a man no older than Tom Kelsey. He probably had known an uphill climb in his profession.

Tom talked to him, sensing the hunger in the man. He talked about his work and his patients. "I will say, the blacks are more grateful than some others," he said. "I have to take my car to a garage for free washing and oil changes because I took care of a certain man's parents. That garage is three miles away." He chuckled. "And there's the waiter who wanted to turn over his tips to me because I cleared up a slight dermatitis which he had, and could prove that it was neither a social nor hereditary disease."

"How do you handle this bothersome gratitude, Doctor?" Hubbell asked him.

"Well, it's a choice. I get hard-boiled, or I get condescending. I tell the garage guy that I'm damned if I'll bother to go

40

three miles for a quart of oil, and I explain to the waiter what a magnificent salary I am earning, that I have no family to use up cash—and he should put his tips in the bank if he doesn't need the money for other things."

"And you end up with two men puzzled that you can be so stupid," said Dr. Hubbell.

"I suppose I do. What should I have done?"

"Not make a personal thing of your services to them," said Dick.

"Do you practice medicine that way?" Tom asked him.

Dick threw up his hands. "Not me! I get so involved with my patients that Judith says I should put my bed in the ward."

Judith smiled. "He'd do it, too, if I'd go there with him."

"You stay right where you are," Tom told her. "And keep baking pecan pie."

"Is it good?"

Tom laughed. "A leading question if I ever heard one."

"I suspect," said Dr. Hubbell thoughtfully, "that the applied research you men do must lead to personal involvement. I should like to research that!" He turned to Tom. "The Institute was only taking shape when I left the hospital staff," he explained. "The talk then was that they would have Center staff men as heads of the departments, to direct the projects and the men who worked with the patients. Do you think that might be a better way, Dr. Kelsey, than having your own staff?"

"Personally," said Tom quietly, "I like the setup the way it is. Independence for us seems to work."

The evening was a pleasant one. Jim Hubbell did not talk about himself, but he was aware of his situation and recognized that the other doctors were aware of it.

The next day when the two men were eating lunch together, Tom expressed his feeling of shock to Dick. "I still keep thinking about him."

"Yes, I know. It is a great loss to the profession as well as to Hubbell."

"I keep saying to myself, 'There, but for the grace of God . . .'"

"It can happen," said Dick.

"I know you said that no one could think the man was guilty. But was he? Medically, I mean. Presumably he was, legally."

Dick carefully cut the meat from the chicken leg on his plate. "What difference does it make?" he asked then. "If he was guilty, or was not? Now, I mean. His life as a doctor has been ruined, as well as his life as a man. Whether he ruined it, or twelve men on a jury did, there the matter stands." He spoke angrily.

Tom nodded, his face thoughtful. "Thomas Aquinas said that when one imprisons a man, one keeps him from doing evil, but also he is kept from doing good."

"And that is precisely where this tragedy lies," Dick agreed.

"It's going to haunt me," Tom assured his friend. "Should we try to do something for Jim?"

Dick nodded. "But there's just one way."

Tom looked up eagerly.

"Carefully," said Dick. "Very carefully."

A short time later, at a Christmastime cocktail party, Tom found himself talking about Jim Hubbell to Carter Bass. They had secured a quiet corner where Carter could sit in a big, gold velvet chair, her hair shining in the glow of a lamp; Tom could stand, his elbow hooked over the mantel corner, and they could talk to each other. First about the three yellow porcelain rosebuds in a silver vase on the chest beside her, then about the food being served, and their hosts. And eventually about Jim.

Did Carter know him?

"No, not really. He was already gone by the time I came here. But since he's been back, I've seen him from a distance, and of course I know what happened to him. It seems especially tragic when you consider what it must have taken in the way of brains and ability for him to get where he was. On the staff at University Hospitals."

"It isn't easy," said Tom. He told of his dinner at Scott's. Carter listened, sipping from the glass in her hand. The large diamond she wore caught a dozen prismed colors from the lamplight.

"The whole evening, and our talk," Tom concluded, "left me with the feeling that I should be able to do something about this man."

Carter smiled up at him, her eyes soft. "You're the kind, Tom Kelsey, to believe you should do something for the whole world."

"Oh, I am not!" Tom denied with some heat. "But here, in my little corner of the world . . ." He held up his thumb and forefinger, measuring off a half-inch space. "Here," he went on earnestly, "surely we can do something. This man is in my corner. And for him that could be the world, good or bad."

Carter studied his face. The rosy tint of the wall behind her glowed in her cheeks and on her throat. "This is your corner," she said softly. "Isn't it?"

"Yes," Tom agreed. "I like this corner, and the way it has become a world for me, too. I like the people I know, the work I do, and the way I am allowed to do it. To put myself into that work. I hear talk that changes should be made . . ."

Carter's head lifted from the gold cushion, her eyes were instantly alert. "Who says that?" she asked. "What did they say?"

Tom was surprised at her intentness. He took her glass and put it with his own on a tray that was being passed. "It probably was just talk," he said.

She nodded. "A lot of talk does go on," she agreed. "Right here." She looked out across the room, at the people clustered into groups. "At the Center certainly. And some in the Institute."

"Yes," said Tom. "Listen to it now." The room hummed and buzzed with voices, laughter, crackled occasionally with argument.

"Do you think there should be changes?" Carter persisted, still intent on what he had suggested.

Tom tossed his head to shake the dark hair back from his face. "Well," he compromised. "I came to the Institute after a hundred brains had devised the thing. At least a hundred. They planned and erected the building, they selected the fields for research. And some excellent work is being done. Your leukemia research, for instance; Dick Scott's cancer. In my own field, the setup alone justifies the system as devised.

"Traditionally, you know, medical care has been made available to the poor in places convenient to the persons providing that care, not to those needing it. In this city, transportation is poor and scarce. Medical care used to be available to the poor only from the crowded city hospitals. Many of the poor stayed away from those clinics, even though they were medically ill. But our Research Institute is only blocks away from the ghetto. Clausen is right in one of the poorest districts of the city. The poor come there for care and treatment. Those cases that seem to be a part of our research into family medicine, or seem to indicate a pattern for certain illnesses, are brought to us. Not sent, brought. Sometimes the rest of Research gets a patient, you have gotten those children, Dick gets them. The burn center got a whopper just this afternoon. The Institute is a working system, and I am glad to be a part of it."

Carter listened to him, smiling. "But what about changes?" she asked again, teasing him, yet serious, too.

Tom knew that she was teasing. "Oh," he said largely, "I'd change the color of the lab walls. And then, of course, there are those restrictions on romance."

Carter laughed. "That still?" she asked him. "You poor, inhibited Lothario. You are one, aren't you?"

"By now you should know."

He liked Carter Bass. He could always talk to her about his interest in family preventive medicine, his wish to get the message through to the young folk—teen-agers, young adults . . .

That evening, driving her home through the quiet city streets—a light snow was falling; wreaths hung in lighted windows; the beauty of Christmas had come again to the world—he talked to her about his recent assignment to lecture in the medical school.

"Does it bother you, Tom?" Carter asked, sensing a note of uncertainty in his voice.

"The lectures, no. I've done three and they went pretty well. In fact, not much about my work does bother me, Carter."

Nothing did. Tom did his work, his attention fixed on the plans he had made, his interest in that work complete.

"Has there been something . . . ?" she asked.

"Yes. Or there seems to be. Ten days ago I went across to

conduct the class. I start with a lecture, prepared and thought out. We always end up with a question-and-answer session. Rather great. But ten days ago . . ."

"What happened?"

He had drawn up into the drive of the apartment hotel where she lived, but he made no move to get out of the car. "I don't know what happened," he said. "I went over and no class showed up. Nobody. After ten or fifteen minutes, I made inquiries. And there on the bulletin board was a neatly typed notice that the lecture—my lecture at my time—had been canceled."

"And you didn't know."

"Of course I didn't know. And I couldn't find anyone who did know. I made my report to the Dean, but it was all I could think of to do."

"A student joke, do you think?"

"It could have been."

"Will it happen again?"

"Not unless my name is forged. I told the class that I would sign all orders. Then—and this was more recently. On Monday of this week I was to be part of a seminar. I received a message by telephone. The voice was typically an impersonal secretary's voice. The seminar, she said, would be held out at the University campus, in such and such a room in such and such a building. That time I checked on the thing, and there had been no change."

"Who called you?"

Tom shrugged.

"And why?" Carter persisted.

He laughed shortly. "Fun and games is as far as I could get."

"I'm glad you were wise enough . . ."

"I only wish I were wise," he said. "Then maybe I'd know

what was going on."

"If anything beyond fun and games," said Carter, gathering her coat about her, and her purse.

Tom took her to the door of her apartment, kissed her, and departed. The doorman took a dim view of a car left in the driveway.

He liked Carter very much, he told himself. "That's because," he said aloud, "she encourages me to talk about myself."

Whatever the reason, he did enjoy taking her to some of the holiday parties, and meeting her at others. She was lovely to look at, and she flattered a man's ego. In the large Institute and Hospital group both of them usually were invited to these parties. Attractive singles were popular.

Also frequently present at these parties and always ready to be friendly was Evalyn Trice, not a single, but popular. She worked as a volunteer at the Institute, and lately usually in Tom's department. She had begun the work through the Junior League, she told Tom, and continued it through her church. She was a pleasant, slender, dark-haired woman, a social figure, he discovered. Her family was an old one in the city; her husband was a successful attorney. She had one daughter.

She teased Tom about his evident attraction to Carter who, in turn, called Evalyn her rival, and declared that she was the woman Tom dreamed about.

He enjoyed this running gag, and warned both women that such talk would get him fired from his job. Personnel would never condone a double-barreled romance within the Center.

Since his friends were almost entirely members of the hospital community, the talk at parties which Tom attended was largely medical. Often, at least when he was a part of it, that talk concerned the Institute.

It was almost a game, he decided, to discuss what the Institute could do, rather than what it already was doing. Suggestions as to its future were made, some of them possible, most of them not. He listened to all that was said; some items he stored away in his mental files for further study, but his own contribution to the talk had resolved into a few dryly humorous remarks about the proscription on romance within the Institute's walls, or even the Center's confines. Silently he argued with what was being said and suggested. He formed likes and dislikes, trusts and mistrusts. He knew definitely what his position was.

But he spoke up only on the matter of romance. "Affairs, to you," he would say. "As a man under orders, I have to avoid sitting at the same cafeteria table every day, or offering a cup of coffee to a nurse three times running."

It became a joke, and people built it up at the parties and at work. Tom wondered if he had started a situation which he could not handle.

"They like something to laugh about," Carter reassured him. "You know? You could be very popular in this city's society, if that should be what you want."

"I don't know much about the city's society, but to be popular—isn't that what everyone wants?"

"Not everyone in medicine," she reminded him.

That was true. "But the world would know about you," he offered for the purpose of discussion.

"Then," she countered, "I suppose the question would be, should we—" her cheeks turned pink—"should *you* let the world in on it?"

"The world," Tom mused. "Look, why don't you come down on my floor at regular intervals and talk to the young people you'll find in the halls?"

She made a face at this prospect. "Don't they know that

tie-and-dye garments can be washed?" she asked.

"Oh, they know everything. Just ask them. You spoke of the world—those kids embrace the world, given the least chance."

On this night, when he returned to his home after the party, he decided that it was fun to be among people. "My peer group," he said dryly, below his breath. But, after partying, he often came home tired, and sometimes his house-keeping got beyond him.

Scooter's Mattie Miller was faithful, and came twice a week to clean and dust, to change his bed, then wash and iron his household linens. But there were other little tasks . . .

Like talking to Caesar, and feeding him. He must remember, within a day or two, to get fresh milk and a supply of cat food. He regarded the animal now as he ate, a handsome creature in black and white, much better off than the waif he had rescued six months ago. "My refugee," he said aloud, amused at himself. He had long wanted to call the cat Sahrman, but he hadn't quite dared. Sometime Sahrman might come to Tom's home, and— Occasionally Tom was afraid of the refugee. Doctor Sahrman, it was, of course. The man himself was persistently on the defensive; Tom had not been able to make friends with him.

He went into the living room and picked up the news-papers and magazines which he had been reading the night before. When the cat was finished, he washed that dish and those left from his own breakfast—he yawned mightily—hours and hours ago. As his mother had used to do, he made things ready for tomorrow's breakfast, not hours and hours away. He filled the coffeepot, put a plate, a cup and saucer, and a glass on the table, covered the dishes with a clean towel.

In her heaven, his mother would be nodding approvingly.

He went upstairs, the cat leaping ahead of him.

His mother had now been dead for almost two years. Tom should have remembered to have a wreath put on her grave. She always had done that for his father's grave at Christmas.

His father. He remembered his father's funeral; he had been ten. And the ceremony at the church, the walking up the hill to the gravesite, sitting and standing beside his mother, decently dressed in black. A small, plump woman, with her dark hair drawn smoothly back under the black hat that Tom did not remember having seen before.

After the service, the assembled friends had all come up for a last word with his mother and Tom. "Be a good boy," each one had said to him. "Take care of your mother."

Tom had been too embarrassed and emotionally torn to say anything, but his mother had replied firmly, composedly. "Tom is a good boy," she had said. "And I'll take care of him now. Later, he will take care of me."

His mother, at least, had fulfilled her obligation. She had nurtured their tiny inheritance from his father, she had worked, first as alteration woman in a dress shop, then in the linen room of a large hospital. She had kept their small house and raised her son, sending him to school, planning for his future.

Tom . . . He remembered the time when he had failed to cut the grass because he had wanted to practice tennis. He had been very good at tennis, and he explained to his mother that it took practice.

Her reply . . . "We are people who must work, Tommie," she had said earnestly. "We must live, and you must learn to be a man. You must have an education. So now we do the things before us, work at the tasks, my son. We can look neither to the right nor to the left."

"But, Mother, there is no fun in that!"

"No, there is not. But there is pride."

He remembered her saying that. Now, ready for bed, he turned off the light, and for a minute stood looking down into the street, brightly lighted with mercury lamps. A wind had risen; a large piece of paper was whirling along the almost empty street. He shivered and got into bed, pulling up the blanket, letting the cat find a snug place at his feet.

During that day . . . and at the party that evening . . . Leaving her, he had kissed Carter. She had talked to him of popularity. It lay within Tom's reach, she thought.

She did not know of the too dearly earned lesson which his mother had begun to teach him. Tom Kelsey was doing well; he wanted to do better. Rain suddenly slapped against the window, and he turned on his side.

## CHAPTER 3

THE DOCTOR DRIFTED into sleep, warm under the blankets of his bed, his feet warmed by the cat who had curled up against them. This was a comforting thing with the sound of rising wind about the house, and the rain beating against the wide window. He hoped it would not turn to sleet or snow before morning.

That was his last conscious thought; he was dead to the world when the telephone rang—and rang a second time before he could prop himself on an elbow, reach for the lamp switch and the persistent telephone.

He croaked when he said "Hello," cleared his throat and tried again.

"Oh, Dr. Kelsey!" said a woman's voice into his ear. "This is Evalyn Trice . . ."

Tom sat up on the side of the bed and rubbed his eyes with his free hand.

Evalyn Trice? He shook his head; he could not place . . . But, yes! The volunteer who served irregularly in his clinic. She worked at the admissions desk, or as a messenger. Mrs. Trice, as slender as a young boy; the pinafore was becoming

to her. *Great day!* She had been at the big party tonight—
he glanced at the clock. Last night. She had worn a bronze-
colored dress, shiny—and she talked about her poodles,
amusingly.

"Mrs. Trice," he broke in on whatever it was she was
saying. "Will you repeat what you told me? I wake up
slowly."

"I'm sorry," she said at once. "It's a terrible hour, I know.
But that's why I got panicky. You see, my husband . . ."

Her husband was a lawyer, Tom thought. Yes! A promi-
nent lawyer. Dr. Bonley had said that he was.

And now Mrs. Trice was telling Tom that they did not
have a family doctor. But tonight Edward had been suffering
severe abdominal pain . . . She got that phrase from her
work at the hospital.

"Perhaps you should bring him to the hospital," Tom told
her.

"You're probably right," Mrs. Trice agreed. "But Edward
won't hear of such a suggestion. Would there be some medicine I could give him to relieve him? What about a hot
water bottle?"

Tom rubbed his eyes again. "No laxative," he said quickly.
"You could—I suppose you have aspirin?"

"Yes, and some Nembutol."

"Good. Give him two Nembutols, and if he is not relieved in three hours, give him another. No hot water bottle,
but keep him warm. And of course see your doctor—or a
doctor—tomorrow."

It was the usual response to a 2 A.M. post-party-belly syn-
drome. Tom hung up, trying to remember if he had ever
met Edward Trice. He probably had; he could even have
talked to the man at last night's party.

He lay down again, Caesar protesting at being pushed

53

around. "Sorry, old chap," said Tom. "I don't like these night calls either. Not on this job."

He wondered why on earth Evalyn Trice had called him. He certainly was not the only doctor she knew. He'd do a little follow-up the next day.

And on that resolution, he fell asleep.

But when the next day came, and it did, all too soon, Tom must think about many, many other things. The Trices completely escaped his mind. He had hardly reached the Institute —he was only halfway through the resident's night report— when word came that Dr. Bonley had been killed.

In a highway accident—as he drove to the Institute that morning. He lived outside the city—someone had entered the freeway, going in the wrong direction—there had been a head-on crash.

Tom could not believe what he heard, or comprehend the fact behind the words.

Bonley—Tom had liked the man. His ability to work and let those under him work. He was a handsome man, not more than ten years older than Tom—he had a family. Oh, this was a shocking thing!

He said so to Sahrman, who came up to him to ask him if he had heard the news. "Shocking," said Tom. "Unbelievable."

Sahrman nodded. "But now would be your chance," he told the other doctor.

Tom stared at him. The news had frightened him. And grief then had come, to lose a colleague, a friend, so suddenly, so needlessly. He was appalled at what Sahrman had said, had suggested.

"Damn you!" he cried, keeping his voice low and tense. "How can you even think of such a thing? A *man* has been killed! Some idiot has killed him, has ended his life's work. Bonley had a family. He has two sons. Young boys who need him. And his wife." He looked across Sahrman's shoulder into Dr. Bonley's office. The morning's mail was still stacked on his desk.

"There's work for Bonley to do right there on his desk!" he cried. "His engagement pad is filled with things he should be doing today. Instead . . . Oh, go on about your work, Sahrman! And try not to speak again as you just spoke to me."

"Okay," said Sahrman. "If that's the way you look at things."

"Well, it is, and you'd damn well better not forget it!"

Tom went about his own work that day and found added to his tasks all the things that came up concerning Dr. Bonley's work and his death. There were many things to do, papers to be found in the doctor's desk; his secretary could help Tom, but she wanted authority from a staff man. He talked to newspapermen about Dr. Bonley's work and his death, all the time in his mind the image of that tall, handsome man, his silvered hair and his deep voice. Tom had liked him. He contributed to the section's memorial fund, vetoing flowers.

And two days later he attended the funeral, clearing a way in the day's busy schedule to be away for the last two hours of the morning.

"Take care of things here," he told Sahrman. "If the Bennett boy comes in, send him up to Seven. Dr. Scott thinks he may be ready for chemotherapy."

Sahrman was watching Tom's face. "You of course think it is the right thing to go to Dr. Bonley's funeral," he said softly.

Tom looked up from the clip board in his hands. Sahrman's smile was knowing. "You should remember," Dr.

Kelsey said stiffly, "that my name was listed with those of others on the Institute staff to attend the funeral."

"I do remember. But you would go anyway, would you not?" It was more a statement than question.

"Yes," said Tom. "I would go."

And he did attend the funeral, wearing his sober charcoal gray suit with a darker gray tie. In the church he sat in a pew with the other doctors, and rode with them to the cemetery, his thoughts on what had happened, and what would happen. His companions talked quietly; Tom had little to say.

It was pouring rain. Literally buckets of water were coming relentlessly from the leaden sky. In the cemetery, the mourners were clumps of mushroomlike umbrellas. Tom was reminded of the play Our Town. He thought about Bonley, pleasant always, with beautiful courtesy to everyone, co-workers and the patients.

In fact, he was the finest man Tom had ever known. Without really knowing him at all, Tom amended his thought. He had never been in Bonley's home. Talking to her briefly at the funeral home was only the second time he had spoken to Mrs. Bonley—Joanne.

The committal service began with dignity and beauty. The white robes of the priest and his acolyte blew in the wind.

". . . suffer us not, at our last hour . . . to fall from thee . . ."

The acolyte stepped forward to sprinkle earth upon the silvery coffin, bare now of the velvet pall which Tom had admired in the church, and the boy stumbed; the priest caught at his arm, for below their feet a crack had appeared, and even as the congregation and the family watched in horror, the earth began to crumble away, and finally to collapse one whole side of the opened grave. The frame sloped and the casket tipped perilously. Tom and Dr. Lewis stepped forward to draw Mrs. Bonley back. Tom spoke to the boys. "Get out as quickly as you can," he said. Someone screamed, someone sobbed. His own voice was drowned in the shouting voices of other men and hysterical women.

In a minute the horror was over. The casket was being carried back to the hearse. Dr. Lewis was supporting Mrs. Bonley, leading her and the boys to the limousine.

Tom was left standing, trembling. He could not possibly have spoken. He never could have told how he returned to the car, whether he got wet or not. But he did reach the car, and got into it, drawing his topcoat about his knees, still shaking. The other men murmured to each other. Tom sat looking out of the window, and for some reason he thought about the time, in his first days at the Institute, when he had sat in the o.r. observation deck and watched Dick Scott do surgery on a man's stomach. The lighting had failed. . . .

And now Tom remembered that time. Then, too, he had been shocked as he was now, ready to protest, to strike out at anyone responsible. Now he felt the same, but why should he connect those two events?

Harold Daives rode back to the Center in the same car with Tom. As the men dispersed on the parking lot, raising their umbrellas, turning up their coat collars, Daives caught his hand through Tom's arm, seeking shelter under his umbrella.

"You're the type to bring one," he told Dr. Kelsey.

Tom made no comment.

"This certainly has been a morning," said Daives. "Only bright spot in all this is that now you'll have a chance for something good. If you want it, that is."

Sahrman had said something of the same thing. But by now Tom had no impulse to curse. Revolted and even frightened, he let Daives precede him into the tunnel, shook out his umbrella and followed him, not having spoken at all.

He returned to the Institute, knowing that it was lunchtime but not at all inclined to eat. There was an accumulation of tasks waiting for him, decisions to be made, talking to be done. Word of the grave collapse had reached the complex, and everyone must speak of it. Even Carter Bass came downstairs to ask Tom about it; then, at sight of his face, she shook her head.

"Of course you don't want to talk about it," she said quickly.

He pushed his fingers through his thick hair. "It's just . . ." he broke off. "Strange things happen," he said. "To me they seem strange . . ."

"What happened this morning would seem strange to anyone, Tom."

"They had a tent. It should not have happened."

"No, it shouldn't have. Look. Have you eaten?"

Tom frowned. "I don't believe I have time."

"You'd better find time for a sandwich, son."

He managed a smile. "I'll send someone after it."

"Sure. Lonnie would be glad to go."

Lonnie did go, and brought back the cheese and ham sandwich, the tall carton-cup of milk which Tom had ordered. Tom thanked him and bent again to the papers which were piled on his desk. Since the Clinic worked with various government programs for the poor, paper work could be overwhelming. He had not yet unwrapped the sandwich when the first telephone call came. There had been others, all routine. But this one—Tom reached for the phone. He listened, his blue eyes widening, then narrowing. Finally he took the phone from his ear and looked at it.

"Is something wrong, Dr. Kelsey?" his secretary asked him.

"I don't know," he told her. "That is, something must be

wrong with me, or with this telephone."

"The call came for you; I just switched it."

Tom looked at the telephone again, and put it down on the cradle. "Maybe I'm crazy," he murmured. "I could have sworn that call came from a racetrack. There were bugles, horses' feet—*They're off!* You know the sort of thing."

"I've never gone to the racetrack," said the girl.

She surely had heard it, though, on radio or TV. Tom had. And it had all been there on the phone. Thoughtfuly, he unwrapped his sandwich, ate it, and drank the milk, his face still puzzled.

He went out into the corridor, he checked the interview rooms, the emergency cubicle, and went on to the wards. He wanted to tell someone what had happened. Anyone he told would laugh at him and say that somebody had been playing a joke.

On him? Why? Well—they got some weird characters here on One. As patients, and as visitors.

He returned to his desk and to his paper work. His secretary said there had been three phone calls while he was gone, all routine. He cared for those calls and picked up his pen.

The telephone buzzed again, and he reached for it. "Dr. Kelsey," he said briskly, and frowned.

He listened for only seconds, his face flushed and his eyes narrowed.

"Is something wrong?" his secretary asked.

Tom put the telephone down hard. "This time I get psychedelic music," he told her. "Loud."

She laughed. "Somebody is being funny, aren't they?"

"Not very," growled Dr. Kelsey. "Why don't you go home, Karen? It's after four."

"But I don't leave until four-thirty." She looked troubled.

Tom nodded. "You're right," he said. "This just seems to

be a long day."

Actually, he wanted to be alone, free to be angry, puzzled —whatever he wanted to be—without some young woman watching his all-too-expressive face. But that damn telephone call . . . He could call the switchboard, but this call, too, must have come in normally.

He got up abruptly and went out of his office. Down the hall, Sahrman was talking to the resident and to Lonnie. Tom wheeled and went the other way; he turned into a side corridor. An old man in a wheelchair came toward him. "You helped my arthuritis a lot, Doc," he said happily. Tom talked to him for a minute, then walked back the way he had come and sat down again at his desk.

But he was always to remember that day and say to himself, "It all began then. And there."

Dr. Bonley had been killed on Tuesday, was buried on Thursday. On Friday morning Tom Kelsey came to work by way of the Clausen Neighborhood Center. He regularly checked that facility, liking the service given there, and wanting it to continue that way. The physicians, residents, and interns assigned to that duty could be good, bad, and indifferent. Tom knew this, and thought they should at least be kept on their toes—expecting a staff visit, he meant.

So many things could come up at Clausen. He liked talking to the patients and to the staff.

His office knew where he was, but even so, Karen protested when he didn't show up in his own office until almost eleven o'clock.

"Dr. Lewis wants to see you right away, Dr. Kelsey," she said reprovingly.

"How right away?" Tom asked. "Does my desk get all the mail for this address?" he asked. Then he glanced at the girl.

"Yes, I do get it now, don't I?" he said quickly. "What does the Director want?"

Up on the top floor of Research, Dr. Lewis held in his hands all the strings, all the threads of the big building and its activities. He knew the name of every aide, staff doctor, intern, student nurse, and what they were doing. He . . .

"He wants to see you as soon as you get back from Clausen," said Karen firmly.

"You told him I was at Clausen?"

"Now, Dr. Kelsey . . ."

He nodded. "I know. I'll go right up." He glanced at the pile of mail again, tugged at the bottom of his jacket, and went to the door. "You could have given me time to put on a white coat," he told Karen. "Maybe he won't know me without my name plate."

When Tom waited at the elevator, Sahrman came along. He didn't speak, just stood watching Dr. Kelsey. He probably knew that the Chief had summoned him. Well, why not? Things on One couldn't be allowed to get too screwed up.

Dr. Lewis was an older man. Sixty, probably. The harpies were always putting him on the retirement list. His face showed his years of hard work in his profession. But he was a good administrator and a good doctor.

This morning he looked up brightly when Tom came into the office.

"I understand you've waited on me," Tom said at once. "I'm sorry."

"You go regularly to Clausen?"

"Frequently rather than regularly, sir. I keep track of the place."

"Good. Like it?"

"Very much," said Tom earnestly. "They are filling a big need, and they work fine with us."

"I agree with you. Sit down." Dr. Lewis tipped back in his chair and gazed at the younger man over the edge of his half-glasses. "We suffered a great loss when Dr. Bonley was killed," he said gruffly.

"Yes, sir, we did." Tom spoke with feeling, and he felt his hair fall across his forehead. He brushed it away with the backs of his fingers.

"As much as we regret his loss," said Dr. Lewis, "his work has to be done. Continued."

Tom chewed at the corner of his underlip. Sahrman had thought of this, and Daives, as well as probably several dozen others. Tom could guess at what was coming.

It did come.

"D'you think you could carry on that work?" asked Dr. Lewis.

"I could try, sir," Tom said hesitantly.

"Someone has to try."

"Yes, sir. But I would like to get one thing straight. I did not want Jim to die so that I could . . ."

"Don't talk nonsense!" cried Dr. Lewis.

Tom took a deep breath. "It wouldn't sound like non-sense to some people," he said firmly.

The Director swung his chair away to gaze at the books which filled the shelves behind him. "I know what you are talking about," he agreed, coming back. "In a place like our Institute, and certainly in the whole Medical Center, jockeying for power is what my grandson would call the name of the game."

Tom smiled faintly. "I'm not very good at that game, sir."

"I didn't think you were. When you came to us, you wanted the boundaries of your job well defined to you. You sounded like a man ready to do that job."

"Thank you, sir."

"But, however much we may regret it, a change has been forced upon us. And right now, before we can make any real plans, we have to fill the gap. So I am asking you if you can carry on for Dr. Bonley."

"Make the decisions," said Tom, as if speaking to himself.

"Yes," agreed Dr. Lewis. "Big decisions and other sorts. In addition you would need to consider overall policy, and decide on particular policies."

Tom could think of an example or two. "I think I know what you mean," he said quietly. "Yes, I could do that, I believe."

"I believe you could, too. You've been with us for seven months; that has given you experience in what the first floor does. You are interested in the work."

Tom looked up, his eyes bright.

"Bonley said to me, several times, that you were a good man. He spoke particularly well of your efforts to provide care for the families who are involved in your department's problems of gathering research material on genetic disorders. It seems you developed ways of combining both things into a single program."

Again Tom took a deep breath. He was glad that he had pleased Bonley. "All right," he said slowly. "I'll try to fill in."

Dr. Lewis nodded. "Thank you, Kelsey," he said warmly. "We'll make things as easy for you as possible."

Even then, they would not be easy. Tom's position would not be permanent; there would be any number of eager beavers striving for the final appointment as Chief of Socio-medical Research. Almost anything Tom did would be judged now as a part of his own striving. And his thoughts flashed to Sahrman. And Daives, who had spoken of his chances.

He started to rise, and sat down again. "There are some

details," he said, speaking hesitantly. "Already. Right now I think of one policy which I have rather formulated and pursued with Dr. Bonley's supervision. My colleague, Dr. Sahrman—" He glanced at the Director inquiringly

Dr. Lewis nodded. "One of our foreign men," he agreed. "In his case, I believe he actually is a refugee. Some of the others are only foreigners working to establish their licenses to practice in this country."

"Yes, sir. Now, Sahrman is a capable doctor. I suppose, in his place, with his education, I too would be resentful of having to spend this rather long time doing work he should be through with."

"Is he difficult to work with?"

"Not really. He does the technical work perfectly. Even with dedication. But he has a quick temper, and what is surprising to me, he does not seem to sympathize with the poor and often grubby people we handle. They sense this—"

"Hmmmn," said Dr. Lewis.

"He does his work," Tom hastened to say. "In fact, he is capable of doing much more work than he does for us. He is a fine diagnostician and surgeon. But he does not like the grubby poor. And so he does not endorse the policy I started to talk to you about."

"Then talk about it," said Dr. Lewis.

"It's a simple thing. But—over at Clausen, and downstairs, too, I have been getting the young people—often members of a sick person's family—to help in the Clinic. I let them help with stretchers, do orderly work; the girls undress and wash old people who can be reluctant before a handsome nurse in a handsome uniform. It began with language barriers. Not only the foreign-born, but some of our own people come from the deep south, and their talk can be hard to understand."

64

"Yes, it can," said Dr. Lewis. "Vocabulary as well as pronunciation."

Tom nodded. "We get all sorts at Clausen," he said. "And that means we get them downstairs. Negroes of every shade in color and behavior. Derelicts from the levee streets, poor whites, the old and disoriented. Hippies. We get hungry teen-agers, and lost ones. Dropouts whose families would dearly love to have them come home. I especially like to put those kids to work. They won't admit it, but they enjoy a shower bath and clean clothes, some decent food. We pay them in that way, largely, with the help of the Auxiliary. We get young people from the so-called communes."

"Here in the city?"

"Oh, yes. They'll take over the top floor of an old loft building, or move into some abandoned warehouse. There is an inner-city church which provides what they call a crash pad. The sick kids will go there, and maybe from there to Clausen. So we reach them.

"Then, in another category, we have the decent poor. Perhaps they are the most heart-touching, sir. A widow with a bunch of children she is trying to keep sheltered and fed. Or an old couple, both sick, but unable to pay for nursing home care on their pension. Oh, we get all sorts, you know."

"And from these, you get the young people to help you?"

"To help themselves, rather," said Tom. "If they can get hep to the healthy body thing, they'll spread the good word. Yes, I do use the young people, wash and tie down their hair, get them some clean threads—clothes, that is."

Dr. Lewis laughed aloud. "I think perhaps you've learned as much as you've taught!" he declared, liking this tall doctor with his mop of dark hair, his earnest eyes, his sensitive mouth. "How long have you been conducting this rehab policy?"

"I began it quite soon after I came here. I wanted to get

some cooperation and interest from the kids who accompany their friends or family members here. They can give us trouble if they decide they should. Dr. Bonley said I could try working with them. Sort of 'if you can't lick 'em, join 'em' philosophy, he called it."

"I think he approved. As I said, he spoke well of you."

"I'm glad," said Tom.

"And if the thing works, I think you should keep at it. Perhaps Dr. Sahrman will come to see . . ."

"I believe the best we can expect there is nonaggression, sir."

"All right. Incidentally, if you've been over at Clausen all morning, perhaps you have not heard that there was a burglary at Dr. Bonley's home last night."

Tom looked shocked. "How could that be?" he asked.

Dr. Lewis shrugged. "It happened. Mrs. Bonley had stayed with a sister for the night. You know, the Bonley home is quite new, and out in the county."

"They have lived there for about three months," Tom agreed

"Yes. But whoever broke in knew where and how to enter through a terrace door. I suspect they knew also that Mrs. Bonley and the boys would be absent. They took the doctor's scarf pin—it had a diamond in it, and had been his father's. He wore it seldom. They took Jim's lodge ring and some cash which he habitually kept on hand in a certain place. They took a mink jacket, one Joanne wore often, but did not take the new one which Jim had given her for Christmas. A better jacket. They—he—she—worked neatly, and did not tear things up because they knew what they wanted and where to find those things. When they left, they turned the bedspread back and folded the sheet and blanket open into a triangle."

Tom shook his head. "That's an incredible story," he said. "An incredible happening."

"Ghoulish," agreed Dr. Lewis. "I've heard of professional thieves reading death notices—but whoever did this job knew the Bonley house, and that she would be away. Knew where the particular valuables were kept."

"There's insurance?"

"Oh, yes. And the company will probably trace the thing down."

Tom went downstairs, thinking hard about the Bonley mystery. He had decided that some of the young people who came to the clinic were responsible for his crazy phone calls —just wanting to bug the doc, or maybe even to be friendly. But the Bonley house . . . Dr. Bonley's widow . . .

He was still shaking his head when he came into his office, and this time he changed into his white coat. Briefly he told his secretary that he was, for the time, filling in Dr. Bonley's place.

"His secretary . . . ?"

"Only if you find the work too heavy. She'll be placed. You've got so you can read my handwriting and know my peculiarities."

"Will you move into the big office?"

Tom shook his head.

"You should, Dr. Kelsey."

"I often don't do what I should, Karen." He hoped she did not realize that he was self-conscious about making too-obvious changes. "I'm only filling in," he said again.

He sat down at his desk and became immediately immersed in the accumulation of work. Almost at once there would be changes in his duties. No longer could he say, "Dr. Bonley will have to decide this." Now Tom Kelsey would have to decide.

The word of his advancement, like the word of the burglary, got quickly about. It was discussed. People came and went, in and out of his office. When he belatedly went down for lunch, a dozen people spoke to him. Even the patients knew, and greeted him with a difference. Not exactly respect or deference. "What'ya say, Doc baby!" could not allow that claim. But there was a difference.

In the cafeteria, a staff doctor introduced Tom to a visiting consultant as "Dr. Kelsey, acting Chief of Sociomedical Research."

And there was a slight difference, though not at all unpleasant, in the way the eminent consultant greeted Dr. Kelsey.

He mentioned this difference to Dick Scott when, among all who came into his office that afternoon, Dick showed up.

Dick had come down, he said, to discuss the Bennett boy. "I think we can safely start chemotherapy again." He looked around him, he went to the door, and looked at its outer surface. "Haven't got around to painting it," he said, coming back.

"Doesn't need painting," Tom told him.

Dick sat down in the chair beside the desk. "I like the couch in the office next door," he said, meaning Bonley's office.

"I do very well without a couch," Tom said. "I don't have as much company, and they don't stay as long."

"Hospitable guy, isn't he?" Dr. Scott asked Karen.

She smiled at him, arranging the forms she was putting under Dr. Kelsey's right hand so that he could sign each paper without moving the individual ones.

He frowned at the top one. "Director?" he asked.

"I checked with Dr. Lewis's office, sir," Karen told him.

"Don't call me *sir!*" cried Tom loudly.

"You do it anyway," Dr. Scott advised her.

"I'll stay over at Clausen," Tom promised. "Calling me 'sir' before I'm old enough, calling me Director when I'm not."

"Making Karen work in the same room with you," Dick added. "Bonley's secretary had her own small anteroom."

"If she complains," said Tom. "Not you, Dick. Karen. If she complains, I'll—"

"Move?" asked Dick brightly.

"No. I'll think about it."

"Damn stubborn Irishman!"

Tom signed his papers.

"Now seriously, Tom," said Dick when he had finished. Tom leaned back in his chair and stroked his forehead with his fingertips. "You should move."

"Dr. Lewis didn't say so."

"It probably never occurred to him that you would stay here."

"I'm only filling in. Did you hear about the Bonley burglary?"

"Yes. A creepy thing. I'd hate to know someone had trespassed on my property, let alone the loss."

"Creepy things happen," said Tom. "What my associates in the halls and wards here call really weird things." Then he smiled wryly. "D'you know," he asked Dick, "my patients—the best they could find to say about Bonley's being killed was that it was 'bad news'?"

"For them that could cover a ghastly murder, couldn't it?"

"It did," said Tom, deep lines between his eyes.

"Your people," said Dick. "As you call them. Won't they consider it a put-down if you don't move into the Chief's office?"

Tom considered this, his eyes drawn to slits. "They might . . ." he decided.

"Then you will move?" asked Dick, thinking he had clinched his argument.

But Tom shook his head. "Not unless my desk here won't hold the work," he said.

Dick walked to the door, promising to continue the argument.

"Okay," said Tom. "Just keep it friendly and short."

He bent again to his work, only to have Dr. Sahrman come in.

"What is it, Sahrman?" he asked, not looking up.

Sahrman did not answer at once, and Tom sighed, laid down his pen, and sat erect. "D'you have problems?" he asked.

"No. But I could not help but overhear some of the things which Dr. Scott was saying to you."

"And my side of the conversation as well?"

"Yes, sir. And I have just one question to ask you, Dr. Kelsey."

"Fine. Ask it."

"It is this: should you not agree with Dr. Scott?"

Tom glanced at Dick, and found him smiling. He smiled, too. "Not when I don't agree with Dr. Scott," he told Sahrman. "And I often don't."

"But, Dr. Kelsey . . ."

Tom began to check and sign the admissions slips which had accumulated on his desk, along with some dismissals and transfers.

"Dr. Kelsey is right," Dick was telling Sahrman. He doesn't and shouldn't give me lip service. I mean, seem to agree when he does not."

"He's impressed with the fact that you are Chief of Cancer Research," Tom said, not looking at the two men.

"Sometimes I am impressed with that myself," Dick assured him. "I think the trouble with you, Sahrman, is that we Americans can be impressed and not show it. We consider that it doesn't need emphasis. Then there is another thing. Here at Research, and this applies to all of us, we are a big glass and steel think-tank."

"Tell him what that means," said Tom, stacking the admissions slips, ready to tackle the dismissals.

So Dick endeavored to tell Sahrman, who spoke and understood English very well but often found slang incomprehensible.

"We encourage differing ideas," Dick concluded. "Dr. Kelsey can disagree with me and still be my friend and an amicable co-worker. This applies to all sorts of matters. Professional things connected with our work—such as the recent discussion as to whether he should move into Dr. Bonley's office. We can equally disagree on the merits of striped shirts, or the value of using extreme methods to prolong the life of an eighty-year-old woman dying of cancer. He doesn't agree with me about large parties, the war in Viet-Nam, or on schools. And he says so."

"I know that he does," said Sahrman. "And it would seem to me that he will, quite soon perhaps, hurt his career by saying so." He walked out of the office and turned down the corridor.

Dick and Tom looked at each other. "Does he deplore or anticipate your crash course?" Dick asked Tom.

Dr. Kelsey shrugged.

"He's a strange sort of guy, isn't he?" Dick asked.

"Well," said Tom, "he's had a hard time."

"Who hasn't?"

"I don't mean that sort of hard time, Dick. For instance, here comes this acting-Chief situation. Sahrman's been here much longer than I have. But he knew, as a foreign doctor establishing his residence, that he had no chance whatsoever to get the appointment."

Dick again moved to the door. "Lewis chose the better man," he said firmly.

Among all the other duties which Tom had taken over from Dr. Bonley was a schedule of speeches and appearances he must make to "sell" the Sociomedical Center to the neighborhood, the city, and the nation. He would need, he immediately found, to fight for his department in the staff meetings which were regularly held. Bonley had promised to appear that same week at a round-table information program on TV.

Tom was sure that he would not make the appearance Bonley would have made.

"You're pretty enough," Dick assured him, "though do try not to scowl. Just concentrate on all you have to say about the health standards of the nation not having a chance to be raised unless medical care is made accessible to the poor."

"In neighborhoods where it is needed," Tom rose to the bait, but grinning in acknowledgment of the bait. "I suppose I bore everyone."

"You're supposed to bore everyone. And be sure to tell 'em that Clausen is the realization of that concept. The ideal health center."

"We need others."

"You say that on TV," said Dick, laughing. "And make the speeches, too."

Tom would agree to the speeches, though he balked on any engagement that was not of professional nature. He staunchly proclaimed that he was no do-gooder.

What was he, then?

"A scientist, interested in raising the national, and local, health standards."

That would be good enough. And it was good enough. After the TV round table, he immediately found himself in demand on his own rights. He would have to make some decisions, he thought, about the time he could afford to give to such things, about his clothes. Appearance was important. Just keeping his fresh shirt supply . . .

Pondering this problem, rather than the reports which were on his desk, he looked up at Karen, who was bringing the midmorning cup of coffee, along with the news that there had been another burglary.

Tom frowned. "Another . . . ?"

"Like the one at Dr. Bonley's," she told him.

"Oh." Tom sipped his coffee. "Someone we know?"

"Well, not really." Karen was a dark, vivid girl with a pretty young body and a freshly pretty face. This morning she wore a pink blouse with her dark blue skirt. Bonley's secretary had been an older woman, but Tom was well satisfied with the work which Karen did and the way she prettied up his office.

Now she was talking fast, telling him about the burglary. It had happened, she said, in one of the tall, handsome houses on Virginia Avenue, three blocks from the edge of the University Hosiptals complex. A number of staff doctors lived in those houses.

"They used the same m.o. as at Bonley's," Karen told him. "That means manner of operation, Dr. Kelsey."

"I watch 'Dragnet' sometimes," he agreed.

"Well—they entered through a basement window, they took a fur stole and a few other things, but not as much of a haul as at Bonley's."

Tom chuckled.

"But they left the bed in the master bedroom turned down

the same way. And, oh, yes, Dr. Kelsey, this house is the one where Dr. Lewis used to live." Karen's eyes rolled ceiling-ward.

Tom set his coffee cup down.

"I think," said Karen, "we girls think, that it was someone who didn't know the Director had moved to the hotel last fall, but did know his habits, that he always goes to the medical society meeting on the third Monday, and his wife baby-sits for their daughter's children. So the house would be empty, and it was, anyway, for the new people."

"Is the new owner a doctor?" Tom asked, feeling the prickles and bumps of coincidence or meaning in these bur-glaries.

"No. He's a musician with the Symphony. Plays a cello, I think. But don't you believe these burglars were the same as robbed Bonley's?"

"Could be, Karen," Tom agreed. "The police probably are considering that angle. I hope they can discover who the per-son is."

"They don't leave fingerprints," said Karen. "Dr. Kelsey, do *you* think it is someone connected with the Institute?"

Tom looked up in surprise. "Why should it be?"

"Well, Dr. Bonley and Dr. Lewis . . . One of the girls thinks it might be one of our hippies."

*Hippies* was a generic term that covered a large segment of the people who came to One. "I don't think that washes, Karen," Tom told the girl. He hadn't given the matter enough thought to be himself convinced. "Our 'hippies,' as you call them, wouldn't know about turning back a bed."

"No, and they wouldn't be neat, either," said Karen, satis-fied to go back to work. "And I guess," she added to her dis-cussion, "it would have to be someone who didn't know that the Lewises had moved."

"Who has moved?" asked Dr. Sahrman, who had come into the office in time to overhear her last words.

"The Director," said Karen, again looking upward to the top-floor office. "Dr. Lewis."

Sahrman was surprised. "He no longer lives on Virginia Avenue?" he asked, having a little trouble with the *v*. "When did this happen? Where does he now live?"

Karen's fingers flew across the typewriter keys. Perhaps she had not heard him. Tom could pretend that he had not. He had enough work on his desk to make the show convincing. But he was troubled about the things that had been happening. The telephone calls, the burglaries—"Creepy," he said below his breath.

"Dr. Sahrman." He spoke aloud. "Would you find it convenient to go over to Clausen about eleven o'clock? With me?"

Dr. Sahrman did not turn from the file cabinet. "I cannot see why both of us would be needed," he said. There was the faintest tinge of—well—opposition? Disagreement?

Tom could not have identified the shading of tone. For the past days he had been uncomfortably aware that Sahrman was not in sympathy with him. Perhaps not actually fighting him, but—"If eleven would not be convenient," he said crisply, "find time during the day, will you, please?"

"Yes, Dr. Kelsey. I shall arrange to be free at eleven o'clock."

Tom nodded and glanced at Karen. She would remind him.

At eleven, Dr. Sahrman came to Tom's office. He wore his overcoat, knowing that Kelsey liked to walk over to Clausen. Tom did. He enjoyed going that mile through the city streets, through what had once been a good middle-class neighborhood but which now had decayed into ghetto and slum. Dirty sidewalks, broken windows, garish signs on stores now empty. Big houses where a dozen families lived, two- or four-family flats, the stone work no longer scrubbed to a gleaming white. The attempts by the city to reclaim this district, the small neighborhood park with a jungle gym and a row of swings, two of them broken. There was a housing development—a high-rise apartment house and some duplex town houses with a real effort made toward respectability, but not always achieving that, or even safety. Tom had been warned that the district could be dangerous. On this misty morning, various people spoke to him. Three youths lounging on a corner were overly cordial. "How ya, Doc man! Ya got any pills for what ails me?"

Tom grinned and made some reply, walking steadily on his way. Sahrman drew the collar of his coat higher about his ears and said nothing.

Tom spoke to a storekeeper; he spoke to two women taking a basket of clothes to the laundromat. He opened the glass door of Clausen Center, and the men went inside.

"These wide, clear halls," he told Sahrman, "are a rarity among institutions for the poor." The floors were clean, light reflected brightly from them, and from the walls.

Sahrman said nothing.

"We have a meeting," Tom explained. "Down this way."

"Complaints," said Dr. Sahrman.

"It would seem so," Tom agreed. "I've asked for some staff people. And of course the patients involved."

"Why should they be consulted?" asked Sahrman.

"Because Clausen belongs to them, not to us." Tom's voice was firm.

He opened the door of the small staff room and found that his meeting was already assembled. Time was not to be lost. Dr. Kelsey and Dr. Sahrman could not both be away from the

Institute for long. At the table were seated an intern, a resident, one of the physicians assigned to the Center, the manager, and the nurse supervisor, Mrs. King, who was the stereotype of her class—stereotype because actually so many women in nursing for twenty years did tend to become like others of like experience. Mrs. King was a large, strong-appearing woman; her voice was a bit louder than it really needed to be. Her hair was waved and set firmly below her white cap, and her uniform was as starched-seeming as cardboard. But she was an excellent supervisor. Doctors came to lean on her type.

Against the wall, seated in a row, were a dozen of the people to whom Tom said Clausen belonged. Young and old, they sat alertly, a little nervously, but with determination in each face. Three of these people were white, the others were black, which fairly represented the population of that district.

Tom said "Good morning" impartially, and took off his topcoat. The intern hung it on a pole coatrack; Dr. Sahrman's coat went there, too.

Tom sat down at the table and asked if they could get down to the business at hand at once. "Every one of us is needed somewhere else," he acknowledged.

The manager of the Center cleared his throat. "I believe Mrs. King can state our main problem," he said.

"I can state it, too," said the black woman who sat, dead center, in the row of chairs. She was large, full-busted, her upper arms straining the sleeves of her pink sweater. She was in her thirties, and promised to be aggressive.

"Would you get it said more quickly, Mrs. Bullock?" Tom asked her. He made a point of learning names where he could.

"I know what's goin' wrong," she told him.

Tom glanced at Mrs. King, who nodded.

"All right, Mrs. Bullock . . ."

Sahrman had not sat down; he lounged against the wall behind Dr. Kelsey.

Mrs. Bullock glanced up at him, then spoke directly to Tom. "I understand you're boss-man here now, Kelsey," she said.

Tom shook his head. "No, Mrs. Bullock. But I am acting Chief of the Research department, and, yes, of Clausen as well."

"Say it your way," she agreed. "You been here how long?"

"Acting Chief for a few days, but I've worked with the Institute and Clausen for seven months. About that."

"Yeah. And I remember when you first come here, you said the rules would be about the same. Right, Kelsey?"

"Yes . . . So far as possible."

Every one of the people in the chairs was watching Mrs. Bullock alertly. Sometimes one or the other would murmur a word or two. But she evidently was in charge of the delegation. "Okay," she said now. "I asked to talk to you, and you said I could."

"Get on with it, Mrs. Bullock," said Mrs. King.

Tom drew a pad of paper toward him and took his pen out of his coat pocket.

"Okay," agreed Mrs. Bullock. She hitched forward on her chair. "Now one rule here at Clausen is that we folks get appointments for seeing the docs, or for shots and stuff. Right?"

"Yes. You ask for, and get, appointments."

"And nobody goes in ahead of you."

"Well, sometimes you have to wait a little."

"Waiting sometimes we understand. But a fella walks in and gets attention—"

"Was he bleeding to death?" asked Tom.

Everyone laughed.

"The rule about appointments should be observed," said Tom. He made a note on the pad.

"Okay, Doc. We hear you."

"Any other gripe, Mrs. Bullock?" Tom asked.

"Yes, Doc, there is. There's this small matter of our seeing the same doctor each time we come in. Ain't that the rule?"

"Unless we lose the doctor, or it's his off day."

"Yeah, yeah, we could understand that. But when I come here with my kid or my mother, or send Leroy over to have his arm dressed—our doctor is Duclos—or so I was told. Our family doctor is Duclos. Right?"

"Yes, Mrs. Bullock."

"Well, each one of us, this past week," said Mrs. Bullock, sweeping her large arm and hand along the row of waiting patients, "we ain't been gettin' our family doctor. It's the old take-'em-as-they-come rule around here lately. Just like it is down at City."

Tom frowned. He sat up straight. But this was wrong . . .

"How did that come about?" he asked Mrs. King.

"I told them to hurry things up," said Dr. Sahrman. "This Dr. Duclos—if he is busy—any doctor can dress a cut on a boy's arm." Only his tone said *black boy*.

Tom was angry. He took two deep breaths. He wrote something on the pad of paper. Then he smiled at Mrs. Bullock and her companions.

"There has been a misunderstanding," he said. "I have been busy. You know about Dr. Bonley's death. Dr. Sahrman, as you also know, sometimes has difficulties with our language."

Behind him, Dr. Sahrman made some sound. Tom did not flick an eyelash.

"I think you can all go home now, Mrs. Bullock," he said pleasantly. "The rules will not be changed after this. Thank you for calling the situation to my attention. A mistake was made, and we are sorry.

He stood while the patients filed out—the clean old man who walked with two canes, the pregnant girl of fourteen, Mrs. Bullock . . . He went over and closed the door, turned and stood against it. His blue eyes were blazing.

"You know the rules as well as they do," he told the staff members present. "We are here to care for the poor and the sick of this district. Efficiency is a help; speed is not. The patients are our first consideration; the staff is second. Visits are by appointment; the patients sees the same doctor each visit. Records are kept on a family basis. The philosophy at this clinic is the philosophy of the Institute: personalized family care. We want the patients to identify with the doctor, and the doctor, whenever at all possible, on a continuing basis, to serve the family."

He stopped and looked around the room. Each face told of the arguing there had been during the past week. "Are there any questions?" he asked briskly.

No one spoke. Tom went to the coat tree and took down Sahrman's coat and his own. Mrs. King helped him with his. "Come again, Dr. Kelsey," she said softly.

"I'll be happy to, Mrs. King." He let Sahrman precede him through the door.

"He sure threaded a lot of needles this morning," said the intern before the door was completely closed.

"I'm glad I don't have to walk back to the Institute with him," another voice agreed.

Perhaps some of the staff would have been surprised to know that Tom did not speak of the matter again to Dr. Sahrman. He talked a little about the burglary of the night before and at the Bonley home earlier. For most of the time, he strode along the sidewalks, crossed the streets, thinking.

For one thing, though grudgingly, and for the first time, he was being glad that he had been given the authority to handle that morning's problems.

On their return to Research, Sahrman went to lunch, and Tom went to his office, where he dictated a brief summary of the complaint.

Waiting for Sahrman, or Karen, to return, though that was not necessary, Tom washed his hands, put on his white coat, and went down along the corridors, looking in on the patients, watching one being interviewed—getting a family history could take time, patience, and humor—and checked the in-patient charts at the desk. The nurse there, and the intern, asked him what had blown up at Clausen.

Tom looked up absent-mindedly. "Only me," he said after a pause. "I was feeling uppity because of my present status as acting Chief."

The intern laughed.

"Is Dr. Sahrman back on the floor?" he asked.

He was.

"Good. I'll go get my lunch."

"You won't like it," the intern promised.

"I don't expect to," Tom called over his shoulder.

He had eaten his split pea soup and his cheese sandwich, but his cookies and custard still remained untouched when his name came over the squawk box.

"We should get pocket beeper service," said one of the doctors he passed on his way to the house phone.

"I don't have any empty pockets," Tom told him.

"There is an urgent outside call for you, Dr. Kelsey," the operator said to him.

Tom had his hand over his right ear to shut out the dining room noise. "I'll try to take it," he decided. As he waited, he waved to Carter Bass, who had just come into the dining room. He could take his cookies to her table. . . .

"Hello!" he said then alertly. "Oh, yes, Mrs. Trice." He listened, surprise, shock, guilt crossing his face.

"Oh, but I am sorry," he said. "Is your husband still at home?" Tom had told the woman to get a doctor on the case. He had not followed up. Though he did not take private patients, he should have . . . perhaps . . .

"Has he been sick for this past week?"—the week during which Tom had been so damn busy. Mountains, literally, had fallen on him. But if Trice really had lost the use of his legs . . . This was bad!

Evalyn Trice was talking. Yes, her husband had continued to feel bad. At first he had felt weak—she had thought it a leftover from his stomach ache—she had called Tom for that, he would remember.

"And I told you to have a doctor see him the next day."

"Edward wouldn't hear of it. But he got weaker, until he couldn't walk. We both thought he had the flu, and he already was staying in bed."

Tom definitely should have checked on the man!

"Now"—her voice dropped so that Tom could scarcely hear her—"I'm afraid his legs are paralyzed, Dr. Kelsey. I'm frightened."

So was Tom. It took a real effort for him to speak quietly to Mrs. Trice. "I am going to send an ambulance to your house at once," he said. "Give me your number there. You come to the emergency room with Mr. Trice. Try to keep calm; things will be taken care of."

He ordered the ambulance; he alerted emergency and told what little he knew of Mr. Trice's case.

Abandoning his custard and cookies, he went back to his office. He had some heart tests on Clausen children scheduled for that afternoon. Kids—and EKGs—he hoped he could make things go well.

They would, he felt. Of course he had dozens of families with heart disease and failure in the picture. He was hopeful that the heart researchers were right, that the tendency to future trouble could be detected early.

The children came in, not half as apprehensive as were their parents. But if Dr. Kelsey said the kids needed to have all this done to them—Joey didn't have no heart trouble, his Momma knew that! Yes, she had what Dr. Duclos called a murmur, and her Momma did have a bad heart—but Joey—

Joey was not at all concerned. His eyes as big as walnuts in his handsome little face, he submitted to being partially undressed; he lay down on the table. Yes, he would too lie still! He giggled a little at the straps, the abrasive salve—he watched the machine with some doubt—but no, it didn't hurt. Dr. Kelsey said it needed as many wires as a radio to get his heart to talk.

This impressed Joey, and he lay very still. The stylus went across the tape, up and down, busily—and the ceiling lights went out. The machine stopped, the technician made a sound of protesting dismay.

"Joey, did you do something?" cried Joey's mother.

Tom gritted his teeth and tried to reassure both the child and the mother. These power failures happened, he said.

They certainly did. The lights flickered and came on. It did seem that in a multimillion-dollar building like the Institute, the lighting could be made reliable!

The heart testing took an hour or more. Midway, Tom got to a phone and asked if Mr. Trice had been admitted. Yes, he was at the diagnostic center.

Talking, Tom frowned at the slip of paper he saw tucked between the telephone and the wall. It appeared to be a sales slip or an adding machine tape. Written on the back, in the manuscript printing so many young people used nowadays, was a weird sentence.

BLACK IS BEAUTIFUL

WNWD

BUN

BEAUTIFUL IS GI GU

Tom read it, then crumpled it in his hand. No child had printed that. He went back to work.

The examinations over, he went into the same corridor, a dozen EKG strips in his hand, and, still curious about that silly, cryptic message, he glanced at the wall phone.

"Well, I'll be damned!" he muttered.

For there, in the same place, was another bit of paper. This was yellow, torn from a larger sheet, but still printed.

SYRINGOMYELIA

I LOVE YOU

THE DISEASE IS DEVELOPMENTAL IN NATURE

Tom stared at the printed words. They didn't make sense. Individually each word and phrase did. A little. But the whole thing . . .

A code?

The Research Institute did not run to medically knowledgeable juveniles. Was some adult playing games? A game? What game? And with whom?

He stood thoughtful, his dark eyes gazing down along the corridor. He could ask someone. Yes, and have his own sanity suspect.

Or . . .

He walked a few feet toward his office. Stopped short. He tore the end from the botton paper clipped to the board which he carried. He took out his pencil, clicked the point free, and he wrote

PUDENAL BLOCK

SCOPOLAMINE

NO DEMEROL

He tucked his scrap of paper between the wall and the telephone.

Before he reached his office, he thought, "I should have printed that fool thing. Everyone knows my handwriting." He shrugged and decided to get some work done, then go over to see about Trice. That case was on his mind.

He began to work—mail—telephone messages—the records from the heart tests—

Within the hour two people came into the office. The resident wanted to know why he did not recommend Demerol for pudenal anesthesia.

Tom stared at him.

"I thought it was routinely used for difficult deliveries, Dr. Kelsey," the young doctor persisted.

"I believe it is. Though it doesn't really deaden pain so much as it creates a euphoric sensation of not caring about the pain."

The resident had departed before Tom recalled his fool note.

When a nurse arrived to ask him if he was counterordering Demerol in spinal anesthesia, he was ready for her. He asked where she had got the idea. Had she had such a direct order? He said a little more.

"I am no game player," he told himself solemnly. People took his contributions too seriously.

He was still trying to work and simultaneously consider the

puddle in which he found himself playing when Carter Bass stuck her head in the door. "End of the day, Doctor!" she said cheerily.

Tom held his head in both hands. "It couldn't come too soon!"

She came in and sat down in the chair beside his desk. "Karen gone?"

"She had some papers to take around and I told her to get on home when she was through."

"What's wrong with you?" Carter asked him.

So Tom told her briefly. About Clausen and Sahrman—Carter had heard of that. Others thought he had handled it well.

"Save your praise," Tom advised. And he told her about the notes. "I had no reason to think the things were meant for me," he said earnestly. "It was someone with an enlarged sense of humor—that has no place in our work. I had no business trying to play a game I knew nothing about."

"But, Tom, as Chief . . ."

"I have to take notice, yes. But I don't have to out-idiot the others on my staff." He was bothered; she could see that he was.

Then he recalled the lighting failure. "I keep thinking someone is trying to bug me," he told her.

"Why?"

"Well, it's that, or they want me reduced to a state of gibbering foolishness. I must have raised their hopes with the Demerol thing. I'll never get rid of that, Carter."

"Oh, yes, you will. But, Tom, if there is some connection between these various things—"

"They are all creepy."

"Yes, they are. And maybe we can find a pattern."

"We?"

"I'd like to help you. Together we could watch, and probably see what is going on."

He smiled at her and began to put papers back into his desk. "I'd like that," he said. "Though there is every chance that I am borrowing trouble when the dear Lord knows I have enough of that already on hand."

He stood up. "Look," he said. "It has been a long day. Would you want to walk home with me and have a drink?"

She smiled. "Why, Doctor, I'd love it! I'll sign out, and you can change your coat. I'll meet you at the big front door."

He liked Carter, he told himself, changing his coat.

The lights of the city sparkled against the glass of the "big front door"; he put his hand companionably through her arm as they went down the walk, between the clipped yews, and waited on the traffic light at the corner. "I'll drive you back for your car," he promised. "You know? I've been thinking about how well we get on together, and how much I like you."

"That's good thinking," she said warmly. "Continue, Doctor."

Above and around them rose the windowed buildings of the various hospital units, so familiar to them that they did not notice them. The wide city streets skirted the complex.

"And then," Tom continued, "I wondered if my mother would have liked you, too."

She glanced at him. "That's a big item in your life, isn't it, Tom? Your mother, and her approval."

He nodded. "Yes. For a time—quite a long time—I thought it was too big an item."

They reached another cross street and turned down along the far side of it, coming to the neat row of red brick and white window-framed houses where Tom lived. He took out his keys and unlocked his front door. "That's a very masculine thing to do," said Carter.

Tom glanced at her. "You do it."

"I don't like doing it."

"Well!" He pushed the door open; Caesar came bounding out, greeting Tom with a loud *meow*, raced down the steps and along the front walk. His black tail waved high.

"Will he be safe?" Carter asked.

"He's a city cat. Everyone else should be wary. By dinner-time—he has a built-in chronometer—he'll be on the kitchen window sill." Having turned on the hall light, he stepped aside so Carter could precede him. The house was warm. They dropped their coats on a chair, and Carter followed Tom to the kitchen, where he got glasses down from a cupboard.

"You're a good housekeeper," she told him.

"Mrs. Miller keeps me that way."

He knew her taste, and the drinks were quickly made. They went to the living room, where he turned on lamps. There was a blue couch and a deep yellow armchair. A brightly patterned rug on the floor.

"My mother," Tom said, gazing across at Carter, "took seriously the fact that she had a son to raise. And she raised me. There was an insurance policy for my education, but, of course, I had to be held to the purpose. My father had died when I was ten. She worked hard to keep us in safety and some respectability. She expected me to do no less."

"Did you?" asked Carter, turning her glass against the light.

"I wasn't a bad son," Tom assured her. "But by the time I reached med school, I discovered that there were girls about."

Carter chuckled. "I'll bet."

He smiled. "There was one girl," he said. "A very pretty girl. And I became fascinated by her."

"And your mother . . . ?"

He nodded. "Yes, my mother rebuked me. No, she scolded me. She was a small woman, came up somewhere between my elbow and shoulder, but I had an almighty respect for her. So when she scolded, I listened. She pointed out to me what this fascinating girl was. What she was, even by my mother's count, was young and gay; she wanted to have fun. But then my mother went on to remind me of what my duties were. I still had several years of training before me, and if I hoped to be any kind of doctor . . .

"She didn't ever mention my duty to her. But that duty was there, I well knew. So real an obligation that I could see how a pretty girl could steer me away from performing it." He sipped from his glass. "There, too," he said ruefully, "I probably was borrowing trouble."

Carter tucked a velvet pillow between her shoulders and looked at the books on his shelves, at the carved-wood duck decoys which served to prop those books upright. "Did I once hear you say you had your mother's furniture here in your home?" she asked.

"Yes. It was hers."

"Then tell me. Did she buy that glowing yellow chair you are sitting in?"

Tom rubbed his palm along the yellow chair's wide arm. "Not really," he said. "That is, she bought the chair at a sale, but it used to be a serviceable dark green. I had it recovered."

Carter smiled at him. "Your mother raised a very nice boy," she said softly. She finished her drink and stood up. "I really must be getting home," she said

Tom drove her back to her car in the Institute's parking lot and returned, thinking steadily about Carter Bass. He liked her, he liked being with her and talking to her. He could be frank and honest, and never fear that she would violate his trust in her, nor take undue advantage.

Now there was a phrase! What in hell did it mean? In this world of give and take between men and women, why shouldn't the woman take any advantage she could get?

He went about preparing his dinner. Tom liked to cook, and his mother had taught him to do the simpler things well. What with the modern convenience foods, and such skill as he had, there was no trick to being a bachelor.

His mobile mouth quirked. Trick, indeed! He didn't so especially want to remain a bachelor. Right at this minute, it would be very pleasant to return to his glowing yellow armchair and hear a girl—a woman—in the kitchen, clanging a pan against the stove burner, slamming the oven door, running the can opener. He was at an age where he should be seriously considering such an arrangement.

The Personnel office had considered that fact when, last summer, the Director had talked to Dr. Kelsey about office romances. Had he had someone like Carter in mind as being dangerous for the new staff man?

More likely, he had been thinking of a girl like Karen, with her pretty legs, her flipping blue skirt and pink blouse, the rolled scarf which tied her dark hair.

Personnel—Tom let Caesar in through the kitchen window —Personnel had said that office romances were costly because the work of the individual suffered. Did it? Would it? If a chick like Karen were involved, perhaps it would suffer. But with Carter—no. She was interested in Tom's work, and would want to help him.

Office affairs were costly because "the morale of the other employees was hurt."

Various females smiled upon Dr. Kelsey. Volunteers, record clerks, nurses, the unmarried sisters and cousins of his friends . . . and Carter. At least he had been friendly. But certainly there was nothing like romance. Not yet.

CHAPTER 4

EACH DAY was different, each day was busy, the tasks and events varying. On one day Tom had had that silly battle of silly memos, and had been disturbed about it.

On the next day there were other, and more important, developments. As acting Chief of Sociomedicine, he attended a staff meeting, and at the conclusion he asked Dr. Lewis if he could be given a few minutes. Dr. Lewis nodded and led the way to the rear and private door of his office.

Tom followed, stealing a glance out through the high windows at the panorama of the city below them. This was a rainy morning, almost springlike. Mists and what could be clouds drifted across the view.

"Do you have a problem, Kelsey?" Dr. Lewis asked, reading the memos which his secretary had left for him.

"This place abounds with problems, sir," Tom replied. "But I haven't brought one of mine to you."

"Good. What did . . . ?"

"I have a request, sir." He paused and looked somewhat anxiously into the weathered face of the Director of Research.

"Is the name of Dr. James Hubbell familiar to you, sir?" he asked.

Dr. Lewis leaned his head back and half closed his eyes. "James Hubbell," he repeated thoughtfully. "A lot of doctor's names go across this desk, Tom."

"Yes, sir, I know. But Hubbell . . ."

"Hubbell," said Dr. Lewis again. Then he lifted his head and looked sharply at Tom. "Is he the one . . . ?" he asked.

Tom nodded. "Yes, sir, he's the one. He was accused and convicted; he served the time allotted as punishment, and now he's out, but he has no job. I wonder if he might not be given some sort of work here at the Institute?"

Dr. Lewis pursed his lips. "Medicine makes for a vulnerable environment, Tom," he reminded the younger doctor.

"Yes, sir, I know. I've only just met Hubbell myself, but I understand he was a specialist in diabetes . . ."

"And good, as I remember. But I think his license . . ."

"Was revoked. Yes, sir."

"Then he can't practice medicine."

"No, sir. Just or not, that is a fact we'd have to deal with."

Dr. Lewis studied Tom's face. "Would Hubbell want to work in a hospital, Tom?" he asked.

"I don't know."

"Giving him a job—if we could and he would want it— Might his presence mean trouble with others? High or low in position?"

"I don't know, Dr. Lewis. Trouble can crop up where least expected. But then, there's been a little trouble for me, too."

Dr. Lewis looked surprised. "Really?" he asked incredulously.

"Maybe not really." Tom laughed. "But I would like to offer Hubbell a chance to get back into the rarefied atmosphere of medicine."

92

"Humph!" said Dr. Lewis. "If you can find any such air . . . Suppose you talk to the man, find out just how interested he might be. I will say that I admire the spirit in which you are doing this, Tom."

"I may be out on a brittle limb myself someday."

Dr. Lewis nodded and picked up his telephone. Tom departed.

Using a corridor house phone—after the weird-o notes, he did this warily—he told Karen that he was going over to University, meaning the big main hospital of the Complex. The evening before, he had talked to Edward Trice's attending resident, and had promised to look at his admission this morning. Technically, because of that admission, Trice was his patient, and the earliest thing Tom wanted to do was to transfer the case to a staff man. This should not take long, he told himself, glancing up at the clock on the tunnel wall.

He did not know Edward Trice as a well man. This fact alone made his present situation difficult. A dozen times he had regretted ever seeming to take on this patient. But the thing had happened, and there was his name on Trice's chart at the nurses' station.

Tom read the whole thing, and whistled soundlessly. Trice did seem to be in a bad way. The muscles of the trunk and arms were now affected. . . .

The nurse had told him that the floor resident wanted to consult, and now that doctor approached, introducing himself to Dr. Kelsey. The man was, probably, in his second or third year of residency, a capable doctor. His name was Brooks. "Have you seen your patient?" he asked Dr. Kelsey.

"No. In fact—" And Tom went on to tell the story of his brief medical attendance on Mr. Trice. "I shouldn't have prescribed over the telephone," he concluded. "I plan to transfer him at once to a staff doctor."

"We get caught into things," said Dr. Brooks sympathetically. "Let's go look at Trice; the paralysis is advancing. We expect it to proceed next to his throat and his speech."

Tom made a sound of regret. "I do wish I had handled the thing differently."

"Could you?" asked Dr. Brooks. "I mean, hit the way you were."

Tom mentioned the coincidence of Bonley's death.

"And Mrs. Trice did not call in a doctor as you advised."

"Yes, there was that. I still should have found time to check on him."

Fifteen minutes later, Tom went back to Research, shaking his head all the way—at himself, and at the prospect for Edward Trice. What would Tom be able to say to Evalyn?

There was plenty for him to do in his own department quickly to divert his mind. In the matter of family research, the ghetto people with whom he worked could present some unexpected, even improbable, hazards.

"They say all they want from Clausen"—he would tell his colleagues, and his friends Carter and Dick Scott particularly—"at least, the three most important things they want are to be treated 'nice,' which I find means like living human beings; second, they want attention within a reasoable time, and third, they want to have a physician they can consider their own.

"But so far as I am concerned, I could wish also that they might bring me a recognizable family tree instead of the puzzle we so often get."

"Do they know about their ancestry, Tom? I mean, if reading and writing is a problem . . ."

"I get that, of course. But sometimes they do know. They just have trouble telling the story so I will know."

"Oh, well, then you're the problem."

He could have been. But this morning he was trying to

make some sort of family chart for a—family?—named Light. Self-respecting, ready to work and pay their bills. But—

A history of aneurysm seemed to run through that family, and Tom knew that he could not expect to research beyond the grandparents. But even then— The second generation was known as the Nickells—a son living in Chicago, two daughters in Cleveland, twin daughters here in the city, patients of Clausen Center. One twin, Glenda, had just died of an aneurysm. The mother, Margaret Light, seemed probably to have one, and, she said her Momma "was took that way, too."

All right. Tom would begin with the mother of Mrs. Light.

Why Light, if the children were called Nickell?

Well, after she came here, she took up with Light. Nick was her children's papa.

There seemed to be no offspring by Light.

But there was Glenda and Donna, the twins. Glenda had married, two children survived her, and four natural grandchildren, one foster child. Glenda's son was in prison for life, so there were no names to add to his line. Or were there? Could the foster child . . . ?

Of course the aneurysm thing was of prime importance. Up on Cardiac, they would very much like to anticipate other cases in the family. There was a large field for consideration. Genes, food habits, other diseases . . . Tom reached for his pencil.

Sahrman used numbers, and letters for sub-categories, to identify patients. That method would seem to simplify things —79-a, 79-b. The children of Margaret Light . . .

"Yes, Karen?" he responded to her firm "Dr. Kelsey." He had told Sahrman that he could use numbers and sub-letters for his records. Sahrman said the names were too long. But if ever Tom caught him calling one of their people by a number . . .

He looked up in wonder at the people who were standing

beside and in front of his desk. Who in the world . . . ?

There was a man, and a woman—and another man. They wanted, this man said, to talk to Dr. Kelsey.

Tom stood up. "I am Dr. Kelsey," he said. He looked around the now-crowded office. "Karen," he said, "I believe we'd better go next door."

Next door meant Dr. Bonley's office, which was larger and could seat several people. There was a couch. . . .

Tom led the way. "We'll be more comfortable here," he explained.

He went behind the desk, which was bare of everything but the telephone. His visitors sat down, the woman and one man on the couch, the more aggressive one, the spokesman, in the chair at the corner of the big desk. Karen lingered in the doorway.

"You might bring me some paper," Tom told her kindly. He tried to make his face reassuring, though he was not, himself, so very assured. His callers did seem to have a chip of some sort on their shoulders.

Karen brought the paper and a folder. Tom glanced at her and at the folder. The name on it was Richardson. Tom opened it and read the top sheet, which was the usual work-up sheet for a patient examined at Clausen.

The big man in the chair cleared his throat. "My clients," he said in a fruity baritone, "name of Richardson—Anene and Robert—they have come here to get some property which is being denied to them."

"Oh?" said Tom, rolling his yellow pencil between his palms. "Well, if property of theirs is here . . ."

"It's here, all right," said the big man in the chair.

"You speak of them as *clients?*" Tom asked.

The big man fished in his inside coat pocket and produced a card. A business card. Tom read it without picking it up from the desk corner where it had been laid.

"Sax," he said. Attorney at law. There were other items on the card. An address, a telephone number. A slogan. The Right Man for Your Rights.

He pursed his lips to hide the sigh. If he had got himself into a hassle with some organization defending—well—almost anything . . . He didn't recognize the man and woman on the couch. But so many people came through Clausen, and even through Research— He considered taking time to look at the case history and the other records.

Instead he sat back in Dr. Bonley's comfortable desk chair and spoke quietly to the lawyer, who was more than ready to challenge him. "Suppose, sir," he suggested, "you brief me on what your claim is, and what you want of me."

"We came here to see the chief man."

"Well, if you first went through Clausen Center, I'd be the one."

"You ain' the one tole me to have my gall bladder took out," said the woman on the couch.

Tom raised his eyebrows and opened the folder again. Admission data, the standard form. The usual items. Family history—HPI—Habits. Review of All Systems—admission by James Bonley, M.D., to General Surgery Ward, Female patient—

He closed the folder. The case was a full year old.

"Dr. Bonley was your admitting physician," he said quietly, looking from one face to the other. None seemed friendly. "As perhaps you know, and most regrettably, Dr. Bonley was killed a couple of weeks ago."

"He didn't op'rate me," said the woman.

"No, I am sure he didn't."

"But he said I should be op'rated."

Tom sighed. "You came here," he said, "to recover property?" Good Lord, she didn't want her gallstones!

"Let me speak for you, Anene," said the attorney at law. "My client," he told Tom, resuming his pompous, attorney-at-law voice, "came to the Clinic a sick woman. Naturally, she wanted to know what was wrong, and she wanted to be made well."

"That covers practically any of our patients, Mr. Sax."

"Yes, sir, I so presume. Now, she was told to get X-ray pictures made, and a test called an EKG—'

"If gall bladder difficulties were suspected, that, too, was routine." As well as g.i. tests, g.u., blood . . .

"She considered it so. She even considered, and her husband did, that it was what you call *routine*."

"I meant a customary procedure."

"Yes, sir. But what was not routine—or so we think—was the fact that when she did have the operation, she was unconscious for six solid days. Now, was that routine, Dr.—er—?"

"Kelsey," said Tom, again opening the folder. Yes, there it was. Pulmonary embolism.

"She seems to have made a good recovery," he said, gazing at the well-fleshed woman—what the history takers would put down as WNWD—well nourished, well developed.

"You are not considering her anguish, that of her husband and her family, during those six days of coma?"

Oh-oh!

"These things happen," said Tom. "Evidently Mrs. Richardson was well cared for during the crisis. She has recovered."

"Yes, sir, but the point is: things did not go right. And we have had doctors tell us that the surgery may not have been necessary at all."

Tom laid his hand on the folder. He must now be careful

of what he said. . . . "Just what did you come here to get today?" he asked.

"Well, we know there must have been records kept—you likely have them right there. And we know that X-rays were taken, and the EKG record . . ."

"The tracing. Yes, there were such things done." His eyes narrowed. This, he was sure, was a planted case. Planted by whom, and for what purpose—maybe even to test Tom Kelsey? Anyway, he wanted witnesses. He touched the buzzer on the desk and asked Karen to summon . . . He listed four interns by name. Would they please come to this office, *stat*.

He looked up at the visiting attorney. "We are a teaching hospital," he said. "Yours seems to be an interesting situation. I have sent for a class to sit in on this."

Attorney Sax could have objected, though to no avail. The Complex definitely was a teaching institution and certain things were implicit with every service.

However, Mr. Sax seemed more pleased than not to have an audience.

The interns arrived, three immediately, and one later, but the gray-green surgical garments he wore explained that slight delay. Quickly, briskly, Dr. Kelsey outlined for them the situation in hand. This was the sort of case, he said, which occasionally needed consideration by a practicing doctor.

"Now I believe the attorney for our patient of a year ago . . ." he nodded his head toward Anene Richardson, then brushed his hair again back and across his forehead.

Mr. Sax distributed more cards and said once more that things had not gone right for Mrs. Richardson. He said that he belonged to an organization dedicated to get the rights of people like this poor woman.

The red-headed intern raised an eyebrow, the tall thin

one leaned against the filing cabinet. The two short ones—a very young-looking blond chap, and a dark, bored-seeming one—stood waiting. Kelsey had more fat on the stove, probably.

"We truly believe," said the lawyer, who also was well nourished, "that we have a right to possess such records as were made for Anene Richardson during the time she was a patient at Clausen and at University Hospital. We asked for such records and were referred to the chief doctor of Clausen Center. You have admitted that you are that one, Dr. Kelsey."

Tom nodded. "Since Dr. Bonley's death," he said quietly, "I have served as acting Chief of Service."

"But you say you have no personal knowledge of the case?"

Tom's hand lay flat upon the record folder. "I don't need personal knowledge, Mr. Sax. We keep detailed records. But whatever sort they are, the courts have held that all such medical records, *all* records, X-ray plates, EKG tracings, all belong to the doctor and to the hospital, not to the patient."

"We—Mr. Richardson," said Mr. Sax, "paid out money . . ."

"According to their ability," Tom agreed. He glanced at his interns. "But the amount paid is not significant. Nor would the fact be important if this were entirely a charity case."

Yes, this definitely was a planted case. Sax was too sure of what to say next. The man was there to make trouble, and perhaps would succeed. Later, Tom would point that out to the class.

Meanwhile, Sax was talking largely, and with seeming logic, about a person's owning what he paid for.

"That sounds reasonable," said Dr. Kelsey, making a note on his pad of paper. "But the ethics, as well as the law, of medicine governing medical care are clearly defined, Mr. Sax. They are regularly expounded in a course given in our medical schools, and open to any lawyers who wish to attend them. The course is called Forensic Medicine. These doctors in training have all attended such a course. I did, in my time, and the law we are taught says that any patient, whether he is paying cash, or is supported by insurance or subsidy, pays the doctor, or doctors, for, and is entitled to, the opinion of the doctor as to what the tests have revealed. He also pays for the advice which the doctors may give as to the patient's welfare. He is entitled to that advice. The patient buys that professional opinion. But he does not buy, and therefore own, the means by which the opinion was reached. He—all doctors—are glad and willing to communicate these findings to another doctor, but they do not, by ethics and by law, surrender ownership of X-ray plates or other records made and preserved on file."

Mr. Sax stood up and leaned across to speak directly into Tom's face. One of the interns moved a little, and Tom's hand lifted from the desk as much as five inches, and dropped. "Are you telling me all this stuff," demanded the attorney, "or lecturing to your class?"

"Both," said Dr. Kelsey readily. "This is a legal matter entirely. I am glad that it is, because, frankly, Mr. Sax, it is much easier to take a stand, and maintain a stand, on a legal point. A moral consideration would be harder to defend." He was calm and pleasant.

Mr. Sax was neither. "That could be arranged!" he said angrily.

"No doubt it could," Tom agreed. He stood up, and the tall thin intern said, "Yeah, man, go!" The other three clapped softly.

Frowning, Tom turned to face them. "Demonstrations in

a classroom are not to be tolerated," he said coldly. "Your opinion of procedure is your own, and to be kept so."

When next he turned his attention to Mr. Sax, that man's broad and well-nourished back was going through the door, his clients having preceded him.

Tom sat down and asked his class to be seated.

Finished with his lecture, which was brief, though he did include a comprehensive review of the Richardson case, he added his opinion that the case had been planted. "We probably shall hear more of it. So I shall make, and would urge you to make, a complete record of what was said, including your opinion on the situation."

"We couldn't use your carbons, Dr. Kelsey?" suggested the man in the scrub suit.

Tom laughed. "I'll see that you have a carbon. But I intend to make my own report for my personal files. I keep one; I began it when I first thought about certification in the College of Physicians. I knew that I would need it. Now the thing has grown in size and value, it has changed in nature as well. Personal as well as professional material is included. And I continue to find the whole record valuable."

The class dispersed; Tom went back to his office, dictated his report, asked for carbons for himself and the interns. He glanced at his personal file, stored in the two top drawers of the cabinet in the corner. The labels of those drawers were turquoise blue.

This finished, he left his office and went to a ward where he had three children with broken bones. They belonged to one family. At first Clausen had thought they might be victims of child beating, but Tom believed there was some bone trouble, hereditary rather than environmental. Each child had suffered previous fractures.

He worked until noon in the ward and studying the

X-rays. He brought the records back to his office, and Karen told him to go to lunch. He did, acknowledging that one-thirty was high time.

There were always people eating in the cafeteria, but by one-thirty the noontime crowd had thinned. One could easily find an empty table. Tom took his tray to the first one available, still preoccupied with the morning's events.

He was eating his deviled egg and looking at his toasted sandwich when someone said, "Mind if I share, Kelsey?"

Tom looked up. It was Rosenthal, the biochemist who wore loud shirts. "No, of course not," he said. "How are you, Mike?"

"In a towering temper," said Mike Rosenthal, sitting down, taking his food from the tray, and arranging it on the table.

"What's happened today?" Tom asked, laughing.

"Doesn't something happen every day?" Mike demanded.

"Well, yes, now that you call it to my attention." Tom began to eat his sandwich.

"I come over here," said the chemist, "to get blood and fluid samples from a psycho, and I discover that the court has ordered him dismissed."

"And you're mad because you have to eat Research food."

"Agggh!" growled Rosenthal. Busily he ate his soup, and wiped his mustache.

"Was it a dangerous criminal?" Tom asked.

"God, no. Pickpocket punk."

Tom chuckled.

"Biochemistry tries to get some work done on these feeble-minded characters," said Dr. Rosenthal seriously. "But how can we if Research doesn't keep them long enough for us to test them?"

"Even Research can't fight the courts, Mike." Tom was ready to tell about his case of that morning.

"Research could set up some sort of defense," Mike declared. His shirt for today was striped widely—green and yellow.

"What do you suggest?"

"There should be more strings between University and this building. Then you'd have more wallop in telling the court to keep hands off."

"Oh, yes, you do believe University should run Research."

"Staff it."

"There goes my job, then," said Tom, relishing his dish of pears. "I'm only Acting, but I glory in things as they are."

Rosenthal was not in a mood to joke. "You know the system is lousy, Tom!" he cried, in his earnestness leaning across his plate of spaghetti.

"I know the system is big," Tom agreed.

"And that's only one reason it's lousy," Dr. Rosenthal assured him.

"Well—" Tom stood up. "I'd better get back and keep it from getting lousier. See you, Mike."

He forgot Rosenthal's temper before he reached One and his office. He was thinking about the date which he had with Carter for that evening. He was taking her to a symphony program which both wanted to hear. She wouldn't promise dinner—but they both hoped they could make an eight o'clock date.

They did make that time, easily, laughing at their caution. "But two doctors really are tempting fate," Carter acknowledged gaily. She looked lovely in a blue, silky suit of some sort—Tom was no expert on women's clothes. But the color called attention to her limpid blue eyes, and the soft scarf at the throat was more appealing than any amount of jewelry.

The concert was satisfying, and Carter invited Tom up to her hotel suite for a drink afterward. "You'll want to check in," she reminded him, "and the bar wouldn't sound too good as a place to be found."

"You think your apartment sounds better?" he asked, and chuckled to see color pink up into her cheeks.

"Give the number, and don't be sassy!" she told him, taking her coat into the bedroom.

"Don't you have to locate?" Tom asked when she came out again.

"If I have a critical. But remember, I'm not the man in charge of a service."

He sighed. "I remember that I happen to be. Temporarily, of course."

"Aren't you consolidating your position?" she teased him.

Tom rattled ice into two glasses and looked around at her, one eyebrow up. "Why is it," he asked plaintively, "that any change in my career seems to disturb some woman in my life?"

She gaped at him.

"Don't you like being called a woman in my life?" he asked, bringing her the glass.

"It isn't that, Tom."

"What then?"

"It's your suggestion that I am disturbed."

"And you're not?"

"I wouldn't have said so. Of course I was glad that you were named Acting."

"Oh, that! I was the only one handy."

"And I suppose there are things you should be doing to make the position a permanent one. Don't you want . . . ?"

"Well, I'd like the money."

"And the tongue in your cheek, sir, is about to push through."

Tom sat down beside her on the couch. He was laughing.

"What other woman in your life . . . ?" she began.

"Oh, the hour grows late, Dr. Bass."

She thrust her elbow into his ribs.

"Hold it!" he cried, looking in alarm at her glass."You'll ruin my Sunday suit."

"But there's all that money to buy a new one. Seriously, Tom, did I sound disturbed?"

"Mhmmmn."

"Me, and who else?"

"The only one I can safely tell you about . . . in my past . . ."

"I know. Your mother. All right, Doctor. Tell me how the changes in your career disturbed your mother."

"Well," he said, "she was an anticipator. About everything. She lived so much into the troubled future that often she could not enjoy or appreciate what was going on in the present. When I was in college, she made plans for me in med school, and when I was in med school, there was the internship coming up. She did not relish the idea of my doing a general internship. . . ."

"She could have spoken to the dean."

"Don't think she didn't consider it. I lived in a state of continuous terror."

She patted his arm. "Poor Tom."

He smiled. "Now my story is getting results!" he told her.

"Stick to that story, son. I suppose your mother picked out your specialty for you?"

"I vividly remember the Sunday afternoon when I endeavored to explain to her about aptitudes and advisers, and such. But I didn't get far. When I began my internship, you should have heard her! As literally as she could without physically moving into the hospital—which was a large city institution—she followed each step I took. And every time

I changed service, she grieved because it was not surgery."

"But you did do surgery."

"Sure I did. Not anywhere near as expertly as my mother thought and told, of course. And she was sure I was moved out of surgery too soon. Before my time was up, she declared, which was nonsense."

Carter turned her head to look at him inquiringly. "She did want you to be a surgeon?"

"And as soon as my internship was over. Well, I persuaded her that I needed residencies."

"And then you did have to select your specialty."

"Oh, yes, but my mother didn't know that. I did my residencies in general medicine, though she thought, of course, that I was working up to replace Osler or DeBakey, or both."

"When did you move into your present field?" Carter sounded genuinely interested.

"Much, much later. When I completed my residencies and was certified in medicine, I made the mistake of going into private practice."

"Was it a mistake?"

"It really looked that way, Carter. I went through the whole deal. I borrowed money, I opened an office, I waited for patients. I made a delivery or two, and learned about the eyes of experienced women."

"But you didn't tell Mother."

"She knew about those women, and had warned me about them. I had to see them to believe them. As for the men—I lanced a carbuncle and got floored by that patient. I refused to do abortions. And I went broke." He sat thoughtful, shaking the last bit of his drink in the glass. "In short," he concluded, "I was a failure."

Carter nodded, the swirl of golden hair moving against

her cheek. "Because you were idealistic," she said softly.

"Nonsense!" Tom cried. "I just wasn't ready to stand alone."

"But now you would be. Would you try it again, Tom?"

"I don't think so, Carter. I like what I am doing."

"Good! I'm glad to hear you say that."

He started to make some comment, but the telephone rang. Carter answered it and held it toward him. Tom was looking at his watch.

He had to go to the hospital, she could tell from his side of the brief conversation, and she fetched his topcoat. As he put it on, he briefly mentioned Edward Trice. "I sort of got into that," he admitted. "I've turned him over to a Staff of course."

"Then he isn't your case."

"No, but I am glad I was called."

He went down the hotel corridor on the run. Carter was frowning as she closed the door. "Dr. Osler," she was thinking, could get hurt in his idealism.

Tom had always liked a big hospital late at night. The halls stretched endlessly, there were sounds, but they were like beads of water as against the steady river-roar of daytime sounds. There were people alertly about, the guard at the door, these days. Tom must identify himself. The nurses at the desk spoke to him in normal tones. Except for that island of light, the hall was dim, not to disturb the patients who should be sleeping. But a stretcher cart could go as swiftly as by day; the three doctors at Mr. Trice's bedside glanced up quickly at Dr. Kelsey's appearance.

The resident identified him as the one who had admitted the sick man, now evidently in extremity. Oxygen tent, i.v. tubes—Tom stood against the wall, out of the way. "I'm glad you called me," he told the resident.

"Yes, sir. The nerves in Mr. Trice's abdomen have become involved. The tall man is Dr. Blandford from Neurology."

Tom looked again at the tall man. Blandford was a well-known name. This specialist, the resident, Dr. Cook, and the Staff attending named Rothfeld worked over Trice. Tom helped when asked. He was told that the wife and daughter were down the hall.

Stimulants were administered, a respirator brought in. Blandford thought perhaps a thoracic man might consult— but there was not time. The course was steadily downward, and Edward Trice died at ten minutes after two. The quiet in his room became cold; Tom shivered in its chill, because, almost immediately, he found himself the patsy.

"I am sorry," said Dr. Rothfeld, stripping off his gloves with the usual squeaking, slapping sound, "that we couldn't do more for Kelsey's case."

The implication was, in everything that was said, that if they had had the case sooner . . . Tom was even asked to sign the death certificate. He refused. "I handed the case over to Dr. Rothfeld days ago," he said clearly. And too loudly, perhaps. The resident looked at him.

"Yes," the young doctor agreed, "he did." He moved to the desk ready to fill in the form. He identified Tom's position in the Complex to the two specialists who were preparing to go home. "He brought the case in because he was a friend of the family."

Which was not strictly true. Tom knew the wife slightly.

"And I sent word to him tonight for the same reason," said Dr. Brooks.

Dr. Blandford and Dr. Rothfeld were courteous to Tom. The neurologist asked about his work at the Institute. "I understand you are doing some exciting new medicine over there," he said.

Suddenly Tom was very tired. "But we still lose patients for the old reasons," he said. He heard himself say it. Later he could not swallow those words.

When Dr. Brooks suggested that he might want to tell Mrs. Trice, Tom agreed. He should not . . . but he did.

He went to the corridor's small waiting room and found Mrs. Trice alone. He gently told her what had happened. "I don't think your husband ever had a chance," he said. "This was a quickly progressive disease."

"Where did he get it?"

"Perhaps Dr. Rothfeld can tell you more about it," Tom said. "But there are diseases, you know, that we doctors cannot cure, or prevent."

There were things to be done, papers for the widow to sign, questions to answer, arrangements to be made. Evalyn was alone; she had sent her daughter home, she told Tom.

Finished, he took the wife home. She seemed dazed, and beyond realization. The Trice home was a tall, narrow one, of sandstone blocks with wrought-iron grills at the windows and doors. There were lights, and the daughter, Elene, answered their ring, opened the heavy front door.

"Papa?" she asked.

"Yes, dear," said Evalyn, taking the tall girl into her arms. Elene was, Tom would say, nineteen. Her hair was honey-blonde, long and shining. She had lovely skin, and would be considered a beauty by anyone.

There also was present a young man with thick and smooth light hair, a reserved manner. He found some things to say to Dr. Kelsey. And each proper thing locked Tom more firmly into the unhappy situation of having once been the dead man's doctor who had lost his case. Didn't these lay people know that the doctor really in charge seldom accompanied the bereaved home?

He was becoming angry and not a little frightened.

The Trice case could hang around his neck like the Mariner's albatross.

Evalyn never should have called him.

But she did.

Tom should not have taken the man to the hospital.

But he had.

And now the dead man was Kelsey's case; he never had had a chance for life, but he had gone for that first week without attention. The hospital would know that, and talk about it.

For six months the hospital had talked about Roxie Turner and Dr. Kelsey. He had made it possible for the girl to walk. It was a miracle! There had been luck in that case, just as there was luck in this one. Tom had not deserved all the praise about Roxie, and he did not deserve to be blamed or criticized about Trice.

He left the Trice home feeling sunk. Grammatical or not, there was only one word to use about his condition. Of course he'd been asking for deflation. His red balloon had blown up too bright and too big. To think he was doing so well at Research, to have the work he enjoyed so quickly crowned with the mark of success. He had been named as acting Chief, he could boss people around. And now . . .

Was this really going to be like other ventures of his, and not work out? Of course he was sunk.

For no reason that he could have defined, he turned his car toward the Institute, parked it, and went into the dim and silent corridors of One's administrative area. He had a key to his office, but he had never used it before. He did now, and went inside, fumbling for the light switch.

He shrugged out of his topcoat and turned toward his

files. It had been his somewhat vague intention to make some comprehensive notes on the Trice case while it was still fresh in his mind. He could type it all on a single sheet of paper, file it, and then go home to bed, hoping to sleep.

He stopped with his hand six inches from the file drawer where he kept a certain sort and size of paper and folders. But tonight—

He stood staring, unbelieving what he saw. The two top drawers of the cabinet had papers sticking out untidily from them. He opened one drawer, feeling like a sleepwalker, still not believing what he knew he saw. The drawer was a mess.

Still staring at the top drawer, he reached for the handle of the lower one. The neat turquoise tab was torn; its edges brushed his fingertips, and the drawer . . .

His eyes were attracted to the floor. There were odd sheets of paper about, one under his desk, three up against the wall—

It seemed as if his file drawers—just these two that contained his personal papers—it seemed that they had been pulled out and dumped—on the floor, perhaps—and examined? He could not tell. Nor could he tell if anything was missing. The whole mess had been gathered up and stuffed, any which way, back into the drawers which were closed, with oddments of stiff file covers and paper sticking out.

What a jumble! Tom sank into his desk chair, to stare at the filing cabinet, to try to reassemble his distraught mind, which just at the minute was as much in confusion as were his papers. Nobody touched his files. Only a few knew he had them. Karen, Sahrman—maybe Dick Scott . . . Who had done this thing, and why?

It must be someone with a key. Unless the deed had been perpetrated before his office was locked for the night. As little as five years ago, a doctor's office could remain unlocked. But here on the first floor, especially because of some of the people who came in, or worked in, these halls—

Tom immediately discarded the idea that one—some—of the Clausen people would have done this. But they would not have confined the destruction to those two drawers. There were a dozen other files, some of them much closer at hand.

Had this thing been done by some enemy of his? Though Tom really had no enemies! He could not think who might have something against him, a feeling so strong . . .

Could it have been an accident? Perhaps Lonnie or the cleaning crew could have pulled the drawers out, spilled them . . .

No. The drawers were heavy, and were installed upon guides against tipping and spilling.

But if this had been done on purpose, what was the purpose? Was someone searching for particular records or notes?

Sax! Sax? Or someone he had sent. Contacted. Looking for that woman's records? But there again, how would he know about the personal files?

It was really weird.

The echo of that term drifted across Tom's memory. The telephone calls, the memos at the house phone—Tom had called those things weird.

Oh, this line of thinking was ridiculous! There was not one reason to connect any of these happenings with the other. If they were connected, there must be a reason behind them. Some pattern. And there could not be.

Tom had come back here tonight only because he wanted to write down the details of the Trice case and perhaps find some answer to the man's death. It was only chance that he had done this.

Wearily he stood up and made enough order out of the

files that the drawers would close without any papers pro-
truding. Later he would get them in proper order again.
Probably that would take a hundred and one nights of hard
work.

Wearily he snapped off the lights and went home.

But he was back at his desk early. Lonnie was surprised to
find him there so early, so busily typing. "Did you have an
emergency, Doctor?" he asked. "Have an emergency?"

"No," Tom answered. "Just a pile-up of work."

"I'll get you some coffee," said Lonnie. "Some coffee." He
shuffled away.

Tom gazed at the doorway where the orderly had stood.
Could he have done this thing? He would have done it
clumsily—as it had been done.

Unless the guilty person wanted him to know that the files
had been turned out. Probably nothing was taken.

No. In either case, Lonnie was not the guilty one. More
likely it had been . . .

He shook his head. He was not ready to put a name to
anything that had happened lately. The weird things . . .

When Carter knew . . .

He probably would not tell her.

He already had talked too much to her about his personal
affairs. He was ready to be sorry that he had done this.
Though he would like to talk to her about Trice, and the
element of chance that the case should have fastened itself
to Tom's name. On the night when her husband first became ill, Evalyn could have called any one of a dozen doctors at the Institute, whom she would know just as she knew
Tom Kelsey. So—he would like to talk to Carter about the
chances in medicine.

He wished now, in this troubled time . . .

He ripped the paper out of the typewriter, rose and put it

into the file. He changed into his white coat and went out into the hall. He had work to do, and there was no time or reason for him to act and feel like a pouting child. He was not one.

He was a grown man, and a good doctor. This fact he should keep safely in his pocket and defend it only if necessary.

## CHAPTER 5

IT WAS some time later—January had escaped and February now held the city in the dark, icy cold peculiar to that month. Snow fell, and was beautiful until the plows came and the heaps of white turned black, scabrous. Tom lost his heavy gloves, which annoyed him much more than it should, though by then he was able to laugh at Karen's suggestion that they might have been stolen.

"Who would?" he asked.

She shrugged.

So he bought some new ones and forgot about the incident. He was not beyond losing things, he was certain.

The work piled up. Winter was a hard time for the poor. Colds, falls on the ice—Clausen was very busy. Often Tom went late and wearily to bed. And on this particular night he decided to eat dinner at the hotel instead of having to cook his own. He should do this regularly, he told himself. He could relax with a half-pint of wine and the evening newspaper. He could have bought five steaks for the price, of course, but what the heck? He was solvent and had no estate to think about.

Into the rosy glow of self-satisfaction he looked up in puzzled surprise at the girl who had come to his table and said, "Dr. Kelsey?"

He scrambled to his feet, shaking his hair back from his eyes. Who in the world . . . ? Oh, of course! Elene Trice. He had seen her only the one time.

"Will you sit down?" he asked. "Could I order you something?"

"Nothing, thanks. I just wanted to speak to you."

She was a tall girl. She wore a loose silk blouse and white trousers. The blouse was largely blue, figured in brown and red. It was sleeveless, and scooped low in the neck. No bra . . . Tom didn't like that fad, and as a doctor deplored it.

Elene was tall and slender, but nicely rounded in the proper places. She had honey-blonde hair, much the color of Carter's. It was long. As she contemplated Dr. Kelsey, she tucked one side of it behind her ear. "Go on and eat," she told him. "Your steak will get cold and icky."

"Well, we couldn't have that," said Tom. "I suppose you want to talk to me about your father's death. I am very sorry that had to come, Elene."

"It was rough on him," she agreed, almost indifferently. "But that isn't why I bothered you. Dad, and his being sick, is Mother's ploy with you."

Tom choked a little and pressed his napkin to his mouth. *Ploy?*

"She got you into that," Elene told him. "I'd like you to consider me for what I am. Me, on my own."

Tom smiled at her. She was very young—but he liked young people and usually got along well with them. "How is your mother?" he asked. "She hasn't been to the Institute lately. At least, I haven't seen her."

"She'll start coming again. Though I could wish she wouldn't." Elene combed her long hair between her fingers. "You see, she's my rival. That happens between mothers and daughters."

Tom blinked. "Rivals for what?"

"For you," said this girl readily, frankly.

Tom looked up. He gulped. He almost sprang to his feet. He was so astounded . . .

"Of course," she said. "You're good-looking . . ."

"Oh, come now!"

"Exciting-looking. That's better than classical beauty. I'm an art student. I know. Your thick hair and your keen eyes, the deep crease in your cheek. If you'd wear a scarf instead of a tie, you'd be really wild."

Tom laughed and finished his steak.

"But you can't deny that you are kind," said this strange girl, "and interested in people."

Tom pursued his lips. "It doesn't pay to knock them about," he agreed.

"So I've fallen in love with you."

"Oh, no!" Tom protested. "You haven't done any such thing."

"I won't make any trouble for you," Elene told him earnestly. "But I would like— Look, can't I work near you? I'd not be a nuisance."

"What is it you want?" the man asked helplessly. Had the wine been so strong . . . ? This crazy girl could not—possibly—

"I want a job," she said reasonably. "You could give me one."

"Oh, Elene. A girl like you should be dreaming about marriage, not working in our sort of clinic."

She rested her chin on her fist and regarded Tom. "I'm

going to be a bridesmaid next week," she told him. "Blue and lavender chiffon, carry spring flowers—jonquils and lilacs and stuff. When I get to that bit, it will be entirely different. Do you know that I've been reading *The Confessions of Felix Krull* by Thomas Mann? It is very good. I think I am logically progressing from Hesse to Mann."

"I haven't the least idea what you are talking about," Tom told her. "Though I was about to mention school. Don't you go to school?"

"Not really. I've been taking some courses in life drawing and ceramics. And I am planning to make a vegetable garden in our back yard. I've ordered the seeds. Melons and corn and stuff. You see, Dr. Kelsey, I don't relate to the things my age group thinks important. Maybe, in a few years, I'll find a way . . ."

Tom ordered her a dessert from the pastry cart and some fresh coffee. As she ate her coconut cake, he listened to her talk and watched her. She did seem to be alone—out of step —and with her father dead . . .

Should he try this idea of hers? It was his place, and his work, to help others. He had done this and more for other young people. Scooter, and a long list following him—he had given them work in the clinic.

He was sorry for the widow and daughter of Edward Trice. To that degree, Evalyn might indeed be her daughter's "rival." Remembering the term, he chuckled aloud, and Elene glanced at him.

"Aren't you taking me seriously, Dr. Kelsey?" she asked.

"Oh, yes! Quite seriously. I was just thinking of my reasons for liking your mother and for liking you. And then I considered myself as one irresistible to the ladies, and naturally I laughed."

"You shouldn't," she said.

"As for being kind," he continued, toting up the bill and getting out his wallet, "why shouldn't I be kind? Look, I am going to walk you home. You must have a coat . . ."

"I hope so. I left it on a chair in the lobby."

Someone could have stolen it; it was a good coat. But it was there in a heap of camel's hair and a leopard printed scarf. Tom claimed his own coat at the check stand and put his hand under Elene's elbow.

"You don't have to take me," she protested.

"At this time of night, on the city streets . . ."

He would not go up the steps to her front door, but he saw her safely into her home, then he turned toward his own. Walking briskly, his heels pounding, he thought about Personnel and the romance situation. Perhaps they had a point. Girls of this day were on the prowl. And if Elene Trice were serious . . .

He reached for his keys. One sure thing, he was not going to tell Carter about this evening. It was the sort of adventure one woman never could understand about another, especially with a man in the middle. Tonight—the whole episode could have been a joke. These kids had strange ideas of humor. "Let's see if you can make the Doc." It had been tried before. Sometimes successfully. Tom thought back over what he had said to Elene. He guessed he'd been careful enough— if there was such a thing as being that careful.

Even if this was a trap— He'd experienced that, too.

He went into his house, fed the complaining Caesar, and let the cat out for his nightly rounds. He changed into a sweater and slacks and made himself a drink. With it in his hand, he sat thoughtful.

He hadn't much self-vanity. His mother had seen that he did not. Her wildest praise of her son, however proud she might be, was to say, "Tom does very well."

So he didn't think for one minute that using a scarf instead of a tie would make him "really wild."

But there had been a few times—he remembered one girl. He'd really liked Dorothy. Maybe she did set out to get him, as his mother decided. But it was a very pleasant trap; he easily fell in love with Dorothy. She was a secretary, a nice-looking girl with long legs and a pretty body. She and Tom liked doing things together; it was purely a matter of he-and-she. They had no money; Tom's practice brought in very little; he was in debt up to his ears for office equipment. Dorothy earned enough to keep a small apartment and to buy the sweaters and skirts she liked to wear. Both she and Tom—they had taken long walks on Sunday afternoons, they cooked hamburgers or made fudge in Dorothy's ridiculously small kitchen. They sat side by side on her couch, snuggled, kissed, and were happy.

But his mother—she had feared marriage between them.

She thought Dorothy was not the kind who would "take things" or would admire Tom as she was sure he should be admired.

"Now, yes," she agreed. "She wants a man. But if you'd marry her, and the babies came, and there still wasn't any money—wives don't understand about doctors, Tom. Some wives don't understand about men and their work. And when there is no money . . ."

Tom thought that he and Dorothy could surmount any of these problems. He really wanted that girl. . . .

Meanwhile, Tom's work went on, with a few unpleasant developments and a lot of good ones. He was called upon to give a report on Clausen and Sociomedical Research at the annual civic-medical meeting at the end of the month. This was always a large and brilliant affair, with men of distinction named and honored.

Dr. Lewis told Tom that he was to make the Clausen report.

"I can," said Tom, almost indifferently.

Dr. Lewis gazed at him, then smiled and went away.

But Karen was shocked at his reaction. This was an important affair, she told him in a half-dozen ways. He would need a dress suit. . . .

"I have a dinner coat," Tom assured her.

He should work up a speech. If the city and the industries of the community were to back up his work at Clausen . . .

"No speech," said Tom. "Just be sure I have the figures."

"But, Dr. Kelsey . . ." She was ready to weep.

"It will be all right," he assured her.

And it was all right. Tom made a good appearance, he spoke with authority, and his audience seemed relieved that there was no bleeding-heart discussion of the Clausen Center. The need, he reminded his audience, had been recognized when the Center was built. If the figures he had at hand were not enough to say that other centers like Clausen were needed, "then I am wasting your time and mine."

He gave his figures. The Center had been open since last April. In its first nine months it had known 24,502 visits from 10,718 patients. About a thousand patients a month.

He said briefly that these patients received, and would receive, complete physical examinations that would cost each person present a minimum of forty or forty-five dollars in private medicine.

"Our patients pay according to their ability. A patient with a small family and an income of more than $10,000 may pay at the same rate as would be charged in a private clinic. But there are not many in that category. Most of our patients have a family income of less than $4,000 a year."

He spoke, though briefly, of the research being done through the Institute tie-up with Clausen. "This research will help the Clausen patients; it will eventually help you and me." He sat down.

"You were wonderful," Evalyn Trice told him when the meeting broke up. "I wish Elene could have seen you in a black tie."

Tom laughed. "I believe she should be able to imagine me in something so conservative. Now, if I'd worn one of the brighter jackets . . ."

"Don't ever do it!" said Evalyn.

"How are you doing, Mrs. Trice?" Tom asked her.

"You are really concerned, aren't you?"

"Of course."

"Well, actually, I am doing quite well. Edward left his affairs in good order. I find myself not knowing how to fill the time."

"Why not start up your volunteer work again?"

"Yes, I could do that. And probably shall, very soon. This is the first social affair I have attended."

Tom looked around at the chattering, well-dressed people.

"I wanted to hear what sort of talk you would make," Mrs. Trice told him as bluntly as Elene might have done.

"Would you tell your daughter," he asked, "to come around and see me? She said she wanted a job, and I've decided to give her one."

Mrs. Trice looked confused. "Oh, but, Dr. Kelsey . . ."

"I know she doesn't need it financially, but she seemed at loose ends—tell her to stop, will you please?"

She didn't say that she would, and Tom thought of the rivalry bit which Elene had mentioned. Pure nonsense, of course.

He was not so sure when Elene appeared at the Institute

the next day and said she had a sort of appointment with Dr. Kelsey.

Karen looked at Tom inquiringly. "The foyer receptionist . . ."

"She's a suspicious soul," Tom told Karen. "Ask her to send Miss Trice in."

Elene came very quickly, her eyes sparkling. "I thought I was going to sneak in through a window," she told Tom. "And then when I got into your hall, I knew I was over-dressed."

Tom laughed. Against some of the clothes that came into their clinic, Elene's well-tailored tweed suit would, he supposed, stand out. Muted plaids, understated colors, and certainly crisp white blouses. "What happened to your psychedelic blouse and the white bell bottoms?" he asked. " How are you, Elene?"

"I'm fine. Now, how about this job?"

"I'm glad your mother delivered my message."

"She didn't."

"But—"

"What she said was, 'Elene, you must be out of your mind to ask Tom Kelsey for a job. What on earth could you *do?* So I decided you had mentioned it to her, and I came on a chance."

Tom rubbed his hand through his hair and shook his head. "I told her that I could find you a small job."

Elene glanced at Karen. "I suppose your secretary would be shocked . . ." she said.

"Yes, she would," said Tom hastily. Karen snorted very slightly.

"But I am pleased to death," Elene told him, drawing her long hair to one side and holding its thickness in her hand. "You see, I am building a dream, and I mean to guide my life by it. Everything outside of that dream will be without virtue or importance. You see . . ."

"Look, Elene," said Tom firmly. "I am only giving you a job. You will sit at a desk—" Elene looked around the small office. "Down the hall," he explained. "You will fill in simple forms and assist wherever you can. The people who come here, those from Clausen, at any rate, often cannot read, or their reading is rudimentary. Government or medical forms are beyond them."

"But that is exactly what I want!" Elene cried. "To be helpful in the work you do."

Tom sighed and answered the telephone, holding up his hand to silence the girl. He knew that he was placing himself in a dangerous spot, just as he had stuck out his medical neck for her father. Any trouble at all with Elene would be ironic. He had no affection for, and only a slight interest in, Miss Trice.

Karen might find a thing or two to say. She did not approve of this appointment the doctor had made without her knowledge. And a thing or two perhaps should be said.

If Management was at all serious about the office-romance thing . . . Tom could not afford to risk disciplinary action or even a warning interview. He was acting Chief, filling Bonley's place, and doing his job. He could ruin for himself any chance . . .

"Chance." The word echoed in his mind. But, yes, chance.

He should talk to someone about this matter. Dick was always available—and other doctors. Should he talk to Dick? They were close friends. Dick would understand the hazards he ran.

Or should he, not imposing on close friendship, talk to someone else? Someone like Harold Daives? The man had been friendly in an entirely different way.

And then there was Carter Bass.

"Look, Carter," he would say, "there is this girl. Nineteen and at loose ends. Yes, of course she is pretty! Yes, nineteen. Good heavens, by starting young, I could be her father! Yes, I know that her father is dead. No, she is not blackmailing me!"

Dick would say, "Send her to Personnel over at the business office, Tom. Don't have a grateful kid in your hair. You need that hair cut, by the way."

Daives? Well, he would leer, of course, and pat Tom's shoulder. "Take 'em where you can get 'em, sonny. I'd do the same in your place."

Tom pushed the telephone away. "Karen," he said brusquely, "don't let me in again for one of Mrs. Cord's endless conversations."

"I'm sorry, Doctor. She insisted. . . ."

"Mhmmmn. Will you get me the records room, please?"

He talked to Records. He sent Elene down the hall. There was every chance he need not see her again.

*Chance . . .*

For a few days he did not see Elene, then, listening to what he himself knew was prudent second judgment, he decided . . .

He told Karen what he planned to do.

"She won't want to work over at Clausen," his secretary told him.

"Why not? It's a nice, clean place."

"She doesn't know that you show up there regularly."

Tom looked disgusted. "I'm going to talk to her."

Karen shrugged.

So Tom went down the hall with his head high. In his position he had every right to make these decisions.

He went into the records room and asked to see Miss

Trice. A half dozen heads lifted alertly.

He was told that Elene was helping out in the well-baby ward.

He went down there, stopping to speak to this person and that. He was well known, and liked, he hoped. Eventually he reached the well-baby ward where children were detained for various reasons—for thorough testing against what might be a family disease, sometimes just to care for the child while the mother was receiving tests or treatment.

It was a noisy place, and big. Cribs were ranged against one wall; there were toys about on the floor. A noisy kiddie car came straight at the doctor, who jumped nimbly. There was a rocking chair for holding a child and administering tender, loving care. There was a table for baths and diaper changing. Here the doctor found Elene, and he stood back, amused, until she was finished and had picked up the delectable morsel of babyhood, ready to restore the child to the crib. She turned and saw Tom, so surprised that he put out his hand, lest she drop the baby.

"You!" she said, and took the baby down the length of the room.

Tom went over to speak to the supervising nurse. "I am transferring Miss Trice to Clausen," he said.

"She's been very helpful."

"I'm glad." He turned. "Elene," he called, "get your coat."

"Why?" She came toward him.

"I have some work for you to do over at Clausen."

"Clausen?" she repeated.

"I— Look, let's get a cup of coffee, and I can tell you what it is I want you to do."

She glanced at the nurse, who nodded. "I guess he's boss around here," said Elene.

"That's right, he's boss." The nurse smiled at the doctor.

He nodded and led the way down the corridor, walking fast. A time or two Elene had to run for a few steps to keep up with him, though she never did come even with his arm and shoulder.

He held the elevator for her, and they rode down to the cafeteria in the basement. She tried to ask questions, but Tom told her to wait until they got their coffee. "If you're ready for it, you can get a sandwich."

She was pouting and said all she wanted was to be told . . . Tom got their coffee and led the way to a small table.

"I have a check job I want you to do for me," he told Elene. She still wore the white apron over her brown dress. Evidently she was not taking the move to Clausen seriously. Tom set his jaw. He would help this girl, but only up to a point.

He drank half of his coffee, then began to talk about what it was he wanted Elene to do over at the Center. "They will be expecting you," he said.

"Dr. Kelsey," Elene broke in. "I don't want to go to Clausen."

He sat back in his chair and regarded her with steady, dark eyes. "If you work anywhere in the University Hospitals, Elene," he said, "you will do what the Chief of that service decides you will do. If you work for Sociomedicine, you will do what *I* decide you must do."

She gulped and appeared yery young. "You look wonderful in your white clothes," she said plaintively, "but I hate it when you get bossy."

"All right, you hate it. Do you want to quit?"

"No-o."

"Then listen to what I am telling you."

She lifted her coffee cup. "All right, slave driver."

"That's better. Now the supervisor will give you more

detailed directions . . ."

"I like the way you say di-rections."

Tom sighed. "Listen to me, Elene. I want you to make a special survey for me. When Clausen was first opened, we checked on the first 3,000 patients, asked them when they had last seen a doctor. Sixty percent had not seen one in five years. Now we want to make another such survey. We want first-time comers to Clausen to tell when and if they have previously seen a doctor. We want a careful record kept of their replies, and we shall evaluate it to see if the need is as great, or if maybe we are caring for the people of this district."

"Three *thousand*?" demanded Elene. "That will take forever, Dr. Kelsey."

"No, it won't. Four months, six. You are to check only newcomers, but even then—old and young, I want the record kept. It is very important."

"Well, if you say so. But why me? Why can't I stay here?"

"Why should you stay here?"

"Because there is always the chance I'll see you. Over there . . ."

"Now, look," he said. "Do you want this job, or don't you?"

She peered up at him over the rim of her coffee cup.

"All right, then. You go over to Clausen and work at it. And stop feeling and saying that there is some special bond between you and me."

"But, Dr Kelsey— Will you care if I call you Tom?"

"I'd care a whole lot!" he cried. "You just don't do that sort of thing in the hospital organization, Elene."

She began to pout again. "I can't see why not."

"Well, protocol is one reason. The chain of command. And dignity."

"Yours?" she asked slyly.

"I should fire you," he said. "I really should."

"But why, Dr. Kelsey? Why?"

"I'll tell you one last reason, which may not be important to you, but I'll tell you anyway. We especially have to maintain protocol, Elene, because the way you talk and act, and evidently feel, you can be a danger to me."

She focused her attention on what he had said. Her lips silently repeated the word *danger*.

"Yes!" he said firmly. "You see, Management—that's the big office which takes charge of all the thousands of workers in the Complex, the doctors, the nurses and aides, the pencil pushers—Management hands out the pay checks, so it has particular ooomph."

"Don't talk to me like a kindergarten flunk-out!" the girl protested

He smiled at her. "I'm sorry. Let's go on. Management has established a definite no-nonsense position, Elene, on hanky-panky, corner smooching, favors granted and expected, between the male and female employees. You don't indulge in office romance if you want to keep your job. I badly want to keep mine."

"Oh," said Elene. Then her face brightened. She had a cute, turned-up nose. "Are you afraid of me, Tom?" she asked.

"I'm afraid of losing my job. You see, my dear, as we get older, we all get to be cowards."

"Oh," she said again. This time she did not smile. "Then your dreams become only that, don't they?"

"Yes," he agreed, feeling the weight of his years. By the time he was forty . . . "Now if you really don't want to work at Clausen," he said briskly, "I can get you a job at another hospital unit."

"I'd like to stay where I am!" said Elene stubbornly.

"Oh, now, look. There's nothing here for you. Except of course, changing diapers."

"That's silly," she told him.

"No, it is not silly. What is it to be, Elene?"

"I'll hang on for a time, I guess. Do things your way."

Tom had not forgotten his wish to put Dr. Hubbell to work in some hospital-connected capacity. He had talked to Dick Scott about the project. Dick wasn't sure. . . .

"We could find something, surely," Tom insisted. "In a lab, perhaps in the pharmacy. If I had once been a doctor, then had my license revoked, I'd hunger for the field."

"But he can't work as a doctor, Tom."

"I'll accept that as a deplorable fact. But I still think . . ."

Dick said he would send Hubbell around. But the man did not come to Tom's office or to his home. At intervals Tom questioned Dick. "Did you tell him what I had in mind?" he asked.

"Well . . ."

"I know. In a negative way. 'Jim, that crazy Tom Kelsey has the crazy idea . . .'"

Dick laughed. "No such thing. I just said you thought you might be able to find him a job. I believe he guessed the rest of it and didn't come around."

That probably was the case, but Tom planned to keep trying. He could ask Dick flat-out for the man's address. But before the courage to do that had been accumulated, he encountered Dr. Hubbell in person.

Tennis was Tom's passion and his indulgence. He was good at the game; he loved it. The hospital had courts for its interns and residents. Last summer Tom had asked if he might play there. The fame of his skill traveled quickly. He was invited to become a member of an old and exclusive tennis club in the city, close to the hospital complex. There were beautiful, hedged-in courts and some indoor ones, as well as a squash court. Tom had never played squash, but he found he liked it very much. He joined the Racquet Club, a personable, unmarried doctor, a "damn good man on the court! He has lightning footwork."

At Christmas, young Tim Scott had received a good tennis racket; Tom talked to the boy about his game, and then talked about squash. Yes, he would take Tim to the club—probably on a weekend. He found playing squash after a long day could be a bit much.

This particular Saturday, with snow piled high and the park beautiful with it, Tom made good his promise.

Judith said they were to come back for lunch.

They were a little late, and Tom came into the house apologizing, Tim talkative about how *good* Tom was. "You should have seen him, Dad!"

Dick protested that Tom was giving his son some champagne ideas.

"Oh, shut up," Tom retorted, going to the fire. "You sound like my mother . . ." He broke off, leaned over, and smiled at the man sitting in one of the big chairs.

"Jim Hubbell!" he cried gladly.

Dr. Hubbell laid his book aside and stood up. "How are you, Doctor?" He was pleased by Tom's spontaneous friendliness, but he kept his own cloak of dignity defensively around himself

Tom accepted this need for defense, and would not force the man. During lunch, however—an excellent lunch of hot steak sandwiches and freshly made cream puffs—he turned the conversation often to professional matters. Finally he asked Dr. Hubbell directly for his opinion on the so-called mild diabetic.

Dr. Hubbell recognized the bait for what it was, but he readily answered. "I am happy to see that the tolbutamide tablets are going to have to be relabeled," he said. "In fact, I have found that the so-called mild diabetic is often in more danger that the person taking a regular, and somewhat heavy, shot of insulin. Because he is the one relying on Orinase or something of that sort.

"In the prison, I worked in the hospital, and my records indicated that such a program resulted in death from heart or related disease two and a half times more often than if the mild diabetic had taken insulin injections or no medication at all. And, reading up on the matter—I've had a lot of time to read lately—I find that my records are duplicated among a more diverse society."

He was interested, even enthusiastic. When Judith shooed them back to the fire so that she could get the dishes washed, Dick glanced at Tom, then he asked Jim Hubbell to tell Kelsey his story, how he was accused and convicted. . . .

Jim began by saying he felt sure Tom had been told the essential details of his affair with justice. The facts as the prosecution presented them could not be denied. He had had this patient . . . He had treated him in a certain way . . . The patient had died. And the man to blame needed to be punished, to be made a warning example for other doctors.

"But why," Tom asked, "did they accuse you of murder? Malpractice, perhaps. That's all the rage these days. But why . . . ?"

"I was never accused of murder, Tom," Dr. Hubbell said patiently. "It was involuntary manslaughter—A charge such as can be placed when someone—well, like Dr. Bonley—is killed on the highway by a car driven illegally."

"That charge has been placed," said Dick quietly.

"Yes, of course. The other driver was supposed to know

how to drive. He was licensed to drive. Just as a doctor is supposed to know how to administer drugs, and when to use them. He is so licensed.

"The whole trouble is, the progress of medicine has been so great—oh, even in the past thirty or forty years—that people, and the courts, come to expect a doctor to produce perfect results in every case. When he does not, it can be decided that he was negligent. And—it is criminal to be negligent."

Tom rubbed his cupped fingers over the head of the Chelsea dog on the coffee table at his knee. "And he should not, ever, be given a second chance?" he asked.

"Doctors deal with human lives, Tom," said the other man. Don't ever forget that."


"He takes the whole thing much more philosophically than I could," Tom told Dick Scott when Jim Hubbell had left, promising to come to see Tom sometime. Yes, he would like a job, but Tom must remember his position and that of the fellow hiring him.

"You could work in the library, you could . . ."

"I could and would scrub o.r.," said Jim, going through the front door.

Dick said nothing, and Tom looked across at him. "A time or two there," he confessed, "I thought you were running a parallel case with me and my recent experiences."

"Well," Dick conceded.

"I believe you have expected me to get into trouble over the Trice case."

"Are *you* thinking of the father's death?" Dick asked.

"Aren't you? And why call the eminent attorney the 'father'?"

"Because that is how I have heard him spoken of lately,"

said Dick, busily reaming out his pipe bowl with his pocket-knife.

Tom stared at him, his underlip pushed out. "And . . ." he said.

"I think we—you—need to be reminded regularly that we—you—are in a vulnerable position."

Tom sat back on the couch and gazed at the ceiling. "Then you are talking about Trice's daughter," he said. "Elene."

"And Carter Bass."

Tom snapped erect. "I can't believe what you are saying!" he cried loudly.

"I don't think I've said, and I don't plan to say, too much of anything, Tom. Other than to point out that you have a good job. You like it. If somebody else wants it . . . If someone wants to get you out of the way, or if someone should want to use you . . ." Dick was keenly watching Tom's face, but he did not get the quick protest he had half expected.

"Tom?" He nudged the man who sat thoughtful on the couch.

Tom looked up and nodded. "A few days ago," he said, "a little more than a week—someone went into my office, Dick. They had a key. But they—*they* in the singular. I don't want to think he/she."

"I understand." Dick's face was more grave than Tom's.

"They knew where I kept—keep—my personal files. A file I started when I was bucking the Boards."

"You keep those things at the office?"

"Why not? I always have."

Dick frowned. "Well—all right. What happened?"

"The drawers had been pulled out, the papers dumped, then scrambled back in again."

"Good *night*, Kelsey! What were they looking for? Was anything gone?"

"I don't know. I haven't had time to check. I would have to straighten out the mess myself. And I've been so damn busy, doing my work and Bonley's"

"Somebody else should be doing yours."

"So far, nobody has. The double load includes everything from giving Bonley's lectures to answering his mail. When a girl came around with a collection this week, I felt I should ante twice.

Dick laughed, but only briefly. "I suppose you realize that if you are the acting Chief—and you are—you could be appointed to that post."

"You mean, that could offer more danger."

"Not if you know that danger is a possibility." Dick rose and fetched his tobacco jar from the far end of the room. "I've a favor to ask you, Tom," he said.

"To teach you squash?"

"Shut up and listen. I'm lying heavily in the hammock I've strung across the generation gap on such things as squash. But there is this favor."

"All right. It's yours."

"Now wait a minute, Doctor. You already sound like a too-busy man."

"Were you going to ask me to do more work?" Tom asked in dismay.

"I certainly was."

With the heels of both hands, Tom pushed his hair back from his forehead. "Let's have it," he said weakly. "And may I comment on your fast footwork in changing the subject?"

Dick chuckled and lit his pipe. "I suppose you know that they are getting ready to establish board certification of men now practicing general medicine?"

"Yes," said Tom. "If I had the time, I'd apply for a chance to take those exams."

"Oh, Tom!" Dick protested.

Tom shrugged. "I'd like to know where I stand," he said.

"Now listen to me. I—the National Board of Medical Examiners—has been considering your name as a member of the examining board for doctors in family practice. The favor I am asking is that you accept such an appointment if it should be offered to you."

Tom stared at him. Then he visibly swallowed whatever was in his throat. He got to his feet, went over to the secretary, opened one of the glass doors, and straightened a book on the shelf.

"Judy will slant it down again," Dick told him.

Tom turned to face his friend. "You didn't mean what you just said!" he shouted.

Dick laughed. "Of course I meant it. We want you to be on that board, to set up rules and examining questions, select proctors—all the details of establishing such a board."

"I think g.p.'s should have to renew their certification and certainly their diplomate every six years!" Tom's tone was truculent.

"That's a good idea, Tom."

Tom sat down on the blue hassock and leaned toward Dick. "You see," he said earnestly, "g.p.'s have to diagnose and often treat everything the other men specialize in."

"Yes."

"They have to keep up . . ." He sat thoughtful. "And then," he continued brightly, "I think if a man flunks some section of the test questions—say the diabetes Hubbell and we were talking about—he should be advised and questioned about that seeming blind spot."

"Other specialties don't get such advice."

Tom smashed his hands together. "I know they don't, Scott! But g.p.'s—they have to know so damn much!"

"Mhmmmn, they do. And their examining board does, too, wouldn't you say?"

Tom sat thoughtful. "This would mean going to Philadelphia?" he asked.

"At various times, I suppose."

"Well—let me think about it, will you? I couldn't take on a third job, I'm afraid."

"Nobody would ask you to," said Dick.

## CHAPTER 6

ON MONDAY MORNING, the halls of Research and various places throughout the Complex buzzed about the announcement displayed on every bulletin board.

Dr. Kelsey had been named Chief of Sociomedical Research.

Karen was torn by so many emotions that the poor girl . . . "Calm down, will you?" Tom told her. "You'll be giving me your jitters."

"Don't you have your own?"

"Misgivings. Not jitters."

"Well, you shouldn't have any misgivings!"

Tom smiled at her.

"How long have you known?" she asked him.

"Since yesterday afternoon."

"But yesterday was Sunday!"

"Yes, and a miserable day it was. Rain, snow, and slush—I came over here for a check. I usually do that. Then I decided to do some work straightening out my files."

"Oh, yes," said Karen sadly.

"Dr. Lewis came in."

"Came in here?" Karen looked around the office. "We're going to have to move," she said firmly.

"Yes. Dr. Lewis told me that."

"He— Tell me about it, Dr. Kelsey!"

He laughed. "I'll tell you. He came here to leave me a note. He wanted me to come directly to his office this morning when he would tell me—what he did tell me yesterday afternoon."

"That you are the new Chief."

"Yes. He asked me if I would be."

"And you said yes."

"Well, Karen—first there was a bit of talk on the subject. For one thing, I told him that I was a better foot doctor than a desk one. I said that if I took on Bonley's job I would want to be on the floor about as much as I have been. I told him that we'd need another man besides Sahrman and that that man should be someone better at administration and paper work."

"Won't you need a secretary?" Karen asked, her eyes widening.

"I have a secretary."

She smiled widely. "Did Dr. Lewis say . . . ?"

"He said that if I wanted to manage things that way, it would be fine. I pointed out that Bonley had done a fine job, and perhaps I could learn to do it his way. But he said for me to see what would work out. Then he added—" Tom's cheeks reddened—"he said, 'You're in the chair now, Tom!' "

Karen was delighted. "I am so proud of you!" she said warmly.

Tom nodded. "I'm so proud of myself that I'll have to beware of the fall my mother used to assure me followed any pride. Now! Will you please see if you can get Dr. Scott on the phone, Karen."

He wanted to ask Dick one question. Had he known on Saturday, when he talked to Tom, that this appointment . . . ?

"Dr. Scott is in surgery," Karen said.

"Okay," said Tom. "I know the answer anyway."

Karen said that Tom should have his meals sent to his office now, or eat in the staff dining room. Tom gave her a look. "Where would I hear the gossip?" he asked.

She blushed.

"You've heard it, too?"

"Well—"

One thing, Karen. No matter how upset you get, keep your mouth shut. Hospitals, their gossip, their scandals, and above all, their politics, is no war for a nice girl like you to get into."

She smiled at him. "I'll stay out of it if you will," she said saucily.

Tom drew a deep breath. "That will take doing," he agreed.

He did hear the gossip and the comments. In the men's room, in the cafeteria—coming unexpectedly up to a floor desk—out on the parking lot . . .

"Kelsey's a good man."

Roxie, the crippled girl, was mentioned.

And Edward Trice.

"He's brand-new here at University. He bumped a lot of good men."

The talk went on, and time went on. The last snow melted, and March brought in sprouting bulbs, a few warm spring days. And Scooter showed up at Clausen, when Tom happened to be there.

Down the full length of the corridor, he spotted the black man. "Where in the world did you come from?" he demanded.

"I been sick, Doc. Got me this sore leg." He lifted the cane he was using.

"But not for *months*, Scooter!"

"Well, it's been a time. How you doin', man?"

Tom laughed and nodded to the resident. "I'd like to see this man's sore leg," he said. "Scooter's been around a time, but not recently, I think."

"No, sir," said the resident, "but we do have him on register."

Scooter was taken into a treatment room and helped to the table. His tight trouser leg had been ripped and pinned together with large safety pins over a not-too-expert, not-too-clean bandage halfway up the calf. This was cut away to reveal a nasty, suppurating wound. Tom wrinkled his nose. "What happened to you, Scooter?" he asked, stepping out of the way so the nurse and the doctor could clean up the area.

"I don't rightly remember how I hurt it, man," said Scooter. "Bumped into somethin', I reckon. It got sore. You know?"

"Did you see a doctor?"

"Yes, sir. But I was workin' out at a fillin' station at Russian Lake, and I went to a doctor there."

"How long ago was this?" Tom had his clip board ready for notes.

"Two, three weeks. Didn't amount to nothin'." Even lying on the table, Scooter had his porkpipe hat tilted forward across his beady, darting eyes.

"It amounts to something now," said Tom coldly. "Do you remember the doctor's name, where his office was, Scooter?"

"Yes, sir. But he don' know too much." He gave the name and address while the nurse bathed the angry wound and the surrounding area with saline.

Tom was indignant that any doctor would let a wound get so badly infected. "Such a physician might be a candidate to

142

have his license yanked," he told the resident, going out into the hall with him. "I'll call him first, of course. Get his story."

"Meanwhile . . . ?"

"Yes, drain and irrigate the wound, put a good dressing on it, and tell Scooter to come back tomorrow."

"Maybe the other doctor told him the same thing."

Tom nodded. "He could have. That's why I'll talk to him before I decide on what happened."

Back at Research, he pointed to the name he had written on his clip board. "Get this doctor on the phone, will you, Karen?" he asked. "I hope he won't give me a reason to report him to the licensing board."

"Something happen?"

He nodded to the phone, and she put in his call.

The doctor, who was available, sounded like an older man, though by no means senile. "Yes," he agreed. He remembered the "boy" with the injured leg. Consulting his files, he confirmed his memory. "I did only a gross examination," he said, "but I'd think he had run into something sharp, and hurt it. That was three weeks ago, Dr. Kelsey. I cleaned and dressed the wound and scheduled an appointment for him to come back in two days. But I never saw the fellow again. Why? Has something developed?"

Tom answered the doctor, thanked him, and made a note on his desk pad. "No need to report anything on that doctor," he told Karen. "I'm glad I had sense enough to go to headquarters before popping off. Now—" Briefly he told Karen about Scooter. "Guy still lies. It's the best thing he does. Get me Clausen, please."

He talked to the resident. Yes, they had told Scooter to return the next day.

"Let me know when he comes. And especially if he doesn't come, Doctor. I want to talk to him."

"Yes, sir. He could lose that leg."

"He could. And he can do us some harm, too, with the things he tells." It was, he told himself, the only reason he worried with, or about Scooter.

The man did not return to Clausen on the second day, but he did come in on the third, and Dr. Duclos sent word to the Chief of Service that their man was there, having worked up a fulminating fever. "He's going to need hospitalization."

As soon as he could, Tom went to Clausen and shook his head at what the nurse and the attending physican showed him.

"Yes!" said Dr. Kelsey. "Now, Scooter—"

"You goin' take me to the Institute, Doc?" asked the sick man.

"I am not. I am sending you to orthopedic surgery in hope that we can save your leg. Or were you striking for a wooden one?"

Scooter's eyes rolled white. "Doc . . ." he gasped.

Tom pulled up a stool and sat down. "Now, tell me, man," he said, "and I want this on the line. What happened to you, and why didn't you go back to the doctor at Russian Lake?"

Scooter told him, inclined to ramble a bit, though Tom kept bringing him back. The nurse and Dr. Duclos watched admiringly. Scooter had hurt his leg running across a parking lot and falling over one of the metal barriers or dividers. That figured. The doctor had dressed the wound, but Scooter decided to come home.

Where was home?

"Well, I can always make a pad in my gramma's kitchen."

Tom accepted this. "How many others live with Grandma?" he asked.

Scooter was vague. There was his Aunt Beulah, and Kathryn's three kids . . .

"And you," Tom said. "With your leg getting more sore."

"And stinkin'," Scooter agreed. "It wa'nt so bad at first, but then Gramma took off the bandage and packed it with dirt. Then, seemed like . . ."

"*Dirt?*" shouted the three people gathered around him.

"What kind of dirt?" asked Tom.

"Oh, jest dirt. She say the clean earth would help it heal,"

Tom looked up at Dr. Duclos. "I'll call Orthopedic," he said. "You get Grandma's address."

A half hour later the two doctors left the Clausen Center, telling the girl at the front desk that they were going to look at some dirt. Tom caught up with Duclos and found that physician convulsed with laughter which he was trying to suppress.

"What's the joke?" Tom asked him; he was still upset over the Scooter thing.

"Did you ever give a thought to the kind of dirt they think"—Duclos jerked his head back toward Clausen's front door—"we're going to look at?"

Tom whistled silently. "Let's not tell them," he said. "We have an image to preserve."

These things happened and, over all, Tom enjoyed them. They had small connection with his being Chief. In his work, material for anecdotes was the rule. But there were changes which marked his promotion. He must attend staff meetings— those things were important, but of no great significance to Tom.

But it was significant to realize that he now stood in somewhat different relationship to the people who had used to stick their heads around his office door and come in. Now these same friendly folk felt they must telephone to see if he was free. Tom did not like that part of his promotion. He had not changed; others should not feel that he had. Yes, he did different work— For one thing, he must try to find another man to help Sahrman, preferably the administrative type of doctor.

Was it because he had been made Chief that the Trice-case talk seemed to increase? From the first, Tom had expected a little trouble there. Now he was getting it. He realized that the talk he overheard and knew about was only the tip of the iceberg showing above deep and dark waters.

Now, occasionally, a doctor or a group would ask him directly about the Trice case. Why had he attended the man? Oh, yes, the questioner believed he had heard that Tom had called in consultants. He had turned it over to a staff man? Really? Weren't you a particular friend of Mrs. Trice?

This suggestion angered Tom. "She works as a volunteer at Research," he answered stiffly, and would say no more. Needed to say no more.

But he hated the rictus of tension which he felt under these circumstances. If that tension was a part of his new job . . .

Some of it was. He found himself carrying the message of his research department to a city board of aldermen meeting when the work he and his workers had been doing on lead poisoning compelled him to ask for, to demand, the demolition of dilapidated slum housing. He had his figures; he could talk to the mayor and to his Board about the certain peculiarities of health found at Clausen, and investigated at Research. "We have found repeated instances of lead poisoning caused by children's eating paint flaking from the walls of these slum tenements. We can and have made graphs of the incidence of these cases."

"Don't the slums turn up other diseases, too, Doctor?" asked the president of the Board.

Tom nodded. "Every disease in the book," he agreed. "We especially find, in uncommon frequency, chronic arthritis, diabetes, and hypertension."

"I thought hypertension was a disease for topnotch executives," said the mayor, laughing.

"And Chiefs of Medical Services, as well, sir. But we get a lot of it through Clausen. Some of it is because of obesity due to a high-starch diet. Then there is the conflict, the friction of too many people living in too compact quarters. Besides that, there are the decent people who find as they get older that they need to ask for help, to ask for food or do without it. Blood pressure mounts with worry and humiliation."

"I suppose it would," agreed the mayor.

The meeting went well, but as it broke up, the mayor himself asked Tom if he had not been Ed Trice's doctor. "Poor devil."

Tom found a quiet tone with which he named the specialists, Dr. Rothfeld and Dr. Blandford.

This sort of thing had to bother Tom. "But it keeps me from getting a swelled head over hobnobbing with the mayors and such," he told himself.

He didn't like the part of his job that led one of his staff to make an intimate revelation to him. The situation was a nasty one, and had to be handled. Tom would rather not have known such things existed on One in Research. This sort of problem he could not discuss with Dick—or could he? Did Dick, Chief of his own service, have similar problems?

Dick did not have the Trice case hung around his neck. In that, Tom could find no acceptable way to defend himself or to combat his attackers. He decided that there were some people, a group perhaps, who were keeping the thing alive.

If that group was made up of his professional associates, the attack was vicious and had purpose. But that purpose was still another mystery. Tom and Carter talked about it a little.

"In your place, and a man," she declared, "I'd throttle the

next one who brought up the matter."

But Dick urged him to go on as he was doing, knowing the truth, refusing to surrender his unflapability.

"If any," Tom chuckled. "Do you hear things?"

"I have. And have squashed the word like a bug."

Tom appreciated Dr. Scott's championship, but he hated being the subject of public discussion.

He had told Dr. Lewis that he wanted to work with the people rather than run the show from his desk, but a certain amount of running the show went with his job, even after he found a man to set programs, schedules, rules and regulations. The chap—his name was Lawson—was very good at what he called traffic engineering, but Tom had to keep an eye on what he did, just as he had to with Sahrman. No regulation, he insisted, was more important than the individual person.

He must work on this—on all aspects of his new task. Complications, big and little, were not welcome, though they kept cropping up. He began, again, to get strange telephone calls, over the hospital intercom, and in the dead of night at home. The call would come, he must identify himself as Dr. Kelsey—then silence. Or weird, screeching noises. How did these people get to the hospital call system? They must work from inside. He was too busy to make a careful check.

Evalyn Trice could be a nuisance, too, he found. And Elene. Never working together, each would suggest that he "stop in for a drink." Or, "Can't we take a walk together on Sunday and talk?"

He evaded all such approaches. He didn't want to connect his name any closer with that of Trice. He had only sympathetic feelings toward either woman, and decided that, by now, even sympathy was no longer required.

Having talked about this a little to Carter, he decided to

speak of it to Dick, not remembering whether he had mentioned these annoyances before or not. But if he had . . .

On a Saturday, unless an emergency arose, he could generally find Dick busy with what he called household golf—his term for cleaning the garage, the basement, digging a flower bed . . . Any friend who came within reach would have to join the game. Tom knew this and sometimes accepted the cost as worthwhile. So, that spring afternoon, he deliberately went out to the Scott home and found Dick struggling with the patio furniture.

"I should have put a ball and chain on Tim," he gasped. "Lend a hand, will you, Kelsey?"

Tom lent a hand. Within the hour they had the glider, the chairs, and the table out on the flagstone terrace. No cushions yet, said Dick. Judith always refurbished them, and had a later date for bringing them out and leaving them.

"Let's sit down and catch our breath," he told Tom.

"What's the next job?"

Dick grinned and examined a tear in his canvas shoe. "What's on your mind?" he asked.

So Tom told him what was on his mind. "I get a strong idea that someone is deliberately spreading the talk."

"Why?"

"Why do I get the idea, or why do they do it?"

"I know why you get the idea, Buddy, but I do not know what anyone has against you."

"I can't think of that myself," said Tom with elaborate false modesty.

"One day," said Dick, stretching his legs into the sunshine, "at the cafeteria, something was said—not much—and I asked why there should be any talk at all about you. I said that you were a nice guy. . . ."

Tom waited.

"Yes!" said Dick, getting to his feet. "And one of the men pointed out that you were pretty young, and new in the organization, to have been given a big job like chief of a service."

Tom sat frowning. "Do they want me to quit?"

"I don't know who *they* are, and I don't know what *they* want. But you have a boss, Tom. Why not talk to him about all this?"

"Tell him that I see ghosts and talk to them on the telephone?"

"Do you think he hasn't?"

Tom liked Dr. Lewis. He had no reason to fear the man. He would do as Dick suggested. Probably Dick had taken some problems of his own to the Chief of Research Services.

On Monday, Tom himself called the top floor office and asked for a chance to talk to Dr. Lewis. Oh, a half-hour should more than do it. Yes, he would be glad to eat lunch with Dr. Lewis. At one? "Thank you."

"I could have taken care of that for you," Karen told him when he hung up.

"I know you could. But I don't want to lose my touch. I may not always have the cutest secretary at the Medical Center."

Karen was cute. Today she had her dark hair drawn back with a broad red ribbon tied into a bow. Her black dress was piped and belted in red, the skirt rippling and flipping above long black stockings and red shoes. She was a very cute girl, and a good worker. Tom told himself that he was lucky.

At one, when he faced Dr. Lewis across ham and lima beans, head lettuce and butterscotch pie, he listed Karen as one of the good things about his job. Then he settled into his chair. "Why I wanted to see you," he said, "was to ask you why you put me in as head of the Service?"

"Somebody's asked you that, I suppose," said Dr. Lewis keenly.

"Well, yes, sir. At least, it is being pointed out that I am fairly new at Research, That I am young—"

Dr. Lewis smiled.

"And," Tom continued, "that there were others as able, surely."

"Yes," said the Chief of Research. "There were others." His tone was dry. "Tom," he said, "are you a religious man?"

Tom flushed. "I was raised to go to church every Sunday. I go rather regularly now."

"Mhmmmn. Then you will recognize this line. 'Whosoever of you will be the chiefest, shall be servant of all.' "

Tom sat silent.

"It is the hardest thing in the world to be that kind of servant," said Dr. Lewis quietly.

Tom could only gaze at this man who knew so well what it was to be "chiefest."

"Don't you want the job, Tom?" Dr. Lewis asked kindly.

Tom gulped and reached for his water glass. "I'd like to think I could swing it," he said faintly.

"You can. You could. That's why I picked you. To see if you'd think you could swing it."

Tom felt his face getting hot, and he tugged at his shirt collar. Could the Chief have been testing him? Placing obstacles? Like those weird telephone calls and the memos? No! Certainly he had not. But there was a good chance he had been watching Tom to see what he would do when such things happened—especially the built-in gossip over the Trice case—just as Tom's friends had watched . . .

He had an impulse to jump up, run out of the staff dining room to seek some dark and quiet spot and think back, try to remember how he had performed. . . .

He took a deep breath. "I suppose what has been happening," he said quietly, "is because I have been put into the limelight."

"Yes," agreed Dr. Lewis dryly. "As limelight goes here at the Center."

"It's as bright as I'd want," Tom assured him. "And, if you'll allow me, it comes along with some pretty heady wine to drink. I—I—well, I believe I'll start over, sir."

Dr. Lewis nodded. "You do that. Did you ever get your files straightened out?"

"Yes, sir. And thinned out, too. I spent several Sunday afternoons on that job. Stirred up some ghosts much better left buried. And I may be too young for my job, but I'm not half as young as I was when I put some of that stuff down on paper."

The Chief chuckled. "Well, if you're looking for another diversion, why don't you help Carter Bass move? I understand you two get along well with each other, even that you like each other.

Tom finished his pie. He was tempted to mention Personnel's stand on romance. "I like her fine," he said quietly.

Tom knew all about Carter's moving. Ever since Christmas, she had talked about it, debating with herself the benefits of living in a hotel and those of having her own apartment. She asked her friends for advice, and they gave it, but she made her own decision. Tom and Dick Scott teased her about doing this, but it was right that she should decide; she would have to live with the results.

A month ago she had finally decided that she would move. There was this new apartment building within a few blocks of the Center. For that month she talked about decorating problems, furniture, kitchen gadgets. Maid service would be available, but she planned to do some cooking. "And towels!" she told them. "At the hotel, I took towels as a matter of course. But now . . ."

"Didn't you ever live alone before?" Tom asked her. "In a house or somewhere?"

"Let me think." She made a big thing of going back in time, and back— "You're probing into my past," she assured her friend.

"Not with any great results," Tom told her.

She flushed. "Oh, I'm sorry. There's nothing to probe for, really. You see, I lived with my father in my grandparents' home. My mother died when I was born. My dad was a doctor —he still is—and he didn't marry again. First, the grandparents took care of us, now he takes care of Grandfather. My grandmother has died. The men have a housekeeper. But that's in Iowa. . . ."

"They use towels in Iowa," Tom drawled.

"But I never bought any."

Now the great day had arrived, and Carter was moving— with enough help, Tom assured her, to move the Congressional Library. "Especially when you consider that you have bought all new furniture for the apartment, and aren't stealing any from the hotel."

But there were clothes—suitcases full of clothes, and garment bags. A huge green plastic bag full of shoes, even a dozen hatboxes.

"Although I've yet to see you wear a hat," Tom complained. He was carrying things down to his car, and to Carter's.

There were hundreds of books. "And *hundreds!*" said Tom. Packed into dozens of somewhat small boxes. "But heavy!"

There was another heavy box into which she had put medicines—"What ails you, Doctor?"—and face creams, lotions, powders, perfume . . .

"If I'm due to fall and break something today," Tom assured her, "it will be with this load of perfumed dynamite in my hands."

"Then don't fall," Carter advised.

"Lord, but you're bossy."

"I'm taking advantage of my rare opportunity," she assured him.

Down the hotel elevator, into his car, a drive of six blocks, into the apartment elevator—there were other friends at the apartment, ready to unpack books and place them on the shelves, to hang coats and things into the closets. . . .

Tom carried his box of breakables straight to the largest of the two bathrooms. Carter came with him to direct the placing of these things. Before she started to take jars and bottles from him, she removed the handsome ring she wore, twisted it into a tissue, and looked about for a place to put it. She went over to the window, opened it, and tucked the small package into the space between the window and the storm sash.

"Will it be safe there?" Tom asked her.

"On the sixteenth floor, nobody is apt to come by outside and see it."

"I guess not." They went to work.

Carter had plenty of help. There were two men who were bringing in the furniture. Carter seemed to know them; later someone told Tom that they were brothers, and one of them had a child at her clinic. There was Lonnie, the orderly from the Institute, who was the most useful of them all. Before the day was over, he was bossing everybody and calling the doctors "Doc."

"I hope this doesn't carry over into Monday," Dick found time to murmur to Tom.

"Monday, we'll all be flat on our backs," Tom predicted.

"On our backs," Dick mimicked Lonnie's way of repeating the end of each sentence. "Take Tim with you when you go back for more books. There's no need for Carter to go back and forth."

"Two cars are a help."

"Tom can drive Carter's."

"Well," growled Tom, "I guess in this crowd of willing workers we did have to turn up a brain."

But, really, he was enjoying the day. Wearing a light blue outfit which everyone else called a coverall, but he called a jump suit—"I was told I could go anywhere in this!"—his height let him set books and bric-a-brac on the top shelves without risking life and limb on a stepstool. Judy and Linda Scott pressed him and his height into use setting china and glassware into place in the kitchen.

"I'm so glad I have been wise in selecting my best friends," Carter told them all, her face smug.

Gradually, with all the work and all the fun, the apartment was furnished, and the help could collapse, tired, but content with the job they had done.

"There's no toilet paper," said Tim, coming out of the bathroom.

"Use one of those damned books," growled Tom Kelsey.

"I'm making a list of things I forgot," said Carter seriously.

"Give it here," Tom told her. "I'm going out for hero sandwiches and some coffee."

"I have coffee," Carter said, "and a percolator."

"I want my coffee brewed and hot," said Tom. "Tim, you and Linda come help your old back-broken Uncle Tom carry all the food it's going to take . . ." His voice drifted down the hall. Carter sprang for the door. "Get pink toilet paper," she called after them.

On Sunday, Tom went back to the apartment—"to see what we did"—and to take Carter out for dinner. He walked through the rooms with what she called a smugly proprietary air; he straightened the silver-framed mirror in the foyer, he tried the pull cords for the brocade curtains in the living room, and nodded with approval at the painted furniture in her bedroom.

"I wouldn't take up moving as a career," he decided, "but in this the results are tangible. Especially my various muscle strains and aches."

"Doctoring doesn't give you strains and aches?" she asked him.

It did. As soon as Monday morning, after he and Dick Scott had compared their backaches and Tom had sat down to study the week's schedule of lectures, clinics—Karen brought him a typed memo.

Tom looked at it and took off his dark-rimmed desk glasses. "Ask the detective sergeant to come in," he said quietly. He worked constantly with the police.

Except for the muscle twinges, things were back to normal.

The detective came in, a close-cropped man in his fifties with the taut, alert face of his profession. He showed Dr. Kelsey his identification, and Tom asked him to sit down.

"I am looking for a certain runaway girl," the officer told the doctor. "I understand you have some of these people working here at the Research Institute."

*These people.* Tom resented the term, always.

"If you mean what the newspapers call the street people," he said quietly, "and your runaway girl is helping us here, it might be better to let her stay here until you are sure identifying her will better her situation."

"I am bound only by the law."

"Yes, I know," said Dr. Kelsey. They had several young people about who probably were runaways.

"Do you let these kids crash here?" Sergeant Messenger asked. "I mean, do you let them sleep here?"

"I am familiar with the term," said Tom. "No, we do not let the aides sleep here. They come here to work. Cleaning up physically is a perquisite, we pay them a little and feed them amply."

"Do they work at Clausen Center, too?"

"No. Over there the situation is a bit different. I could explain . . ."

"I think I understand. Now this girl . . ."

Tom recognized her at once. She was helping in the diet kitchen, a very young girl with a tight, defensive face.

"Tell me," he said, "when you find this girl—or any girl— what do you do for them? How do you treat them?"

"Believe me or not, Doctor, we are looking out for their welfare."

"I believe you," said Tom pleasantly. "I was just curious. These kids show up—they stay with us for a time—they disappear. I am curious about what happens to some of them."

"You probably help the ones you get here," said the policeman. "As for what we do—well, depending on circumstances, we sometimes return the kids to the parents. Sometimes they go into Juvenile Court—if there is some charge against them like drug possession, car theft—or, and this happens when they are reluctant to return home, we send them for counseling."

"I see," said the doctor.

"Is that bad?" asked the policeman.

"No," said Tom. "No. If you treat each case as an individual problem—I suppose it is the only way."

"Isn't that the way you treat your medical cases?"

Tom laughed. "Yes," he said, "it is." He buzzed for Karen. "We have your girl here," he said quietly.

Things were back to normal; the normal amount of cases came to Research and must be handled, the normal amount of success and failure was to be anticipated.

By that evening, Tom was admitting that his chief bother for the day was trying to keep pencils on his desk. Yes, he knew. Each morning, Karen set a little jar of them, all freshly sharpened, on the blotter.

"But I never can find one!" he declared.

She said she would watch. And the next day she agreed. The pencils did disappear. "But you have dozens of people through here each day," she reminded him.

"The whole joint should bristle with sharp-pointed yellow pencils," Tom grumbled. "Unless somebody is making a collection."

"Who'd collect pencils?" Karen asked.

"Who'd do a lot of things?"

He did.

"I don't dare consider the things I have to do," he would tell himself at night. Some of these things he enjoyed, some fascinated him, some he despised and dreaded to have repeated.

"I don't think I enjoy being the boss," he told himself solemnly. The work he liked. The pursuit and eradication of lead poisoning, Sahrman's sickle cells—

But when it came a matter of charges against one of the supervisors . . .

"She steals," Dr. Lawson had told him.

Tom sat shaking his head.

"I have the evidence, Dr. Kelsey. Things disappear from the personnel's street clothes, from purses, from the supply room. Various ones have been doing a little detective work . . ."

"On whose authority?" Tom asked sharply.

"Well, their own, I suppose. To begin with, at any rate. She's been seen going through raincoat pockets."

"Does she steal pencils?" asked Tom, then he flushed. "I have trouble keeping some on my desk," he explained. "Forgive me, I wouldn't suggest . . ."

"But you'll have to handle this matter, Dr. Kelsey. We can't have the complaints going over to Central Personnel without our attempting . . ."

No, they could not. Tom must set a time to talk to the supervisor, and to talk to those charging her with theft, also to those who offered themselves in the supervisor's defense. They mentioned her years of service, and the fact that she had a mother to support.

Tom had to be the one to sit in judgment. The supervisor must be moved. "For the good of morale," he told the woman. "Whether you did any of these things or not, you are experienced enough in hospital work to realize . . ."

The woman was ten years older than he. He disliked having to judge another person. . . .

He disliked most intensely, realizing, as he must, that cliques had formed in the Institute and at the Clinic—perhaps throughout the entire Complex. He did not, and would not, inquire into the basis for those cliques. But they were there. He could not say they were anti or pro Kelsey. Generally, people were friendly or at least courteous with Tom. But various rulings were popular, or not. Various changes were accepted, or groused about. Sides were taken.

To a degree, this sort of thing was routine in all hospital setups. Tom supposed the bigger the hospital, the wider the breach between the pros and cons. Probably he was not a feature. He determined himself to stay out of any alignments.

He could have ideas and opinions, but, except where his own Service was concerned, he could keep still about those opinions and ideas.

Though of course if a man had friends, and talked at all—Take Elene Trice alone. A man could stub his toe just saying *hello* to that girl in the hall.

She was still working over at Clausen. Tom saw her there. He saw her on the street. The nice clean-cut boy friend still seemed to be around, but Elene flirted with almost every other man available. With Tom of course. That had become a running gag. But she flirted with Sahrman almost as gaily, and trouble could result from her doing it. So Tom probably would have to take some stand on Elene.

There were other friends. Elene's mother, Evalyn. She was apt to expect favors.

There was Carter, who truly was his friend. Tom liked her a lot, and enjoyed her company. He would have enjoyed eating lunch with her each day, dropping in on her clinic as often—only of course he could not do this. For Carter's sake and, he supposed his own.

He even had to weigh and balance his friendship with Dick Scott. Since that friendship was not based on hospital politics, he must carefully avoid any appearance or suggestion that it was. Oh, it was a complicated life he led! A very thin tightrope he walked.

Even Lonnie—Tom had grown to depend on the orderly, to trust him. But Lonnie was only one of several, and the Chief must show no favors.

Favors? To heap extra work on a willing man? Well, yes, he supposed . . .

His most annoying problem was Elene Trice—especially annoying because he would not under other circumstances have given a second thought or glance to the girl. She was young, immature, an exhibitionist. He could have passed her on the street without a second glance; these tall, long-haired, oddly dressed young girls were not his type.

But Elene—he must always remember her dead father. For this reason he had let her pick him up in the hotel dining room. For this reason, he had found a way for her to work at Clausen. He had listened to her talk, but only up to a point. Then he had taken fifteen minutes to tell her bluntly, plainly, that her dream man was definitely not Dr. Kelsey. She must rid herself of all such ideas.

So—the irritating girl had selected Steven Sahrman as a substitute. She herself had explained the transfer to Tom. "I am going to pursue my dream with him," she said. "It is a very satisfying arrangement. We need each other."

Tom didn't remember that he had made any comment in reply. But he did remember what Elene had said; this was followed by an occasional glimpse of the two together at the coffee machine, walking along the Boulevard, arms about each other's waist, standing at a street corner, the girl leaning against a light standard, the man too close to her, his head inclined, his eyes upon her face, talking to her, talking . . .

This was all wrong! Elene had the frank, aggressive manner which came from the knowledge that her position in society would protect her from her own foolishness. Sahrman—his whole background, his history, would make him take what he could get, where he could get it. He was a good-looking devil—but—

"What are you going to do about it?" Carter challenged Tom. "Marry the girl? Then stop feeling responsible for her. You're not. You cannot even *seem* to accede to every kookie girl who makes passes at you, Tom Kelsey."

He laughed.

"Girls make the passes these days," Carter assured him.

"And I'm a fair target?"

"Aren't you?"

"Oh, for Pete's sake, Carter!"

"You're single, you're a doctor, you are young. You have money."

He laughed again.

"Just keep those things in mind, and watch it, brother."

"I shall," he agreed. "I do. But this business—I don't suppose I can interfere?"

"Professionally, you mean? No, you cannot. Unless Sahrman's work suffers. I don't suppose Elene does enough work to make any difference."

"And I don't want to take the position of being her friend and defender."

"You bet you don't. So just put your head in the sand, Doctor. Any step could be the wrong one."

"Maybe I could even mix a metaphor or two."

Carter shook her head at him. "That was a low blow, my friend."

"I'm sorry."

"I don't think you are, but to go back to Dr. Sahrman and the fair Elene. Is it beyond possibility that he might be the right one for that girl?"

"You're not talking about marriage?"

"Well—these Europeans consider only one other alternative."

"I don't believe he's right for her under any circumstances."

"You can't stay out of it and get in with both feet, too, Tom."

"No. I can't."

So he would attend strictly to his own business. Avoid Elene, and talk only sickle-cell to Sahrman.

Personnel was right. Romance had no place in the Institute.

And according to its rules, Tom could not take notice of this romance without being ready to fire the principals. He'd fire Elene in a minute, but Sahrman—the man had already put in a couple of years trying to establish his American license. This should not be thwarted lightly.

So—Tom would be blind—and deaf. And certainly he would keep silent on the subject.

He was doing just that, and working with Sahrman as well. Sahrman had turned up some cases of sickle-cell anemia over at Clausen, and the two doctors were charting out a family investigation of the affliction. They were bent over large sheets of chart paper when Evalyn came into the room. Tom said good morning pleasantly without diverting his attention. Dr. Sahrman was more elaborate to Elene's mother. He told her how becoming her volunteer pinafore was.

She smiled at him and said that was why she did volunteer work. "Dr. Kelsey . . . ?" she said tentatively.

Tom straightened and took off his glasses.

Mrs. Trice smiled at him. "I know you are not in charge of the volunteers," she said. "And you probably won't miss me, but I wanted to tell you that I am going on a short trip."

"Well, that's fine, Mrs. Trice. How long . . . ?"

"Over the weekend, and maybe a day or two longer. I am going with friends to Hot Springs."

"Is Elene going with you?"

"Oh, no. She will stay with friends here."

"Well—have a good time. You deserve a change." She was right. She need not have told Tom at all. He returned immediately to the sickle-cell matter. He wanted, he said, to see each case as it turned up—the original little boy was related to a great many people living within the Clausen area.

He put Evalyn Trice so entirely out of his mind that, on that early Sunday morning, he had to be reminded of her trip. He was barely out of bed, and still in his robe and pajamas, though he did have his breakfast coffee and egg before him, when the telephone rang.

He glanced at the clock as he went to answer. Who, at this hour . . . ?

It was Elene, and he made a face as he managed to say quietly, "Yes, Elene. What can I do for you?"

She was excited, and even weeping, he thought. "Calm down," he told her. "Tell me what's happened. Is your mother sick?"

That was when she reminded him of her mother's trip. Elene had, she said, spent the night with Tessie Sellers—whoever that might be—and she had decided to go home for her raincoat . . .

That figured. Tom's front window streamed with rain.

"And—and—" gasped Elene. "We've had a burglar!"

She said some more, getting more excited—and each thing she said ended with, "Oh, Tom, do come over! It's so close to your house—and I'm scared to *move!*"

She was alone, she was at home. Tom said he would be over, but he would have to dress.

He put the phone down and stood for a minute contemplating his—his *quandary*. A burglary at Trice's—Elene—alone—at the house . . .

He should have told her to call Sahrman. . . . "No!" he shouted loudly, and was ashamed of himself. He went back to the kitchen, ate a piece of cold toast, drank his cooled coffee. He supposed Elene had called the police.

But had she?

Tom could call them. Or he could go upstairs and climb into some clothes . . .

He found corduroy slacks, a thick pullover sweater, brogue shoes—he was pulling them on when he thought of Carter.

164

Yes, sir! That was a good idea. He reached for the telephone beside his bed and, against his will, remembered the night it had rung, involving him in the affairs of the Trice family.

He dialed Carter's number; her phone rang and rang. He gave it six times, and shook his head. She could be away for the weekend herself, or gone to church; perhaps she had been called to the Institute. Her leukemia kids could stir up things, and she had a tricky heart situation . . .

In any case, she wasn't available to go to Trice's with Tom. He'd have to go alone. The police would be there when he arrived, or very soon after. . . .

He ran downstairs and out to his car. The rain had subsided to a gentle patter; the streets were washed clean and shining. The spring flowers and young tree leaves made a pretty picture. He pulled up at the Trice curb and was relieved to see a police black and white in the driveway. Maybe Tom need not go in . . .

But, since he had come this far, he did go in. Elene admitted him, gladly, and told the police officer in the hall who he was. "A close friend of the family. I called him when—"

Tom looked about; there was no immediate sign of robbery or forced entry.

"They got in by breaking a basement window, Doctor," the policeman told him. "A very neat burglar, and he knew the house, where to find things."

It was the same procedure as had been followed at Bonley's, and at Dr. Lewis's former home. Furs were missing, some jewelry—the good stuff, diamonds. Some cash which Mrs. Trice always kept on hand in one of the small drawers of an old desk in an upstairs sitting room. In her bedroom, the spread had been folded back, the sheets and satin quilt turned back into a neat triangle. Tom stared at it and shivered.

Hadn't there been other burglaries marked by this same

method? he asked.

The policeman on duty did not know.

Tom knew of three, all connected with the hospital. All entries into a home known to be empty. "How many people knew you and your mother would be away?" he asked Elene.

She looked at him, blank-faced. "Why, just about everybody," she answered.

He supposed her mother had told others beside himself—and *Sahrman!*

Sahrman had known that the Bonley home . . .

He had, Tom remembered, been surprised to know that Dr. Lewis had moved. He—

Well, he probably had been in the Trice home. He possibly had been invited to Bonley's, and even to Dr. Lewis's. Kindnesses to a doctor in a strange land were not surprising.

"Remind me never to ask him to my house!" Tom told himself grimly. Then he was angry at the way his suspicions had turned. He could as readily be suspected, or Lonnie, or—

"It stumps me," said the policeman.

Tom should let it "stump" him.

CHAPTER 7

ELENE WANTED him to stay with her, but he would not. She was to lock up the house, he said. He nailed a board across the broken basement window and checked on the door up into the house. Elene was to go back to Tessie's; her mother would expect her to be there.

Besides, he had other commitments for this Sunday. He had come over when she called him . . . "Though all you needed was the police. If I were you, I'd call your mother and tell her what has happened."

On this Sunday, Tom had been invited to go out to the Scotts' river cabin, and he meant to go, rain or shine, though the rain did seem to be clearing up.

He went home, cleared away what was left of his breakfast, heated the coffee and drank some. Muttering about fool girls, he tidied his bedroom, found some lighter casual clothes, and drove away, stopping at the Institute for a quick check. Clausen was not open on Sundays. Then he headed for the river. "This is going to be a good day," he told himself. And Tom hoped he would reach the cabin in time for lunch. He was starved. He'd talk to Dick about the robbery—and the coincidences—and—

What he really talked about, mostly, was the interview he'd had with the Personnel Director on the matter of office romances.

He and Dick were working on the canoe, Tom under it, Dick ready to caulk any cracks or pinholes Tom could see against the sky. Ten feet away, young Tim was scraping paint on the john boat.

"That interview conditioned you," Dick told his friend. "You keep watching for situations."

"Well, I don't have to watch. They keep bobbing up, so of course I have the warning on my mind. Lately I've had Sahrman and Elene Trice to keep it there."

"Mhmmmn," said Dick. "And then there's you and Carter Bass."

"Oh, but that's different," declared Tom. "Carter and I are friends."

"She hopes not," said Dick, daubing compound. "Why didn't you bring her out today?"

"I called her to go over to Trices' with me. She wasn't at home."

"So you went unprotected."

"That was the damnedest thing . . ." Tom mused, and the talk changed to the burglaries, their weird similarities. . . .

But the next day, by coincidence surely, the Personnel Director came to the cafeteria at Research for his lunch, and elected to join Tom and Dick Scott. He explained that he made a practice of visiting the smaller cafeterias. "I like to keep my finger on the pulse, as it were."

"Don't touch Kelsey's," Dick advised him. "You'll find it jumpy."

Tom looked up in protest and saw Mr. Franzel's eyes on him speculatively. "Is something wrong?" he asked.

"No," said Tom bluntly.

Dr. Scott laughed. "You conditioned the poor guy a year ago," he explained. "You warned him of the dire consequences of office romance, and he sees cupids and flower-twined hearts wherever he looks."

"I can always take my cheese sandwich elsewhere," Tom promised his friend.

"Oh, don't do that!" Dick protested. "You'd probably not better yourself."

The Director was smiling. "I was pleased when I knew you had been named Chief of your Service, Kelsey," he said. "Are you having some trouble with the boys and girls?"

"I hope not."

"We can joke," said the Director, "but office romances can become troublesome matters in an organization the size of the University Hospitals Complex."

"When do they become troublesome?" Tom asked. "I suppose interference with duties would be the main thing."

"Yes, of course. And gossip—excessive gossip, that is. Things said that patients could overhear, and that would destroy morale and confidence."

"I see," said Tom. "What do the officials—the Board, would that be?—what do they do when gossip gets out of hand? I can think of other embarrassing situations—like calls from a suspicious wife."

"Or from an equally suspicious husband," agreed Mr. Franzel.

"Yes, of course," Tom agreed. "Or husband. How do you deal with a romantic and potentially damaging affair? I'm new at this executive job, you know."

Mr. Franzel glance at Dr. Scott, who also was Chief of a service.

"I like the ostrich attitude myself," said Dick

"Does it work?" Both Tom and the Director asked the question.

Dick shrugged. "So far it has," he said.

"Sometimes it does work," agreed the Director. "We had a situation—one of our junior accountants began going about with a nursing supervisor. There was some talk, and a bit of silliness. We ignored both things, and after what was really only a short time, the whole thing blew over."

"Did their romancing affect their work?"

"It didn't last long enough. We watched that carefully."

"And if it had affected it?"

"Oh, well, then we would have fired them."

"Both of them?" Tom looked troubled.

"Yes, Dr. Kelsey. For one thing, we are not a court, deciding upon fault or innocence. Second, we cannot tolerate any interference with the efficient operation of the complex. In your case, you would have to consider the efficient functioning of your Service."

"I see."

"Obviously," Mr. Franzel continued, "Scott's ostrich operation is a relief, but it works only up to a point. Other companies, and for that matter some units in this corporation, adopt a ruthless attitude from the start."

Tom got up to fetch a dish of ice cream, his face and mind troubled. The entire discussion had taken place with Elene on his mind. He felt sure that it would crush the girl should he fire her. He had moved her out of Research, but she still saw him and talked to him whenever she could. Just yesterday she had called him to her home.

The burglary had shaken her, as it should have. But losing her job—such a little job—should not really upset her at all. She was a foolish girl, and young, and perhaps needed a lesson taught her at this time.

The trouble was—Tom threaded his way back to the ta[?] where Scot and Franzel were talking about fishing—the trouble was, Tom's judgment about Elene's situation was clouded by his own sense of guilt concerning her father's death.

Dick guessed his thoughts, and as the two men went upstairs again, he asked Tom, "You were thinking about the Trice girl, weren't you?"

"She's a bloody nuisance, Dick!" Tom cried hotly. "But the trouble is, she'd be an even bloodier one if I'd fire her."

"I've a thought to inject which won't solve anything, but it might give you something different to think about. Have you considered what you would face if Lewis's 'corporation' here—" his hand swept out to embrace the stairs and the entire building which held Research—"if this corporation thought you or your Dr. Sahrman were involved with that girl?"

Tom stopped. He looked up at Dick who had mounted a step or two. His face was white. "Not me!" he protested. "He couldn't hear a thing like that!"

Dick shrugged. "He might not believe it," he said. "But he could hear it all right." He started up the rest of the stairs.

"Dick, wait!" said Tom, hurrying after him.

"Don't think about it so much," Dick advised him. "And I can't wait; in ten minutes I'm due in surgery."

Tom went on to his office with two resolves. He would forget about Elene Trice, or he would get her out of his Service. He could do either thing, and he would.

He began forgetting her by having three people in a row ask him about the Trice burglary. Yes, he had been there. Not when it was discovered, but he'd been called.

And there was the whole heap in front of him again. People asked or guessed why he had been called. Her father's

ith would be remembered, and the talk about that . . .
Oh, the devil with it!

He told Karen, abruptly, that he was going up to Cancer
and watch Dr. Scott operate.

She was surprised. Was it something special?

"I don't know anything except that he is operating. You
could reach me . . ." He went out and up to the observation deck of Dick's o.r. This, he thought, would give him
something ordered to watch. No flap, no doubts. Dick knew
what he was doing, and did it.

Tom leaned forward on the bench. The scene was as he
would have pictured it had he stayed downstairs and imagined
the whole thing. The rather small room, somewhat crowded
with apparatus and gear. The table—the patient—Tom could
see his forehead and gray hair under the tent of the anesthetist's shield. The anesthetist and his tanks, tubes, suspended
bottles, and monitors. The surgeon, his assistant across from
him, the intern, the surgical nurse—

They were doing chest surgery, and had reached the cavity.
Tom hunched forward. Dick was a joy to watch.

And then—

Instantly he was on his feet, running, a doctor whose re-
flex was to go in and save. He was out through the door, running down the stairs to o.r., to help anyone who had been
hurt in that flash of fire. A doctor who could be needed.

It had started in an anesthetic container—a flash and a
muffled explosion—and Dr. Kelsey running—

The fire was out by the time he reached o.r. And the
patient, accompanied by several gowned, masked people, was
being moved into the adjoining o.r., where surgery would
continue and the operation be completed. Only the assisting
resident had been burned. If Dr. Kelsey would please care for
him . . .

Tom did care for the man, who would be all right. His arm, shoulder, and cheek were burned. The flare had gone that way. And he was soon in good condition.

"We're so glad you were right outside the door," the Floor Head told Tom. "How did that happen?"

"I was observing. But if you think I have guardian angel qualities, go right ahead," Tom told her.

"I sent word in to Dr. Scott that you were here," she said.

"Good. Now you can tell him that everything will be fine." He went back again to check on his new patient, who had been put to bed, a good bit groggy from what had happened. "You'll be fine," Tom told him. "Dr. Scott will see to that." He glanced at the nurse. "I'll go downstairs again," he said, "where I belong."

"Come back the next time we need you," she said, still gazing at him with wonder.

Tom smiled at her and entered the stairwell. Cancer was on Seven; it would take several flights of stairs to steady him down. In the elevator he would have met people. It wasn't the emergency—Lord, he was doctor enough to care for a burned man!—but the emergency itself—that it would happen—

Was he, Tom Kelsey, actually living in a Hitchcock movie? Those pictures were done in a murky light, with swirling mists; the things that had been happening to Tom—they cropped up in the full light of a gleaming hospital corridor, in the shadowless light of an operating room.

These things were done . . .

*These things were done* . . . Cold prickled along his arms, twisted the nerve reflexes of his abdomen.

*Done* . . .

By whom? Not just that swift explosion of an hour ago. Though, God knew, a fire in o.r. was a *thing!*

And added to all his other things, his spilled files—all of

it. So far no pattern of these weird events had developed, and probably no pattern would. There probably was no connection beyond coincidence between this explosion today and his yellow pencils, or the folded-back covers in a burglarized house.

There could be no connection! That flash of fire, which he could still see against his eyelids—

He stopped short where he was, between the second and first floor, with his own footsteps still echoing. But that fire in o.r. was *dangerous!*

If there was a pattern, the thing must be stopped—and at once! The guilty apprehended and restrained. If Tom Kelsey were victim, or, if only by coincidence, present and aware, as he had been today, he must move in and care for things.

He may not have found a pattern in the events that occurred around and about him, but he was certain that someone was being warned—or terrorized.

But to what purpose? And who was behind all this? That was the important question.

It was at the end of that week—March was flirting with spring. One day would be soft and sunny, with fragrant breezes. Another following would be chill, the clouds moving in. Tom had walked to Research that morning, liking to do this, though if he went over to Clausen and back, then home again . . . Oh, what were a few shoe soles? He worked out harder on the tennis courts. Having enjoyed his walk, he came down the corridor that morning whistling softly. Karen would not be in this early, but Lonnie was.

He ran after the doctor, his string mop flapping.

"Take it easy," Tom told him.

"Dr. Lewis said . . ." Lonnie stopped and gasped for breath. "Dr. Lewis would like to see you, like to see you."

Tom turned to look at the orderly. "He told you. . . ?"

"He came in here—I was here—he told me, he told me."

Tom looked at his watch. He still was fifteen minutes early, though of course in medical work even office hours were flexible.

"I'll hang up my coat," he said. He scratched a note and left it in Karen's typewriter, felt of his blue tie-knot, and went out to the elevator.

Yes, Dr. Lewis was expecting him.

The conference lasted ten minutes, and Tom came out of it feeling strange. It showed in his face when he came back into his office. Karen had arrived and was still getting set for the day.

"What's wrong?" she asked Dr. Kelsey.

Tom frowned. "Nothing." Nothing was wrong. Dr. Lewis had been scrupulously ethical. "I hope you will agree with this decision, Dr. Kelsey. I would like to see Dr. Sahrman do a little work over at the diagnostic hospital under Dr. Lindsay."

What could Tom say?

He said those few things. That this was sudden.

"He is supposed to get a variety of experience," Dr. Lewis pointed out.

"He is doing some good work for me on sickle-cell anemia, Dr. Lewis."

"I shall find you a good replacement. What do you think of Dr. Duclos?"

Duclos was one of the physicians at Clausen.

"Those people over there will miss him."

"He'll be going over to Clausen regularly, won't he? They will see him if they come to Research."

So—the change was made. Sahrman was moved to Diagnostics. Duclos would come in here, and a woman physician was to replace him at Clausen.

Tom liked Duclos.

He and Sahrman . . . the volatile man had really not been too good working with the poor, though he was improving.

Elene would think—Tom himself would think—that Sahrman was being taken out of her range—which was silly. Tom could have fired Elene much more easily.

Tom had talked to Dr. Lewis about Sahrman—had he ever mentioned Elene in that talk? He could not remember. Was there gossip going around which Tom had not heard? Did Dr. Lewis think there was conflict between Tom and Sahrman? Well, occasionally there was conflict, but not about Elene. Not much about her, at any rate.

Tom should never have given her a job.

He never should have answered Evalyn's call about her sick husband.

Tom had talked to Dr. Lewis of "ghosts."

Did he think that Sahrman was conjuring these to plague Tom, and was he removing him for that reason? If so, it could be wrong to do that, even if Sahrman was the culprit. If—

Oh, the devil with it all!

Sahrman blamed Tom for the transfer. He came storming into the office and expressed himself volubly, sometimes in English that was as hard to understand as his Hungarian.

Tom sat back in his chair, rolled his pencil between his hands, and waited for the man to run out of steam.

"You're dead wrong," he said then. "I had nothing to do with it."

Sahrman's eyes flashed. "I do not believe you."

Tom shrugged and mentioned the variety of experience. This change, he said, was made for Dr. Sahrman's benefit. That is, he tried to say it.

But Sahrman was kicking up such a row. . . In Tom's office, out in the corridor—he talked to everybody. He even went up to Dr. Lewis. And there he mentioned Dr. Kelsey and Dr. Bass. Dr. Kelsey and Elene. Dr. Kelsey and Mrs. Trice . . .

He came downstairs again and told about the things which he had said. His dark eyes sparked, his hands waved. People listened. It was quite a show, at which he often had a sizable audience of fascinated nurses, orderlies, patients, and aides. He talked to everybody—the volunteers, the messengers, other staff men.

"Of course," said Sahrman, "being on the executive level is a great help to Dr. Kelsey. He gets a better parking space, better keys to better places. He becomes privileged with the ladies."

While on Sahrman's level—if one cared to lower his eyes—one only got transferred. What, he demanded, did a researcher know about an executive position?

It was Dr. Lawson who told him coldly that he had better pack up and move over to Diagnostic, check in with Lindsay, or he would have no level at all. "You'd better get yourself straightened out," he said, "and do the work assigned. If you want your license, that is."

Sahrman said he would take his sickle-cell work with him.

"You know you won't."

Sahrman dropped his head. "Yes," he said sadly. "I do know. I have no rights."

Karen told Tom about this. Tom shook his head and tried to settle down to his own work. It would have been much easier to have kept Sahrman here. . . .

But drifting through his mind, and occasionally coming into bright focus, he wondered about this executive level business. There had to be levels in hospital work as well as in other organizations. Hospitals were corporations, in Franzel's view—though not in Tom's, ever. But in certain circum-

177

stances, one did have to consider the corporate picture.

Sahrman's angry charges had scattered over a wide field. Researchers should not be executives at all. Doctors like Kelsey should let the ladies alone. . . .

Tom smiled wryly at this. In his opinion, he made a strange Don Juan!

But to go back to the corporation image. When romance was injected, or gossip about romance, even ruthless corporations would give some warning. Wouldn't they?

Sahrman had been transferred, not fired. Could this have been done as a warning to the man?

Or were "they" warning Tom, through Sahrman?

It was conceivable, though not palatable, that Research— this "company"—would want to protect its operation, even its reputation, and so removed a Management man at the hint of an affair. Would they want to keep a trained, and therefore valuable, executive under the same circumstances? Even though they did this reluctantly? Probably they would warn that valuable man.

How?

That night Tom went home and spent hours picturing such a warning as coming to him. He concluded that there would be an easy, informal session with his peers at Research. The men might joke about his being too popular with the ladies. They would mention a "rumor going around."

That probably would be all. It then would be up to Tom to straighten things out.

He tried to laugh at his fevered imaginings. In the next days he worked hard at the Institute; he played squash hard in the evenings—

And found himself jumpy when he received the next notice of a directors' meeting.

Could he be fired on Sahrman's word that he had been dallying with as many as three women who worked for the Institute?

He hadn't been. He was innocent. But could he prove it?

Nothing actually was said at the directors' meeting which could even quiver Tom's antenna. Sahrman's transfer was mentioned without comment. Dr. Duclos' move to socio-medical was stated. Yes, that seemed to be where he wanted to work.

"He's a good man," Tom was able to proclaim, and not even think he was also evaluating Sahrman.

It was a relief to get out from under the cloud with which he had walked that week—until he bumped into Jack Lenox over at the Administration offices. Tom had no business with Administration; he was only taking a short cut. Jack worked there, and had come out into the hall for his own reasons. He spied Tom and called to him.

Tom waited. Dick Scott did not like Lenox and called him uncomplimentary names. Tom had no strong feelings. He seemed to see the fellow frequently. They would exchange a few words and separate. . . .

This morning Lenox seemed to have made a chance to sympathize with Tom over the "Sahrman row."

"What makes you think there was a row?" Tom asked him.

"He's a pretty noisy guy, isn't he?"

Tom shrugged. "He's Hungarian; he has words to say on any subject. I didn't know they could be heard clear over here."

"The man thinks he has a grievance, doesn't he?"

"Oh, Lenox, I don't really know. We any of us could stir up a grievance if the mood was right."

"You could around Research, I suspect."

"Now what do you mean by that? We're just one happy family."

"If you get away with that, would you tell me that the whole structure isn't wrong?"

Tom frowned. He stepped aside for a group of people and decided he would not ask Lenox what was wrong with the structure of Research.

He had no need to ask. Jack Lenox told him—with gestures and diagrams. Not only the Research Institute, he told Tom, but the Complex itself was wrongly devised. It should be a cylinder. He tried to show a cylinder with his hands, then got out an envelope and took Tom's pen from his pocket.

"I know what a cylinder looks like," Tom assured him.

"Good. Though maybe a prism would be a better symbol." So he drew a prism and looked up at Tom. "Multiple facets, you see," he said, "but without any independent outshoots."

*Ah-hah!* Tom knew where he was heading. "Like our Shriners Hospital for Crippled Children?" he asked innocently.

"Like the Research Institute," said Lenox firmly.

Tom escaped then, feeling again the prickles which meant recognition of a message being sent his way. He went on to Pediatrics to look at a couple of Dick's sarcoma patients. He had a boy from Clausen—a young man, actually—with what almost positively was a sarcoma of the soft tissue of the upper arm.

It had been said by a private doctor that the boy faced an amputation. His mother, who knew Dr. Duclos, had, in searching for him, reached the Institute. Dr. Duclos had appealed to Tom, who now planned to talk to Dick about the case. Dick did some venturesome things with cancer.

Tom finished at Pediatrics and took the long walk back to Research, having forgotten Lenox and his prisms. But he remembered him again when the boy arrived at Research and Tom accompanied him up to Seven.

As he and Dick waited for the patient to be made comfortable in the cobalt wing, Tom told about meeting Lenox.

"You're not going to tell me he's had his hair cut!"

Tom laughed. "Nothing so drastic. Really, what he said wasn't very important, except that I keep getting messages."

"You're hypersensitive."

"Am I?"

"Well, really you are. But I thought you knew that there was a tight little core of people, especially in Administration, who deplore the autonomy given our institute. They would just love to keep a finger in our pie."

Tom stood thoughtful. "I wouldn't like that," he decided.

"Lenox and his friends think you have not been properly indoctrinated."

"But Research, Dick . . . It has to have direction, of course."

"And intelligent evaluation. But—now take our patient here. Anyone over at Surgical, Medical, or even Administration would tell you firmly that soft tissue sarcoma can be treated only with amputation."

"But you . . ."

"The technique is not original with me. A fellow in Houston—a professor—first decided that some limbs could be saved with radiation-surgical treatment. I accepted his theory and have put it to use. I excise the tumor and use radiation— even cobalt—on the remaining tissue. I have good results, often. It's not sure cure, but it is worth trying and researching. Some of my cases have gone for a couple of years without amputation or recurrence. A couple have subsequently had to have amputation. And I had one stinker—there is serious nerve damage from the treatment. But, still—" Dick tapped his forefinger on Tom's coat lapel— "you don't think your teaspoon is going to empty the ocean of disease in the ghetto, do you? But you still use that teaspoon, don't you?"

"I'm a dreamer."

"And Administration hates dreamers, don't they?"

"I don't worry to amount to anything about Administration," Tom assured his friend, who laughed and said, "Come along. We'll look at our patient."

The examination, the consultation with Dick's staff, took an hour. Dr. Duclos was brought upstairs to advise the sick boy's mother, and to reassure her. The doctors had decided to remove the tumor the next day, then radiation would begin.

Tom went with Dick to his office to sign the necessary papers of transfer from one department of Research to another. "Though this kid never really was my patient," he pointed out.

"Will you please stop making waves?" Dick asked him. "Your conscience is hyperactive, Doctor."

Tom looked up at him. "Do you suppose that's my trouble?" he asked hopefully.

"Could you kill it off?"

Tom laughed and shook his head. "I suppose not."

Dick walked with him to the door. "Can I expect you in o.r. tomorrow?"

"Not if you're going to blow up the joint."

But Tom would be there. He did all the things his profession and position required of him. There he felt sure, and safe.

He did not have to find work to do, certainly. It was the time of year for board meetings and reports. This meant getting Dr. Bonley's records into shape, adding his own.

The Clausen district covered an area wherein lived 62,500 people. The funds to operate the Clinic were given by the Government department of Health, Education and Welfare. This meant meticulous records. The corporation for Clausen was first founded through the Human Development Corporation, and then it became independent, as it was when Tom Kelsey became Chief Medical Officer. Independence meant, however, that it was operated by a sixty-member board of directors, and the Clinic was directed by a thirty-member health committee.

The paper work, the attendance at board and committee meetings, took a lot of Tom's time. He stopped being concerned about himself simply because he had no time or strength to give to such an insignificant consideration.

Evalyn Trice, a hospital volunteer with typing skills, had been assigned to help Karen and Tom get the records made up, duplicated, bound, and stacked ready for the various meetings. Tom found that Evalyn was a pleasant, reliable person to have around. Karen liked her and Tom did. She was friendly and attractive; she would do anything she was asked to do, stay extra hours, talk about finances. . . . When it started, the HEW funds for Clausen had totaled $351,000. This past year, the amount was $881,000. The coming year, for which Tom must prepare an estimated budget, there would be $1,500,000.

"It boggles the mind," said Karen.

"Nobody knows what a million and a half dollars is," Tom assured her.

"But after that," Evalyn pointed out, "you won't get as much, and I'll bet that boggles you, too."

"I can't imagine the place self-supporting," said Karen, gazing at the sheets of figures.

"It will be," Tom assured her. "Medicare, Medicaid, fees charged."

"And we can take up an office collection to round out the corners," said Evalyn, pushing buttons on the duplicator. "You know? I fairly loathe the smell of this machine."

"I'll buy you girls a bottle of Arpege when we are finished," Tom promised. "A small bottle."

Often, having got to know and like Evalyn, he was tempted to talk to her over a cup of coffee about Elene. About Tom Kelsey, too, and the things that "boggled" him occasionally.

He hadn't got around to doing it when things began to go wrong.

It was April, and the weather had decided to go back and take a second look at winter. With crab apple trees pink bouquets on the hospital lawns, and lilacs beginning to bloom, it snowed.

"This is a day when I should have stayed in bed," Tom told Karen when he came in that morning. He shook the moisture from his coat, and smoothed his wet hair. "Imagine snow two weeks after Easter."

"It won't last."

"It had better not. Now, what do you have. . . ?" He lifted his head. There was a commotion of some sort going on in the hall. He went to the door and looked out.

There was a woman—a young woman—thirty perhaps— very pregnant, and she was down on the floor writhing in pain. Lonnie was bending over her, and a nurse was coming up fast.

"Where did she come from?" Tom asked. The cart was being fetched. The woman apparently was in advanced labor.

"She just came in from the street," said Lonnie. "From the street."

"Well, take her to an examination room," Tom decided, "and call o.b. for a doctor. I don't think we have time to send her anywhere."

They did not. Tom signed the admissions sheet with his hands still wet from scrub. He had hardly got into gloves when the baby was born. "Doctor . . ." said the intern, his voice squeaking.

Tom nodded. "Her pulse was like a windmill," he conceded. "Take the baby out. Is it all right?"

"Seems to be. But the mother . . ."

"The mother is dead," Tom agreed, still using his stethoscope. Then the o.b. man arrived, a Dr. Blankenmeister, whom Tom had seen before. He was one of those middle-aged, smooth-faced men that were typically doctors and difficult to remember as individual personalities. Tom briefed him swiftly as to what had happened.

Dr. Blankenmeister went to the table and turned to look around and up at Dr. Kelsey. "But I know this woman," he said.

"You do? Was she trying to get over to Maternity? It's a vile morning out. . . ."

"I couldn't say what she was trying to do this morning," said the o.b. man. "She has been our patient several times—four children, I think. Her record would be on file."

"Her heart must have just failed," said the intern.

"It did," Dr. Kelsey and Dr. Blankenmeister answered at once.

"She was told," explained the o.b. man, "I told her myself, to have no more children. As I recall, her name is Bradley or Bradford, something like that. Didn't she have time . . . ?"

"She just walked in and collapsed," said Tom, "in advanced labor. She made quite a row."

"Yes. The last time I saw her—I was conducting a class. Ten weeks ago. Yes. She was in her sixth month then." He tipped his head back and looked at the ceiling, trying to remember. "We get a lot of women through our clinic," he explained to Tom. "But I remember this one because I'd had her before. The last delivery was most delicate. And I told her then to stop having babies. When she showed up at the

Clinic, I ordered her put to bed. But she wouldn't stay, and we haven't any way . . ."

"I know," Tom agreed. "And when she did come back . . ."

"Yes. She came in through your door. Too bad for you she didn't come into Emergency."

"Patients sometimes make almost any entrance Emergency," said Tom.

The o.b. man glanced at the sheeted figure. "See that she's neatly cleaned up," he said. "Coroners are fussy."

"But she had medical attention!" Tom wanted no part of coroners. "You get me her record, and I'll notify her family."

The family was notified. The family came to the hospital, and eventually to Research—the husband-father, and the woman's brother. Big men they were, rough in manner and speech. Their mood was ugly. Couldn't a doctor be found who knew how to deliver a baby without murdering the mother? they demanded.

The intern talked to them. Dr. Kelsey did. Dr. Blankenmeister came across again. Mr. Bradford declared that he was going to sue the doctor, the hospital—everyone concerned.

"But the woman had a heart attack," said Dr. Blankenmeister.

"She could have come here for that reason rather than to deliver," said Tom.

"She was told . . ." said Dr. Blankenmeister.

Of course the husband would not listen to any reasonable talk. He departed, promising to send some lawyers back.

"I only hope the hospital has its own supply of legal talent," said Tom, thinking of a man named Sax. "What did I do with my suit coat?" he asked.

"You had on a white coat when you worked over the woman . . ." the nurse told him.

He had, and at Dr. Blankenmeister's suggestion, he had stuffed the stained garment into the laundry hamper. The birth had been a precipitate and untidy affair.

But Tom's tweed jacket . . .

It had disappeared into thin air.

No one could find the coat. He went over to Clausen with a white jacket under his topcoat, and returned. Where was his memo pad? he asked Karen.

She looked at him blankly. "I put down messages . . ." she told him. "Three, I think, during the morning."

"Has Evalyn been working here?"

"She has. She's just gone to the little girl's room, I think. But she wouldn't touch your memo book."

It was a nice one, leather-bound, a gift from Mrs. Bonley when he'd been named Chief. It had Tom's name in small, neat gold letters.

It was nowhere to be found.

"The gremlins are back," he told Evalyn when she returned. She said she had not touched, or maybe even seen, the book.

"What gremlins?" she asked.

"Let's go to lunch," Tom said wearily. "And I'll tell you." He glanced at Karen. "Keep a list of every thieving caller I have," he ordered.

"Me and Lonnie, too?"

"Every one of you," he said seriously.

He had completely forgotten all his resolutions about staying away from the ladies. Evalyn was good company, she was sympathetic, she seemed to understand his position at Research and with the Complex.

So, over ham and cheese sandwiches and some really good pickles, Tom told her about the gremlins. His "ghosts."

Trim in her pinafore and white blouse, her vivid face

showing her interest, he told her of the things that had happened to him. From pencils to file drawers . . .

She could not believe it!

"Some of it is coincidence, probably," Tom told her. "Those memos stuck behind the telephone were probably not meant for me."

"But your files . . . And the jacket and memo book this morning . . ."

"They are significant enough to give me a spooky feeling," Tom agreed. "And if there is some purpose behind these happenings . . ."

"You want to find out what it is," said Evalyn. "Of course you do. May I help?"

Tom laughed. "If you can. I've got nowhere. When I've mentioned the ghosts to others. . . Dick Scott laughs at me."

"I'll look around and listen, ask questions. I've worked in the Complex for five years. I can stick my nose into a lot of interesting places."

"Don't get it bumped," said Tom. "Are we ready to bind the reports?" He would talk no more about gremlins.

CHAPTER 8

LAWSUITS, and threats of lawsuits, a spate of busyness at Clausen; new residents were due to come in there, some there were being elevated to staff standing, with changes in attending doctors explained to their regular patients. Tom was busy —at Clausen, and at Research. In the latter place he had a half dozen projects going, with interviews, lab schedules to be set up and checked upon, people coming and going. He had continued to work "on the floor" as much as he could— which was about half of his time.

He had, against disapproval from many sources, continued to let youthful volunteers help in his unit. These were people of his "neighborhood." A few were young men and women of obviously better background than that of his indigenous ghetto people. He had one young man; the name he used was Oscar Alexander. He certainly had attended college, if he had not actually acquired a degree. He crashed at one of the sleeping places afforded in the neighborhood around Clausen, he had volunteered to give blood at one time, offering the information that his type was a rare one.

He now was working part time at Research, especially interested in the blood taken and used for some of the work being done there. A couple of times, Tom found him reading on the subject. When Carter got back from the hematology seminar she was attending, Tom was going to get her together with this Oscar Alexander.

Dr. Kelsey felt that he was in a position to help various people by letting them help him. He could perhaps, and occasionally, serve as a guideline for these same young people. He used that argument to those, notably Dr. Rosenthal, a a staff biochemist, who protested with Tom about the use of these youthful volunteers.

"If they want to learn about medicine, there are plenty of ways for them to go to school, and learn!" said Rosenthal.

Tom thought a lot about his "kids," who seemed happy to be useful. They would do anything from washing pipettes and test tubes to cleaning up a mess on the floor. They pushed carts, they carried heavy solution jugs. They let Lonnie supervise them, and never once had he heard any one of them make fun of the big orderly.

Which was more than he could say for some who knew better. Rosenthal, again, for instance.

It was really too bad that it should be Rosenthal who walked in on one of the clashes Tom infrequently had with his kids. That one didn't amount to much. Oscar Alexander had been told to take a box of books and records to a storeroom. Tom had come down along the corridor, found the open box on a bench there, and Oscar nowhere to be seen.

He asked Dr. Lawson, he asked the intern—Evalyn Trice came past and said, "Oh, Oscar is in the lab telling someone how to do something."

That figured. Oscar was free with advice and instructions, and often as not, Oscar was right. But—"If you see him again, will you tell him to get to my office? On the double!"

"Yes, sir!" said Evelyn, her eyes widening.

Within ten minutes, Oscar came into Tom's office, a very tall, very thin young man with silvery blond hair curling into a drake's tail at the back of his neck. He wore, what all these helpers wore—a white, apronlike smock over his yellow knit shirt and tight-as-skin green trousers.

"You want to see me, Doc?" asked Oscar.

Behind him, Tom could see Rosenthal in the outer office giving some papers to Karen—he could have sent the analyses over!—and listening avidly to what Tom was having to say to one of his "hippies," though Oscar was not one.

"I wanted to see you," Tom said quietly. He went on, still quietly, to mention the box of records and books. Open, that box had not been destined for a bench in a crowded corridor.

"But, Jesus Christ, Doc . . ."

"Don't use that tone or that language here, Alexander."

Resentment sharpened the young man's features, his eyes sparked. But he would hold his cool for a time. "I've been sleeping in a church, Doc," he drawled. "Remember?" He rested one clenched hand on the desk corner and leaned toward Tom.

"Stand up straight when I am talking to you!" said Tom crisply. He could still see Rosenthal's green and white striped shirt out at Karen's desk. "Now I know you're a smart lad, Oscar. So I expect you to understand when I tell you to shape up, obey orders, or stop coming around here."

The young man who called himself Alexander straightened, tipped his head to one side, and looked down at the doctor behind the wide desk. "How old are you, man?" he asked, his tone vaguely amused.

Tom smiled. "Not twice as old," he said equally, "but certainly twice as experienced as you are, Oscar."

The youth narrowed his eyes. "Now let me figure that,"

he drawled. "M-hmmmn! That certainly makes you past thirty, doesn't it, Doc? Which means that only the right side of your brain is working."

Tom nodded. "That could be," he agreed. "John Kennedy at forty-four was President. Werner von Braun developed rocketry with the right side of his brain. Then there was Einstein. Koch. Semmelweiss. The doctors Menninger . . ."

Alexander made a rude sound. "I'll carry your damn books!" he said angrily, and slammed out of the office, brushing Rosenthal's shoulder as he passed him.

The chemist came into Tom's office rubbing that shoulder. "Your types can play rough, can't they, Kelsey?" he asked.

"Did you have something for me this morning, Rosenthal?" Tom asked, pulling a stack of folders forward on his desk.

"Oh, I was in the building—dropped off a report with your girl"—his head jerked backward toward Karen's desk—"and got in on what I suppose was a routine hassle between you and one of your street people."

"It was routine in that these untrained aides have to be trained," said Tom. "Don't you find that true, Rosenthal, in your department?"

"I don't use street people."

But in a sense he did, though with a difference which Rosenthal would explain, should Tom give him a chance. He would not. Rosenthal was ready to make entirely too much of the incident with Oscar. Tom closed one folder and opened another.

Evalyn Trice came into the office with a handful of the yellow flimsies used for interoffice communications. "Oh— oh!" Rosenthal greeted her. "I hope you don't have trouble for the good doctor, Mrs. Trice. He's had enough for one morning."

Evalyn laid the papers on the desk and looked questioningly at Tom.

"Dr. Rosenthal exaggerates," he said.

"Let Dr. Rosenthal tell you what happened," said the pesty man.

"Will you do it out in the hall?" Tom asked. "I'm swamped."

They went no further than Karen's office. Tom should have got up and closed the door, but surely even Rosenthal could not make much of a narrative out of his brief run-in with Oscar—though the man tried . . .

"Oh, I wouldn't worry about it," Tom heard Evalyn say soothingly. "Dr. Kelsey enjoys these encounters. His communication with the kids is very good."

Tom looked up to see how Rosenthal received that; the man was shaking his head as he went out of the office—finally. Evalyn followed him, and may have said more to him. She had encouraged Tom's use of the young people in the unit.

It was an hour later—Tom had almost cleared his desk and was debating whether to make a round of the floor or go over to Clausen—when a girl was burned in the lab some three hundred feet of corridors away from his office.

She was young—a student, a senior in the nursing school, who was assigned to their lab. She was young, but in no sense a "street person." She was in school on a fellowship, and was doing some specialized work in laboratory technology.

That morning she had been purifying bayberry wax with hot alcohol, and was heating a half gallon of the fluid over an open gas jet for the process, when the beaker broke. This caused an explosion, and the girl's lab coat and her uniform under it were ignited. Flames enveloped her arms, head, and body.

Other technicians at work in the larger lab across the hall heard the explosion and came running; they attempted to beat out the flames. Lonnie had heard it, too, and he got there first; he kept pushing people back and warning everyone to stay away from the flames.

When Dr. Kelsey got there, having run and pushed his way through the corridors, a medical student working in the wards had thrown a blanket over the girl. Tom helped him roll her on the floor and beat out the flames. Lonnie fetched a stretcher, and she was immediately taken up to the burn unit on Six. It was too late. Anything might have been too late.

Tom was shattered by the deplorable happening. Surely, surely, he lamented, something could have prevented . . .

"You must not blame yourself," Evalyn Trice told him. "Though I suppose we all feel guilty. I do, and Lonnie certainly must."

"Lonnie?" Tom asked.

"Yes. He kept pushing people away. He wouldn't let anyone near. That med student—what's his name?"

"Conrad," said Tom wearily.

"Yes. He was big enough—and bigger than Lonnie is *big*—he grabbed Lonnie and pushed *him* out of the way. I don't know where he found that blanket . . ."

"He was in the ward. He heard the explosion and smelled fire or smoke. He used great presence of mind."

"Yes, and then you came at almost the same time."

"We are going to have to keep the corridors more clear," said Tom. "I myself had to do a lot of pushing, and I hurdled any number of wheelchairs and crutches."

"The main thing is, you two men got through and put the quietus on Lonnie."

"You keep blaming Lonnie," Tom said curiously. "Why?"

"Well, someone might have helped that poor girl. He could

have helped her himself."

She blamed Lonnie, and kept blaming him, to all who would listen. At the inquiry which was held.

This disturbed Tom. Lonnie was a good worker. Why should Evalyn . . . ? He'd have to talk some sense into that woman.

He didn't do it right away, because even as the inquiry meeting was breaking up, the doctor from up on Burns, commiserating with Tom about the accident, said something to him about his having a loyal defender in Mrs. Trice.

"I don't think her testimony had any weight," said Tom. "I'm sorry she was there."

"She was there evidently to protect you," said the other doctor, looking quizzical.

Tom was annoyed. "Now why should I need . . . ?" he demanded. "That poor girl was working in the lab on my floor, yes. The laboratory director had assigned her, and told her what to do . . ."

"And Mrs. Trice? Well, the scuttlebutt is that you and she see a lot of each other."

Tom stiffened. "She works as a volunteer on One," he agreed.

"Mhmmmn. And while I am sure you are not a girl watcher, Kelsey, I suspect a lot of our volunteers have their eyes peeled for hunks like yourself."

Tom hated the expression; he hated the whole situation, real and suspected. Any "scuttlebutt" was way off base. Though, because of it, he would avoid Evalyn for a day or two.

That afternoon, he left his office early; he was going to get some exercise, he told Karen.

And after his game, when he came out of the shower room at the club, he found Dick Scott in the lounge reading the evening paper.

What on earth was he doing . . . ?

"Waiting for you," said Dick. "If you won't invite me for dinner, I'll invite you."

Tom frowned. "What's going on?" he asked.

"I'll tell you over that dinner."

"Well, all right. I'll be with you in five minutes."

He took Dick home with him. He had steaks at home. Potatoes could bake while they had a drink. Tom prepared to mix a salad.

Dick deferred his talking until the steaks were cooked. "I'm not one to ruin a T-bone," he assured his friend. Tom tried to get a lead. Was his problem Hubbell? The accident on One? Dick had had his own explosion and fire up on Seven.

By the time they were seated and the steaks half eaten, Tom had built up some defense against whatever it was Dick was going to say.

Dick recognized this, but it did not diminish his enjoyment of the meal. "You'll make someone a good wife," he told Tom, gnawing at his steak bone. "My own wife won't let me clean the bone in our dining room."

"Why did she let you out tonight?" Tom asked.

"I just called and said I would not be home. Explanations come later."

"For her, maybe. For me, how about now?"

Dick leaned back in his chair. "All right," he said. "I suppose the subject matter is friendship."

Tom dropped his fork. This he had not expected.

"Friendship," Dick repeated. "Mine and yours. I think there is one. And, second, we shall touch upon the seeming friendship you have developed with one Evalyn Trice."

Tom flushed "Scuttlebutt!" he cried angrily.

Dick nodded. "There's plenty of that, I suppose. I am speaking for myself—what I have seen and know for myself."

"Why do you call it a *seeming* friendship?" Tom demanded. "Evalyn . . ."

"Yes," said Dick. "Seeming. There are those, Tom, who feel that your neglect let her husband die. Evalyn may be one who feels that way."

Tom was shocked. The color drained from his face; he got up from the table and walked into the living room.

"Come back and finish your dinner," Dick called after him, "and talk about this."

Tom came back. He even picked up his fork, but he did not eat. "That whole thing is settled," he told Dick. "Evalyn has accepted her husband's death as inevitable. She has been told about the disease . . ."

"She's said that to you?"

"In the little we've talked about it, yes. She works on my floor, and she is very helpful."

"And very subtle, also, about any plans she may have for revenge."

"I don't know what you are talking about," cried Tom angrily.

"Then, my friend, I am going to tell you. One of the things she is doing is to try to keep me from telling you. For instance, I came to your office earlier today. She was there, filing papers or something. Karen was out. Evalyn told me you had a man from HEW inside."

"I did."

"Evalyn didn't tell you I was there. She didn't tell you I had been there?"

"No-o."

"She didn't tell Karen either."

"I wish you'd make your point, Scott," Tom told him. "You get around to saying a thing the way you operate as a surgeon. Sometimes delicately, sometimes not. You peel away layer after layer of flesh until you are ready to handle the thing you want to say."

Dick's eyebrow went up. "Very nicely said. Well, let's cut through to the point then, Tom. Which is, you are seeing too much of that woman; she is taking advantage of you."

"Evalyn Trice," said Tom, his lips tight, "did not set the fire you had, nor mine back in that lab."

Dick's hand swept out in a wide arc. "Of course she didn't," he agreed. "Those things happened. An act of God, or the devil himself."

"Then what . . . ?"

"She has assumed a proprietary air to you, and about you, Tom. She decides what message to give you, what not. She couches any comment or report about you and your work in terms . . . Well, they irritate your friends, Tom, and they should irritate you. You don't need that woman explaining you; you don't need to have her shielding you—if that is the term. You . . ."

"I like her," said Tom bluntly.

"She counts on your liking her. She hopes you are overlooking the fact that she is ten years older than you are."

"She's not!" cried Tom. "And what significance does that have anyway? She can type, she can file, she can use the copier . . ."

"All the time in close contact with you, able to watch you, to drop her word of praise, comment, advice."

"What in the devil are you trying to say to me?"

Dick took an orange from a bowl and began to peel it, his fingers and his knife precise.

"Your Mrs. Trice," he said slowly, "is not, I will agree, old enough to be, or want to be, motherly. But she does get bossy, doesn't she?"

"She wouldn't presume!"

"Oh, I don't mean about the way you run your unit. Of course not, though that may come. Just now she seems to want to get rid of Lonnie, and I'll bet she's told you to get a haircut."

Tom's fingers threaded through his thick black hair. "Carter has said the same thing to me. And your Judy as well."

Dick laughed. "I'll bet they both have. But Mrs. Trice . . ."

"Look," said Tom. "You mentioned our friendship. Can't we drop this discussion? Please?"

Dick broke his orange into sections. "No," he said slowly. "I don't think we can, Tom. Or should. Because I think you are in danger, and I would like to talk a bit more on the subject. Before this you have worried about how the Boards might estimate you in relation to the women in your life."

"What women? Carter Bass in California? Evalyn Trice running the Xerox?"

"Okay. Okay. Though there is a talkative daughter, too, I believe. But let's go to another subject that has worried you. You say there have been strange happenings. You've worried about them. You've talked about them. Gremlins, ghosts . . ."

"You're not suggesting . . . ?"

"I am only suggesting that you not talk about them to Evalyn Trice. It gives her an advantage she would not have if you'd keep silent."

Dick was too late. Tom already had talked about his gremlins to her, and she had offered to help solve the mysteries. This implied further confidences . . . "Evalyn Trice," said Tom carefully, "is an especially helpful volunteer. She has been a tremendous help getting out my annual reports, which was a big job this year because of Bonley's death and my taking over another man's work."

"Someone else could have been that great help. Bonley's former secretary, for instance."

That was true. Tom had even considered calling upon her. "But Evalyn was right there," he said, "and able to do the work."

"A fact which she called to your attention?"

She had, but Tom was not about to tell Dick so. He got up to let Caesar come back into the house. "I am shocked at everything you have said and implied," he told Dick. "And my first conclusion is that I talk too much."

"To me, do you think?" asked Dick, his eyes smiling.

"To everyone," said Tom stubbornly. "Any problems I have should be my own to solve or to forget."

"That's a good resolution. So stick to it, will you?"

But Tom was greatly troubled. Evalyn had been very kind to him. He could think of several instances of her especial kindness. Perhaps she had come to think of him in a proprietary way—but Karen did, too! Like any good secretary, she shielded the Doctor. Occasionally she and Evalyn clashed.

"Oh, thunder!" he said aloud. "Don't bring these worries around please Dick? I'm not going to be suspicious of anybody. I am entirely too busy doing my job to consider your underground tunnels of emotions and purposes."

Dick stood up. "Keep that busy," he advised. "Now will you drive me back to the club, where I left my car?"

"After we wash the dishes."

"Who, me?"

"It's one of the hazards of having bachelor friends. I'll even let you do the broiler."

"When do you expect Carter back?" asked Dick.

Tom kept his promise to be too busy to get into trouble. This was not difficult in Sociomedicine, what with the unit at Research and Clausen both under his direction.

He did have time to get Evalyn assigned to the receptionist's desk, and out of his office. She protested, but Karen pointed out to her that Dr. Kelsey did not assign the volunteers. If she was a bit smug doing this, if Evalyn resented it, Tom pretended not to see or hear.

He was busy, and Evalyn came far down the list of the personnel under his jurisdiction. Over at Clausen alone he had eight physicians at work full time and four half time. There were two dentists, full time, two half time. These busy doctors were well paid, and not often was one of them enticed from his post. The medical staff was young, which made for some instability. Half of them were black. If this balance changed by so much as one man, Tom had a situation on his hands. A man holding so delicately balanced a scale in his hands should be too busy to play any games of any sort.

When Jack Lenox, meeting him in the tunnel one morning, asked him "What about this being an examiner for the College of General Practitioners, Kelsey? I'd think you would be too busy." Tom agreed.

"I am too busy, and for a lot of things," he said.

"How do you manage?"

"Frankly, I don't know. Though, so far, I seem to be doing it."

Lenox swung into step beside him. Tom was going to Children's.

"That kind of managing can age a man fast," said Lenox.

"Oh, I had a good start on that before I ever came here."

"You've been here about a year now, haven't you?"

"Just about."

"I remember when you came. Do you still like the way things are set up over at Research?"

"What's to like or dislike?"

"Well, what I meant was, how is the system going? Entirely to your pleasure?"

The men flattened against the tiled wall to let a cart go

through. "About the only complaint I have," Tom told Lenox, "is about the restrictions Personnel puts on intermural romance. That ties a man's hands."

Lenox looked at him oddly. "You know, Kelsey," he said. "I can't figure you."

"Welcome to the party," said Tom, turning toward the stairs up into Children's. "I can't figure out a lot of other things."

He left Lenox, but there he was, thinking again. Not about the child over whom he had been asked to consult. The baby had gone through Clausen and been in the ward at Research; her parents were unwilling to make any decision about her without Dr. Kelsey's advice.

He should be thinking about spinal bifida and similar important things, not about the way Research was "set up." Why did that engage so much of Lenox's attention? Sometime Tom would ask him. He reached into his pocket for a scrap of paper on which to make a note, and he stopped short, right where he was, in the busy first-floor corridor of Children's Hospital, with admissions and dismissals cluttering up the place.

He stood staring at the paper in his hand. It was a small card; he had never seen it before. Not that card of a grinning skeleton. It was part of one of the "sick" cards some people thought funny. No doubt a hilarious message had been on the missing part.

The thing was: how had the card got into Tom Kelsey's coat pocket? He'd put that white jacket on about an hour ago. It had been hanging on his coat rack. A fresh one was hung there every morning, complete with name tag, a ball-point pen and a thermometer in the breast pocket. He didn't know exactly who was responsible for that clean jacket. Karen, or Lonnie, or some special person whose dull life was spent hanging clean linen jackets on coat trees.

Tom lifted his head and tossed his hair back from his face. What was he getting into? So he found half of a card in his pocket? He had probably picked it up somewhere, off Karen's desk, or the floor desk—somewhere. Why should he think the gremlins were busy again? He had gremlins. Maybe everyone did. They came and went, big ones and little ones. He could remember his mother saying, in all seriousness, "Now, who stole the cinnamon?"

She always found it, with a logical explanation of its disappearance.

And Tom's gremlins had a logical explanation, too. Someone might have been deviling him on purpose—they just might—but who would that someone be? From time to time, he had considered certain ones. Sahrman, when he worked in his unit. But Sahrman was gone, and the weird things kept happening. Elene mischievous and perhaps somewhat vindictive. She had given up her job at Clausen, saying that she might be back.

Dick suggested that Evalyn herself might be vindictive in a more subtle, more dangerous way. Dick was a pretty calm and level-headed guy, but Tom felt sure that he was reading Evalyn all wrong. The woman was lonely; she might be a bit foolishly fond of Tom Kelsey—she'd get over it. Tom could just as logically suspect curly-locked Jack Lenox, or himself.

The things that happened, happened. That was all there was to it. This morning—he looked down at the card in his hand. He had picked it up somewhere, and now he would throw it in the closest waste can. He had forgotten what note he had planned to make upon it.

He went upstairs, consulted with the doctors, who all knew that there must be corrective surgery for the baby. Tom talked to the parents, and took the father back with him to

Research to get all the papers in order.

And there he ran into trouble. Somewhere the records had not been exact. Tom himself could not check and recheck every case. But he should check such things, because trouble, in the long run, always ended on his desk. And there he sat that afternoon, with the anxious young father seated facing him, and he had to tell the fellow that he had had no right to bring the child to Clausen at all.

"It seems that you have not lived in the Clausen district for the required year, Cecil."

The brown face was earnest. "A year ago, Dr. Kelsey, I was in Viet-Nam."

Tom ran his hand down over his face. "Yes," he agreed. "But your wife . . ."

"She live with her mamma. We still live with her mamma."

That was what the record said, but the Government—the Federal grants were given—to provide medical care for the residents of a certain fixed district. Patients had to live in that district and be able to prove that they did.

This young couple could not prove anything. The neighbors would say that the wife stayed with her mother, who did live in the district, but they would not testify that she had lived there for a year. Her mail was sent General Delivery. She paid no rent, or had any other record of residence.

This was a knotty problem. Oh, yes, the infant's spine would have the needed surgery. Just at the minute, it might be that the cost would come out of Tom Kelsey's own pocket. He must immediately have some meetings with various sections of the Clinic, and here at Research. Admissions, records, social follow-ups—someone had failed to do the job properly in this case. Tom had failed to keep them up to one hundred percent performance.

His conclusion, of course, was that absorption in his own

little troubles, gremlins and the like, was hurting his work. And he need not ask himself if he should let it.

He sent the young father back to Children's, assuring him that all would be cared for, and he bent his attention to clearing up the difficulty, getting care for that baby, establishing the family's residence, and surveying the state of his own work.

Also, as he made notes and dictated memos of meetings, he remembered another time when he had been unhappy in the way his work was going.

He had failed in private practice and gone into group medicine, wanting only, he told himself, to be allowed to work—to see patients and care for them.

But in that clinic, a member of that group of doctors, there were people about him—which meant adjustments, some disagreements, some frustrations. Against his will, he had found himself not always happy doing the work he told himself he wanted to do.

In his home as well there were annoyances and disappointments. His mother, dwelling on the fact that private practice had not worked out, kept close tab on the work he now was doing. She had questioned him endlessly, advised him, urged care and close attention to his work. He should be nice to the other doctors, she said, treat the nurses right, and always be polite to the patients. "Watch yourself every minute!" said his mother.

Which was good advice, but which led to tension. Dorothy, his girl at that time, wanted him to take things more calmly, not to bring his work and its worries home with him.

But of course, said his mother, a man worried about his work!

By nature, Tom was one of those men. Not to "worry" in the true sense of the word, but constantly and conscientiously to consider his work, his patients and their cases, to read up on similar cases, to let the patient talk to him, to study every facet of a case.

Tom would have listened to Dorothy, and lessened his tension—to his own benefit, he realized now—if he had not been forced to criticize the performance of some of his colleagues. There was one chap who took his responsibilities more lightly, and Tom disliked the man's offhand diagnoses. One of the members seemed downright incompetent, and this worried Tom. There was an instance of a superficial examination which failed to turn up a serious situation.

Tom had been unhappy about these things; he had not liked the snobbishness and the class discrimination practiced. In answer to his protest, he was advised to accept and carefully treat patients who could and would recommend him to other patients. A doctor had just so much time, he was told, and a doctor had a living to make. Leave the indigent to the charity wards of the hospitals; their clinic had a big overhead which must be cared for. If Tom planned to marry, he had better get hard-nosed about these things.

All of which was true, but—

Tom fumed about these matters, a little to Dorothy, and more to his mother. There was one man, the incompetent one, his name was Myers, on whose cases Tom declared he would not substitute. Then an evening came when a call had come to his home, his mother answered the phone, and Tom was horrified to hear her say, "I am sorry, but Dr. Kelsey will be busy. Dr. Myers will have to find someone else."

Tom was furious. He snatched the phone away from her; he dialed Dr. Myers' answering service, found out what the call was, grabbed his bag, and left the house without a word to his mother.

When he returned, she, pleased as Punch, fed him and

showed her approval.

Tom sighed and wished he had his mother with him now. She would be, as she had always been, a good balance wheel for her son.

But—and he smiled ruefully—he knew that if she were around and he would take his problems to her, she would sit back in her rocking chair and point out to him that she had spent a good many years raising him to be a man—to be able to do his own work and to make decisions.

He supposed he was able. Though a man did need a woman —want one.

He was glad that Carter was returning the next day. He would have met her plane if she had told him the flight number and the time. But she had only written, hurriedly, "I'll be back Thursday."

She had been attending a six-week seminar on the possibility of using certain chemicals toward early detection and possibly the cure of leukemia, perhaps other forms of cancer as well. It must have been fascinating work, and certainly it would be valuable but Tom had missed Carter.

On Thursday afternoon, he called her apartment and welcomed her home, then invited her to have dinner with him.

"Oh, come here," she said eagerly. Her voice was as throaty and exciting as he remembered it. "We have so much to talk about."

"I'm going to ask you for help," Tom told her.

"Oh? What kind?"

"I'll tell you."

He called a florist and had flowers sent to her, and at six-thirty he presented himself at her door, kissed her when she opened it. She looked wonderful; her fair skin had a fine glow from the California sun. "I thought you were working," he accused her.

"Oh, I was. When I get dinner on the table, I'll tell you about it."

She did, all about the way children could be tested for early detection of dormant leukemia. They ate chicken breasts and rice pilaf, a salad of fresh pears and cheese, good coffee. "Better than my cook can make," Tom told her.

She smiled at him. "Tom," she said, "do you remember what I did with my ring the day I moved in here?"

"Yes," he agreed. "You put it between the two windows in your bathroom."

Her eyes darkened. "It's gone," she told him. "I went to get it when I was ready to leave, and it was gone! I looked everywhere. Even in the plumbing. Just everywhere. I got into a real panic."

"Have you looked . . . ?"

"Since I came home? Oh, yes. I—do you suppose someone took it? Before I left? Maybe the day I moved?"

"They must have."

"But who, Tom? Who?"

"Well, let's see. Window washer?"

"They wash the windows in September and March."

"The day you moved, there were a lot of people in and out, and I suppose all of us went into the bathroom. Except maybe the furniture men."

"Oh, they wouldn't steal my ring!"

"If it's gone, somebody took it. Now, let's try to remember. The Scotts were all here. And Lonnie."

"And Albertina."

Tom looked at her blankly.

"She made the draperies," Carter reminded him.

"Oh, yes. And of course I was here. I saw you put the thing between the windows. I came back the next day, too, didn't I? And after that."

She smiled at him. "Yes," she agreed. "You did."

"Do you think I took it, Carter?"

"I think someone did. It was insured, but I thought maybe you would help me look for it or figure out something to explain its being gone."

He went down the hall to the bathroom. The storm window was tight. The inner one could be raised, but the small space between the two frames was certainly empty. They discussed possibilities, and Tom said again that he seemed to be the logical one to have stolen the ring. "I'm sorry you were upset, Carter. You must have suspected me."

"Oh, stop it, will you?" she asked crossly, as a family member will get cross and feel free to express his irritation. Tom liked that.

It was only when he returned to his own home and Caesar that he remembered he had gone to Carter for help. The ring had put a lot of things out of his mind.

The ring?

Had the gremlins moved into her apartment? On his shoulder, perhaps?

CHAPTER 9

Jim Hubbell was working in the laboratory up on Pediatrics. Tom had got him the position, and Dr. Hubbell was glad that he should not be assigned either to Tom's floor, or Dick's. He would rather not be among surgeons. But the children accepted him; he had a gentle hand when he took blood. He was content, or seemed to be, to sit at a bench and sink at the far corner of the room, make endless tests, write down endless records. It was enough that he was privileged to enter a hospital, to hear its sounds, smell its smells, catch a bit of talk, see the crises arise and be handled.

He performed his job's routine duties with meticulous care, and Tom Kelsey stayed closely in touch with him. Lonnie, the first floor orderly, often used by Karen to summon Dr. Kelsey rather than phone the lab and point him out, and Dr. Hubbell—Lonnie came to know the man, and would visit him on his own.

It was through Lonnie that Jim Hubbell began to break out of his shell. Relying on the anonymity of his white garments —hundreds of people wore the same thing—he would, after a time, come down to One, and with Lonnie would go to the cafeteria for a sandwich and coffee. After another period of time, he would go along the corridors of Sociomedicine in search of his friend.

There came a day—someone was complaining about the way Dr. Kelsey's hippies could smell. Putting a white apron over their clothing didn't always help. This was about to create a situation.

Jim Hubbell heard Lonnie tell the offenders that they should rub baking soda on their aprons, especially under the arms, under the arms. Yes! On the outside of the coat, of the coat. There was baking soda in the diet kitchen, he said, or the lab. Hubbell followed the group and watched the experiment carried out.

And it worked!

But the miracle, as Tom Kelsey saw it, was to hear Dr. Hubbell laugh loudly at the whole performance, a really happy sound. His experiment was working.

Slowly, of course. The man was earning a little money, and he lived in what he called the ghetto. This was in one of the urban redevelopment areas; the old slum tenements had been torn down, and high-rise apartments, low-rise town houses and apartments had been built. Jim Hubbell lived in this district, as did all sorts of other people, good and bad, black and white, those worth helping and not.

Dr. Hubbell's own family was gone. He used that word. The money he earned paid for his living quarters, clothing, and food. The rent which Dick Scott paid for the big house Hubbell owned went for maintenance, taxes, and alimony paid through the court to his former wife. He never heard from her; she could not have remarried. That much he knew.

He was a decent man living among vandalism, crime, and some illness. His ghetto was not in the Clausen district, and for this reason Jim came to Dr. Kelsey's home one evening to talk about illness in his ghetto. There was enough of it, he said, to cause concern. Not an epidemic, perhaps. Probably better food habits or other hygienic measures would correct whatever was wrong. That night the two men talked about symptoms, stomach cramps, fever, swollen abdomens.

Hubbell, of course, had done nothing about the situation. But across the ventilation shaft of his apartment building, on the street, in the store, he heard the people talking. There seemed to be a lot of this particular ailment.

After that hour in his home, whenever Tom would see Hubbell, he would ask him about the illness. Yes, Hubbell agreed, it seemed to be continuing, perhaps increasing. He believed there was no problem in identifying the disease; now his project was to learn its source.

"Would it help if I came down and looked around?"

"You are always welcome in my home, Dr. Kelsey."

"But that's not where the trouble lies, is it?"

"No, sir, it is not."

"But you'll work at this, won't you, Jim?"

Hubbell shrugged. "I have no facilities . . ."

"You already work in the laboratory. Don't be hyper-stubborn about this. I'll speak to Dr. Bass; you're doing hematology for her, I believe. After hours, the benches are empty, aren't they?"

"Yes, sir, except for an emergency technician and the crew on call."

"You do want to do this?"

The man's eyes glowed.

"All right, then," said Tom. "Work at it. I'll make the lab part available."

So Jim Hubbell worked. And Tom regularly checked on what he was doing, and talked about the project. Hubbell told him that the people of his ghetto, the ones who became ill, patronized cheap eateries; Jim went to them and secured samples of the food they ate—secretly. These people were suspicious of, and hostile to, investigations.

"Tell them you're a doctor."

Jim looked at his friend. "I am not a doctor, Tom."

"Okay. Okay. What else will you do?"

"I'll buy some meat at their butcher shops."

"Could you use some money, Jim?"

"It doesn't take much. These people don't have much for food. And their shops—even the so-called supermarkets, the chain stores—are not like those in other parts of the city. The food is not as good, nor as fresh. It can cost more."

"Why?"

"To pay for vandalism, thievery—all sorts of extra overhead."

Tom rubbed his fingers through his hair. "What else do you do?" he asked. "You're keeping good records? We may have to take this to the health authorities."

"I've considered that." He showed Tom his cellophane envelopes and the tags he had devised. "I'm going to have to look into the matter of soul food," he told his friend. "That's where I can function, and you couldn't."

"I know how this discrimination thing works," Tom assured him.

"The whites can come to these eating houses, the bars, the holes in the wall. Sometimes society folk go down, mainly to taste and eat soul food. They make a thing of their slumming and talk about the food being natural."

"Is it?"

Hubbell shrugged. "A lot of pork is eaten," he said. "Ribs or chitterlings. I buy it, even taste it, and get my samples."

"Don't make problems for yourself, Jim."

For the first time since he'd known him, Tom saw Jim Hubbell show anger. "The problem is there!" he cried tensely.

"Yes, I know. But discrimination isn't always confined to a difference in color."

"That's right. Class and class. Knowledge and no-knowledge. When I go in for chitterlings, I don't talk as I do to you. And I'm careful about taking a sample of grease from the stove."

"Do you get that?"

"I have such samples. I'm narrowing in on the pork, I think."

"Well, be careful."

"I am. I shall be. I'm getting to know a lot of people through this. I use tact and scientific care. Both are required. And, I must confess, a deal of self-sacrifice. I am used to clean floors, clean dishes, and clean clothes. But if I'm to pursue this, and it does seem that I am pursuing something, I have to go into the homes of the people who are sick, and sometimes the only way to get a sample of their food is to eat some of it myself. Then to spill some on my shirt, or some such thing."

The man was interested. At night he worked at the empty lab bench. He identified the people who were sick, made charts, drew maps. He brought, or sent, two families to the hospital, through the emergency ward, though Tom would have admitted them to his unit.

The illness, Jim had decided by then, was confined to a certain area, and to a few families—less than forty. But enough.

It was through the two patients sent to Emergency, and from there to the hospital wards, that Rosenthal got on to the investigation. Though not once had Jim called himself a doctor to these people when he found the man and woman desperately ill, he did tell their neighbor to call the police for a University Hospital ambulance. The neighbor, wanting to keep out of "this," said a man named Hubbell had called.

Rosenthal, the biochemist, came straight to Tom. Were the patients Clausen-connected?

Tom immediately knew what had happened. "Were they my admissions?" he asked quietly.

"You know damn well they are Hubbell's admissions."

"Oh, now come on, Mike!"

"He sent them in. I just came over to tell you that I am bringing in the city health doctor. There will be one hell of a fuss!"

"I expect so. Do you know what you have?"

"Of course we know. Fulminating food poisoning. Could be salmonella."

"Try trichinosis, too."

Rosenthal glared at him. "Are there other cases?" he demanded. "You mean we've got an epidemic down in that part of the city?"

"Your city doctor wouldn't admit one. But hold on a minute." He picked up the phone.

Dr. Hubbell came down to his office, looking apprehensive. Managing to keep Rosenthal silent, Tom told him what the situation was. He mentioned the matter of admissions. "You or me, Jim," he said. "The biochemistry department is concerned, as they should be. Rosenthal here has called in the city health department."

Jim nodded. "They should be called," he said.

"You've been working on this thing for ten days or more. You can tell Dr. Rosenthal what you have, and save them some time."

So James Hubbell, no longer a doctor, quietly did tell. He identified the illnesses, he identified the causes, and outlined the cure. He fetched his lab book, his charts, his maps. There were stores, restaurants . . .

No, he would not give his book to Dr. Rosenthal. But it would be available.

Rosenthal was in a state. "He literally went off in all directions," Tom later told Carter.

"What did you do?"

"I'm learning," said Tom. "I called the newspaper before Rosenthal could, or the city Health Commissioner."

"There will be an awful fuss."

There was an awful fuss. The reporters came. The hospital talked to them, the city Commissioner talked, Tom Kelsey talked. And a lot of stuff was printed. Inevitably, and because Tom thought this all might be a break for Jim Hubbell, his name came out. Tom also alerted Dr. Lewis as to what was happening. The Director had known, of course, that the former doctor was working in a lab at the Institute.

Several reporters came to find out what was going on. Pictures were taken, though Jim refused absolutely to pose. One picture was secured of his back bent over his lab bench.

There was one feature writer who sought out Tom Kelsey. Poor Karen watched and listened in astonished fear. This writer was going to make a thing of Hubbell's being a paroled murderer.

"He's a doctor!" said Tom firmly. "And you can quote me."

"Would you say he was practicing without a license?"

"I would not, because he is not."

"Maybe," said the reporter, "he should be."

"There I will agree with you!"

"There's been something said about a cure, and prevention . . ."

Tom smiled. "Better food inspection of the ghetto markets and restaurants," he said quietly. "A center like Clausen for that district. It doesn't take a medical license to prescribe those things."

The feature writer and Tom had shouted at each other, but the article the man wrote managed to convey the message to the city. A public-spirited man had done something for the welfare of the city as a whole.

And the letters poured in. The reporter brought a great box of them to the Institute for "Doctor" Hubbell. His newspaper printed pages of them. Generally they demanded a health center like Clausen for that inner-city district, or a Model City agency which would train men and women to refer people to the proper medical agencies. And nearly all of the letters demanded that this doctor be allowed to practice his profession. The shortage of doctors was mentioned, this man's unselfish interest in the public health . . .

So the feature writer talked again to Tom, who sent him to the office of the local medical society. Within days he published an article demanding that ways be sought to restore Hubbell to medical practice.

"We must find a way!

"If the other doctors won't, the people should find that way! Laws could be changed, exceptions could be made!" Dr. Tom Kelsey, Chief of Sociomedical Research at University Hospitals, Chief Medical Director of the Clausen Center Clinic, was quoted as saying, "I'll help." A picture of him featured this article.

"You'll get your own box of mail telling you to cut your

hair," Dick Scott promised.

Tom got up, opened his closet door and looked at himself in the mirror. "It is a bit bushy," he admitted.

"Many a balding man would envy you that cloud," laughed Dick.

Dr. Daives made a chance to ask Tom if he really was as crazy as he sometimes seemed.

Tom Kelsey lived in a row house. These were connected dwellings, four or six of them to a unit, well kept, and attractive. With Mrs. Miller to clean for him, his home was pleasant, and no problem to the doctor. He lived in comfort and could forget the place except during those hours, after work, when he inhabited it.

Until one morning, when Karen had him paged out on the floor. He picked up the wall phone. "What's up, Karen?" he asked.

"Mrs. Miller called, Dr. Kelsey. She wants you to come home at once. I told her it wasn't possible, but she said to ask you."

Tom looked at the corridor clock. "How are my appointments?" he asked.

"You have a class at two, and three appointments beginning at three-thirty. You were planning to go to Clausen at eleven."

That was flexible. "I'll finish here," he said, "and go past my house on the way to Clausen." It really was not "on the way," but he could make it. On the drizzly day, he had his car with him.

He finished what he was doing, and went to his office to change his jacket. Karen said she had no idea what was wrong with Mrs. Miller.

Tom's head turned sharply. "Was something wrong?"

"She was in a dither about something."

"Why didn't you tell me that?" The woman had a crippled son . . . He was out of the office, out to his car.

He found Mrs. Miller still in a dither, her face bone-white, her hands trembling, tears ready to flow.

"What on earth is wrong?" he asked.

"I—Doctor, will you come next door with me?"

"Next door?"

"Yes. To Church's." She held up a key.

The Churches—a couple and their small child—lived to the west of Tom. He knew them slightly. The man was a sportscaster, now out of town with the city's baseball team. His wife and baby . . .

"Has something happened over there?" Tom asked Mrs. Miller.

"Mrs. Church—she and the baby are at the hospital. Not your hospital, Dr. Kelsey."

"Yes. That happens."

"The baby had an operation. A—hernia?"

"Yes."

"Mrs. Church is staying with her, and she asked me to look in, pick up the mail, things like that—water her plants . . ."

"Go on."

"So this morning, when I came here—I went over there. I didn't think you would mind."

"Of course not. What happened?"

Mrs. Miller stood up. "So come with me and see."

He followed little Mrs. Miller, and he found what she had found. Someone had entered the Churches' house. Drawers had been opened, cabinet doors—change from a box had been spilled across the kitchen table, but the money was left behind. Upstairs the mattresses had been pulled from the beds, the contents of the medicine cabinet had been spilled into the sink below it.

"We'll have to get Mrs. Church to tell us if anything has been taken," Tom said. "The clothes closets seem neat enough."

"Doctor, come look here," said Mrs. Miller.

Tom went with her, downstairs and outside. The basement window had been broken enough for the latch to be opened. Mrs. Miller pointed to footprints in the soft ground outside the window—the prints of a woman's shoe and a man's.

Tom shook his head. He must call the police, let them fetch Mrs. Church, or talk to her. He looked at his watch. He might have to skip lunch.

The police came, talked to them both, and said yes, the doctor could leave. . . .

Mrs. Church, approaching hysteria, was fetched in a squad car. Her baby had had surgery that same morning, she told Tom.

"She'll be taken care of," Tom assured her. "And the police won't keep you long. I'll drive you back myself."

A quick trip through the house made Mrs. Church decide that nothing was missing except some cartons of cigarettes and several bottles of whiskey. "My husband is always given that sort of thing for Christmas," she explained.

Tom took her back to the hospital, leaving Mrs. Miller to close up after the police were finished. Yes, she promised Dr. Kelsey, she would straighten Mrs. Church's home. "But who did this, Doctor?" she asked. "And why?"

Mrs. Church asked him, and again he shook his head. It was a senseless thing, to all appearances.

Just as the other burglaries had been senseless. This one had similarities and differences. Was there some connection? Mrs. Miller had mentioned Scooter, but Tom discarded that. The police would not, should she mention him to the detective. Tom would not interfere.

Mainly because he did not have any ideas of his own. Bonley's, Trice's—Dr. Lewis's former home. And now this, next door to him. "They" could have mistaken the Church home for his. To some extent each burglary had some connection with Tom Kelsey. He knew the victims, and would be concerned. . . .

His attention focused. *Next door! To him!* His gremlins came swarming. Was someone trying to frighten him?

The next day, without thinking about, and certainly not examining, his motives, Tom sought out Sahrman over at the Diagnostic Clinic and invited him to have a drink with him. The end of the day was in sight; only a block or two from the Center there was a cocktail place with delicious hot seafood canapés. . . .

"Why do you ask me to do this?" Sahrman broke in. Rudeness had always been his way.

"Well," Tom said. "I have known you for some time, but I haven't seen you lately. I happened to be over here, and I wanted to see you. You were always a good worker; I wish you were back on my service."

"Your service," repeated Steven.

"Yes. I thought you might come around sometimes, if only to see how your sickle-cell project was getting along."

Sahrman laughed and turned down the cuffs of his white shirt, fastened the links. "You want to talk to me, eh?" he asked. "Things have happened at Research, have they not? A fire, I believe. A girl killed. Could it be that the refugee is a suspect?"

"Oh, for Pete's sake, no!" cried Tom. "Why must you always be so touchy?"

Sahrman bent his head to look down at his shoes, then he stooped a little farther to look at Tom's. "Could you," he asked, "put on my shoes and wear them?"

Tom sighed. "I'm sorry," he apologized. "I can only guess what wearing your shoes would be. But I would honestly like to help you."

"Honestly," repeated Dr. Sahrman. He picked up a stack of chart holders and started for the hall door. He opened it, then closed it again and stood before it. "Dr. Kelsey," he said slowly. His dark face was intent. "I will tell you a story. In my homeland, of which I sometimes think, naturally— in my homeland there was once a wife who very much wanted to make her husband successful, to make him a man people would notice and talk about. Now, there was to be a big celebration. It could have been a hundredth year anniversary, or even a five hundredth. Perhaps some great man was to come to the town. In any case there was to be this celebration, and this wife very much wanted her husband to have an important part in it. She nagged him. Speak up loud, she would tell him. Wear your good clothes. Stand straight! Things like that. She also went about trying to influence others, telling them to remember that her husband was a fine man and a hard worker. That he was handsome and would make a good appearance in the procession. Well, she did these things, and soon the day came when the plans were announced. Her husband's name was on the list, but way down at the bottom of it. Her good man of good appearance was to see that the horses were watered.

"Now, of course, the wife was very angry. And do you know what she did? She cut off all the buttons from her husband's clothes to keep him at home on the day of the celebration." Sahrman gazed at Tom for a long minute, then he opened the door behind him. "Excuse me, please," he said. And he went out.

Tom stood for his own long and surprised minute in the

small office. Then he, too, went out into the hall. Sahrman was nowhere in sight, and Tom went to the elevator and downstairs. He was thinking of the man's story, remembering it word by word. Deciding on its meaning, and relating it to present circumstances was not so easy. The attempt to reach that meaning preoccupied Tom all the way back to Research.

That night he went to see Carter, having called her first. She met him with the offer of a drink. Coffee?

"What's on your mind?" she asked, leading him to the living room, tucking herself into a corner of the big couch. Tom sat in a wing chair facing her. His eyes were still preoccupied with Sahrman and Sahrman's story.

Almost at once Tom told her the whole thing, first telling her about the burglary next door to his home—that had happened yesterday.

She would have dwelt on the event, but Tom wanted to talk about Sahrman and tell Carter the man's story. "It was an allegory," he said. "It had meaning—to him, at any rate. I can't quite figure it all out for myself." So he told the story. "I had gone over to see if there was something I could do for the guy," he explained.

"Why did you go?"

Tom looked at her in surprise. "I've been meaning to look him up."

"And the burglary had nothing to do with your decision to go today?"

Tom flushed; his eyes became troubled. "I wasn't conscious of any reason . . ." he said, more to himself than to Carter. "I felt he had not been treated squarely when he was transferred. He was sure he had not been. I've heard stories . . ."

"Yes. He's been seen with the Trice girl."

"I know. She should stick to her own boy friends. Or at least one of her own age and class."

Carter's mouth twisted wryly. "Class, Doctor?" she asked.

"Look." Tom leaned forward. "All day, every day, I consider the social aspects of every damn thing I do. When I relax, it can be into about as snobbish an attitude as a man can know. So—yes, I meant class. Background, education, preparation for life. Elene Trice and Dr. Sahrman—well, let me tell you what happened, Carter. Please?"

She smiled and wriggled her feet in the red Keds she wore with her jeans and white blouse. The setting sun caught itself in her hair, which was twisted and pinned atop her head, with small, feathery tendrils against her cheek and neck. She looked young, and feminine, and—lovable.

Tom coughed, and told Sahrman's story. She laughed at the wife's frustration. "I wish she had told you what the husband did," she said.

"It probably is not a modern story. But today he would go and display his manly form, turn into the sensation of the parade. Though, seriously, Carter . . ."

"You plan to do something for Sahrman."

"Yes, I do."

"I suppose it hasn't occurred to you that Sahrman does not want to water the horses."

Tom frowned. "Maybe not," he conceded. "But—"

"Should you interfere, Tom? Should you do anything at all?"

He stood up. He walked to the window and looked down at the street. Car lights were beginning to cast rosy ribbons along the Boulevard and through the park. "You don't like Sahrman?" he asked not turning around.

"I hardly know the man, dear. I am thinking of you, and

what little one man can do against a complex system."

"The University Hospitals, you mean?" He came back to his chair.

"Oh, I go farther than that. The AMA, the United States Government, *and* the Health Department. There is just one thing Sahrman wants."

"I know. The license to practice medicine. And I suppose you're right. Though I was able to push things along for Jim Hubbell."

"Yes, you were. And that should be triumph enough for you, Dr. Kelsey. Don't go and get drunk with your sense of power."

An hour later when Tom reached home and parked and locked his car at the curb, started up the steps, he found Elene Trice huddled under a knit poncho sitting on his doormat. He could not believe . . .

"What on earth are you doing here?" he demanded.

"Waiting for you." She pushed her long hair back from her face and stood up, or tried to. Tom's warm hand helped her, and she clung to it. "Can I talk to you?" she asked, her tone piteous.

Tom sighed. "You may come in for a half hour," he agreed. "Then you are going home."

"I can't go home."

"But you are going home. Because I'll drag you there by force, if necessary."

He unlocked the white door, he turned on the lights, and Elene went inside. She wanted to go to the bathroom, she said. She had been waiting for him for hours, and she was freezing.

"The temperature is close to seventy," he told her, "and nobody is freezing anywhere on any doorstep. But you go up to the bathroom." He turned on the light in the upper hall and immediately wondered if he would be able to get her out of the house within his half hour. She was a tall girl, and force might not be enough.

She looked terrible; her eyes were smudged, her long hair like—like vermicelli. Her clothes . . .

Sighing at all the things that were complicating his life, he went to the kitchen, poured milk into a glass, put it and some cookies on a plate, and brought it back.

Elene came downstairs again; evidently she had washed, and combed her hair. She looked better. She surveyed his living room, and finally chose the big yellow chair. Yes, she would drink the milk, she agreed. But cookies, maybe not. She had hypoglycemia, she told Tom.

"Have you seen a doctor?"

She swallowed some milk. "Oh, yes," she cried. "That's how I know I am in such awful trouble."

He sat on the blue couch and tucked two pillows behind his head. " Half an hour," he reminded her.

"You're awfully proper, Kelsey."

"I am not thinking about being proper. I need my sleep. It's already past ten o'clock. So talk."

"All right. But get yourself some Saks cold cream soap for your bathroom, will you? It lathers like crazy, and that deodorant stuff—*yekkkh!*"

He waited. Elene drank the milk and ate one of the cookies. "All right," she said then. "I'll tell you. I'll tell you that my desperation, Dr. Kelsey, has led me to do things that are going to bring disaster to myself and my family."

He sifted through her extravagance. "You're in trouble. Pregnant?"

"Pregnant, no. Trouble, yes. I am going to lose—I guess I already have lost Jimmie."

"Jimmie?"

"Yes. My boy friend. Or he has been—oh, ages."

Tom thought he must be the nice clean-cut boy he had seen at the Trice home when Elene's father had died.

"I won't be able to go to college this fall," Elene was saying. "My mother has been planning that. You never saw such sweaters and blankets and stuff. It's really too bad."

"Why can't you go?" Tom prodded.

"Oh. Well, I just can't. I would have to have a physical, and my v.d. would show up."

Tom sat erect. "Your—what are you talking about?" he shouted. Because, all at once, he was sad, and shocked, and angry.

Elene shrugged and twisted a lock of hair around her hand. "I'm talking about v.d.," she said. "Venereal disease. Syphilis to you, Kelsey."

Tom felt sick. This crazy girl— He stood up and paced around the room. "Who?" he asked. "Sahrman?"

Now she seemed to be enjoying his agitation. The girl did not have one lick of sense! "I don't think it was Sahrman," she said. "Probably the bum I picked up one snowy night."

Tom bent over her. "Don't you know this is serious?" he shouted at her.

He tried to talk to her. She must enter the hospital, he said, and be treated. At once. It was Elene who finally reminded him that the half hour was up.

He took her home. She left him, promising to bring him a cake of Saks soap.

## CHAPTER 10

THERE WAS GOSSIP, of course. Tom supposed there was, but he was too troubled and too busy to care. If he didn't hear the talk, if the matters discussed were not brought to his attention, he need not do anything to quiet that talk, he thought.

He did not hear the talk the evening of the medical society dinner. He did not attend that dinner—forgot all about it, he explained the next day—so he was not one of the group who gathered in Carter Bass's living room afterward. There were a dozen people present, the Scotts, Carter, of course—all doctors, and their wives.

And the talk inevitably was shop. It dwelt on medical things, on the Complex, and on the Research Institute. Some of the group held glasses in their hands, as many drank from coffee mugs.

Mainly the talk, at first, dealt with a lawsuit, filed that same week against Dr. Mercer of the burns research clinic. This was being a controversial topic all over the big hospital complex. Mercer was well thought of; if he claimed a young woman was psycho, she probably was.

"Oh, but you can't go around asking for committal just because a girl comes in and raises a fuss in your ward."

The daughter had been allowed to visit her very sick mother; she had made trouble. Dr. Mercer had asked her to leave; she would not. She became so vociferous about it that the doctor had become angry and had had her committed to a mental institution. She promptly filed suit, and was released. The doctor of the Kidney Unit had co-signed the committal papers without seeing the daughter at all. "If Mercer says . . ." he had argued.

And now the Institute, the two doctors, were the subject of a nasty lawsuit.

"Tom Kelsey," Carter spoke up, "says the woman has a case. Dr. Mercer has had no experience in psychology."

"Kelsey probably knows what he is talking about," said someone. "He is a good doctor."

"Yes," Dick Scott agreed, "and he's been doing great work at the Institute. Simply great."

"The only fault I find with the fellow," said the orthopedist, "is that he trusts absolutely no one."

"Well," said Carter, "things have happened to Tom."

"They seem to," agreed the orthopod. "He did a simply marvelous diagnosis for a crippled girl . . ."

"Roxie," Carter agreed.

"Yes, I believe that was her name. That was when Kelsey first came to Research, before he was Chief. But then, he turned right around and bungled that lawyer's case."

Dick and Carter exchanged glances of exasperation. "Both cases could have happened to anyone," Dick declared. "Trice should not have been forced on Tom. And who in this room can cure lateral paralysis? That case was just one of the many things Carter says have happened to Kelsey. Really, it is incredible. One Sunday his personal files were spilled all over the place. There have been three or four strange burglaries with rather close connection to him; the victims were friends or neighbors. Oh, all sorts of things have happened to him, ever since he came here."

"You mean there is some pattern of persecution?"

"I don't know that there is a pattern, or even if it is persecution. Tom had got to thinking these things are aimed at him."

"And of course he is suspicious," agreed Carter. "Even of himself. Of me, and perhaps even of you."

"I don't blame him for complaining," said one of the women.

Carter stood up. "Don't get the wrong idea," she said earnestly. "Tom is not a boy whining about fancied persecution."

"Far from it," Dick agreed. "He is a capable grown man being hampered in the work he wants to do."

Carter defended him, but the things said had disturbed her enough that, within a day or two, she went down to Tom's office and asked him if he was being overly suspicious.

He looked at her in amazement. He took off his black-rimmed glasses and got up out of his desk chair. "Sit down, Dr. Bass," he said concernedly. "You don't sound well to me."

Carter frowned and laughed, all at the same time, which made for an interesting expression on her pretty face. "I heard myself say, a night or two ago, that you were suspicious, even of me."

"Well, if you'll tell me of what I am suspicious . . ."

"Oh, there was this group at my house. We'd been to the medical society dinner . . ."

"I know. I forgot about it until it was too late to dress

and go. So I got myself talked about." He sat down again.

"Mention was made of your gremlins . . ."

"*Carter!*"

"No. Not really. But mention was made of the things that seem to happen to you, and that have happened ever since you first came to the Institute."

"And someone said I was overready to suspect harassment."

"Persecution," she amended.

Tom tipped back in his chair. "A case could be made," he agreed. "But, no, I don't think I am unduly suspicious. And certainly not of you."

Carter gazed at him, her eyes thoughtful. "I don't think I believe you," she said finally.

Tom smiled and shook his head at her. "Don't let it concern you," he said.

"But I am concerned. And so are you."

"Sure, I'm concerned. It's my neck. My job."

She leaned toward him. "Tom, you don't believe that!"

"Of course I believe it. I think there is some plot, some plan to get rid of me."

"Oh," Carter protested, "there can't be a *plot!*"

"Why can't there be? When you consider all the things that have happened, and continue to happen."

She bit at the corner of her pretty lip. "Do the gremlins go on?"

"Oh, yes. The phone calls. Graffiti on a scrub room wall. Some of the messages lately have been quite to the point, Carter. They say, 'Kelsey, go home!' "

Carter stared at him, her blue eyes round, darkening. "That scares me to death!" she whispered.

"Well, it scares me a little, too. Sometimes."

"Do you believe there really is a plot, Tom? Why should

anyone attack you? You're a very nice guy."

"I certainly am!" he agreed heartily, and Carter giggled.

"Not that nice," she assured him.

"The attack is not on me personally," Tom told her. "My job, perhaps. There certainly is something going on, but the cause, the purpose, is hard to pin down. It reminds me of the shack clubhouses little boys build. And those who build one jealously contrive to keep out any new kids. They have nothing against those kids, just a clannish spirit of self-defense."

"I don't think that fits into you and your situation."

"Maybe not. It's the best I can do."

"Do you suspect anyone?"

"As you say, I suspect everybody, anybody. Myself, and even you."

The men at her home had said that, and she had agreed. "Aren't you going to try to find out?" she asked.

"Oh, I truly hope so!" Tom said fervently.

"May I help you?" Evalyn had asked that, and now he regretted saying she could. He regretted telling her about the gremlins. Carter, of course, was different.

He stood up because she had risen. He took her forearms into his hands. "With your help," he said softly, "we will find out what goes on, won't we?" And without warning, he bent his head and kissed her.

Carter was startled and pleased. "Tom!" she gasped. "Your secretary . . ."

He nodded. "She's used to me and my ways," he assured Dr. Bass.

And Carter left his office, giggling again, which did raise Karen's eyebrows.

But Tom did so much thinking that day, about Carter and the kiss, about her offer to help him, that he called her that night and asked if he could stop in at her house.

She laughed at the term and said that of course he could come, though it was getting late.

"I know it. I had a Board meeting."

"Did something happen?"

"At the Board meeting?" he asked in surprise. "I'll let you listen in on one sometime. Wall-to-wall statistics."

"Sounds wonderful."

"Mhmmmm. May I come? I've done some heavy thinking today, and since you started it . . ."

"Come right over. I'll leave the porch light on."

He laughed and hung up the phone.


She welcomed him with a cold drink, and he regarded it and her appreciatively. "This is what I came for, really," he told her.

"I knew that. But I took off my hair curlers anyway."

She was wearing a housecoat sort of thing, yellow and white striped, and her hair was brushed back, tied with a yellow ribbon. Tom flipped it with his finger. "Let me see your license, Doctor," he said; "you don't look old enough to be practicing."

"Just as I said, you're suspicious." She sat on the couch under a lamp, and Tom took his drink to a chair which stood near the big window. By turning his head, he could look out at the park and the lights of the streets. He tasted his drink, then sipped it slowly.

"You've been thinking," Carter prodded him.

He turned back to look at her. "And I know it is almost eleven o'clock."

She waited.

"I've been thinking for hours," he said finally. "About me, and the gremlins, the plot you suggested . . ."

"I only . . ."

"I know. We both have considered such things, and today I kept thinking about those things, and the people who might be involved. And I decided that if the villain was Sahrman . . ."

"It could be."

"Perhaps. Or it could be Evalyn Trice . . ." He glanced at her and nodded at the way she was ready to accept that suggestion. "Or," he continued, "it could be Elene Trice."

"Do you still see that girl?"

"She worked over at Clausen for a time. I saw her a few days ago. But let's stick to our subject, Carter."

"Sure," she agreed.

He chuckled. "Well, if it is one of those three, I can get them out of the hospital field."

"Do you suppose the solution is as simple as that, Tom?"

He lifted his glass again. "I could hope so," he said. "Though it would mean losing a friend or two."

"I can tell you don't think the matter is so simple. You've detected things, haven't you?"

"Yes. Or I think I have. In any case, I am pretty certain that a simple solution isn't ahead for me. There seems to be some complex, underground—or at least, hidden—movement."

"Against you, Tom? And that is ridiculous!"

He nodded and finished his drink, gazing down at the street, his thoughts again enfolding him. After a time which amounted to minutes, he got up and took his glass back to the kitchen. Carter could hear him rinsing it. She smiled softly and waited for him to return.

When he did come back, he moved restlessly about the room. He picked up a book and riffled its pages, he smoothed his hand over a crystal owl on a table, then took out his clean handkerchief and wiped any possible finger smudges away.

Carter watched him, a tall, slender man with a mop of unruly black hair, deep-set, very blue eyes. His mouth was sensitive, and his body graceful as a trained athlete's. By now she knew that he was a man of humor, of deep consciousness—a vulnerable man, but a strong one, too. Ready to laugh, or to be angered, and to act on either emotion. He—

Having returned to the window again, Tom began to talk about his aim in life. "There is just one thing I want," he said slowly. "Oh, not just *one* thing. I want many things. A much better backhand than I have, a house of my own a little way out into the country, with trees about it. Many things. But my *aim* in life, Carter—" he turned to face her—"my one aim is the continuance of my work and of myself as a man. That I want; that I must have!"

Carter smiled at him gently. "That is a very good aim," she said. "Who would ever need to oppose it?"

He came swiftly across the room to her and sat down on the couch so that he faced her. He took her hand between his. And his hands were strong, lean hands, warm. "You know," he said. "Women are just great. Simply great. The women I've known. You. My mother. And the girl I almost married, and didn't."

"Dorothy," said Carter softly.

Tom's face lighted. "Yes!" he agreed. "I've talked to you about her."

"A little. Are you still in love with her, Tom?"

"No," he said readily. "Maybe I never was really in love with her. I wanted a girl, my own woman. I was happy when we were planning to be married. But that didn't work out. . . ."

"You don't want to talk about it?"

He sat back against the cushions, still holding Carter's hand. "There isn't much to say," he explained. "She was a fine girl. When— Have I told you about the group of doctors I was working with at that time?"

"Only that you did work in a group."

"Yes, I did. And they were all right. I suppose much the same as you'd find in any such group setup. Some were better doctors than others; some were better men. All of us human. I wasn't experienced enough then—maybe I never shall be —to accept the jealousy I discovered within the group. But I think the worst shock to me was over the gossip, the scandalmongering that could go on in that clinic."

"Not about you, Tom?"

"Yes, as a matter of fact. About me."

"Did you deserve it?" she asked, smiling.

"I don't think so. I didn't think so then. Women and their doctors, you know . . ."

"Women doctors don't have that problem, buddy."

"You're lucky. I was doing internal medicine, passing my Boards and all. I was busy. Too busy even for Dorothy, or my mother, let alone other female interests. But—well, these dames . . . They'd ask for me especially when they came to the clinic. Even if they didn't know my specialty, or even my name, they'd say silly things."

"Like 'I want that tall, dark-haired one with the sexy eyes.'"

Tom jumped. He turned and leaned toward Carter. "Women are *fools!*" he shouted.

"Ten minutes ago we were great."

"Well, you are. Great fools."

Carter laughed aloud, and he joined her.

"Dorothy," he said after a time. "Dorothy realized my lack of self-defense against these men who were stirring up talk about me. It was a warfare, a game, of which I didn't know the rules and had no equipment with which to play. She persuaded me to get out of the group and go into private practice again."

Carter put her hand on Tom's arm. He was wearing a dark blue jacket, soft to the touch. "Do you know?" she said. "I believe I am jealous of Dorothy."

Tom laughed and put his arm about her shoulders, drew her to him, and he kissed her hard—harder than he had done in the office. She settled against his shoulder, her fingers stroked his cheek. "Nice," she murmured.

Tom released her and stood up. "Very nice," he agreed. He looked at his watch. "The big hand is at nine and the little hand is at one."

She stood up, too, laughing. "Did I tell you," she asked, leading the way to the door, "that I'd been paid the insurance money on my ring?"

"No wonder I like to kiss you. You're rich!"

"Not really," she said. "I put the money into the bank. I am sure that the ring cannot be lost. It will turn up."

Tom stared at her. "Could this be . . . ?" he asked, and broke off. "Oh, no! It just couldn't be the gremlins at work again!"

"To take my ring . . . ?"

"I was here. I saw you put it between the windows. When it disappeared, you could have suspected me—you could suspect me now of taking it."

For a second Carter put her head down against his shoulder. "Go home, Tom," she said faintly. "Go home."

CHAPTER **11**

THEN IT WAS June again. Hot again. People, in the winter, often came to the Clinic to get warm. And in the summer the air conditioning was equally appreciated, Tom told Karen. "It's sometimes hard to identify these comfort seekers."

"I'd do the same thing," she assured him. "It is stinking hot outside today. Now if you'll just sign these, Dr. Kelsey . . ."

He reached for a pencil. When checking forms, he liked one in his hand. He stared at the ceramic jar which, that morning, was well filled with yellow pencils. "It's full!" he told Karen, looking up at her.

"Yes, sir. It's been full for the past several mornings."

"The purple pencil stealer has all he wants, I suppose."

"More than he wants. This morning there were six pencils on the blotter of your desk."

Tom shook his head. "Some things," he told the girl, "I cannot figure out!"

The next morning his leather-bound memo book and a large pile of pencils showed up on his desk. Karen left them for him to see, and he fetched Carter down from the second floor. "What do you make of this, detective?" he asked her.

Carter asked Karen what *she* thought.

"I don't know," said Karen. "Sometimes I wonder if I walk in my sleep and do these things."

"I won't have you sleeping here in the office," Tom told her.

Carter thought it was Sahrman. She had, she said, considered all the possibilities, and Sahrman lasted longest as a suspect.

Tom did not entirely agree, but her conviction could have been one of the reasons that he went to see Steven Sahrman that night. The refugee lived in a one-room apartment about a mile from the hospital center. It was in one of those fringe neighborhoods, neither good nor bad. Tom had been there once before when Dr. Sahrman had been on his service and had called in sick. This night he wanted to talk to the man about Elene Trice.

Tom had arranged for her to enter the hospital for tests and v.d. treatments. He thought he had persuaded her that only the early treatment of syphilis could promise a cure. She had said she would enter—and then had not. Tom couldn't find her at home; he hoped that Sahrman would know and would tell him where the girl was. If he didn't know about the v.d., Tom would tell him, confident that, as a doctor, Sahrman would help him locate her.

Sahrman was at home; he politely welcomed Dr. Kelsey. He offered him a glass of wine, which Tom accepted. And then, by way of starting the talk he wanted to have, he mentioned the pencils. For a while, he said, they had been taken from the holder on his desk. Then, after an interval when none was taken, now, for two or three days, "I've found a heap of the yellow things, all neatly sharpened, in the middle of my blotter."

"So?" asked Sahrman, who still was being wary with his caller.

"So I ask myself," said Tom, "who's crazy?"

"It could be anybody," said Sahrman. "It could even be you, Doctor."

"Well, I hope not, but it could be."

"Did you come here to tell me to stop taking pencils and returning them?" Now Sahrman's dark eyes glowed, and his tone was icy.

Tom held on to his temper. He had other things to ask this man. "No," he said readily, "I came to see if you could tell me where to find Elene Trice."

Sahrman's head lifted. "Is she lost?"

Tom nodded. "In a way, yes, she is. The girl is sick, Steven. I told her—she agreed to enter the hospital for tests, but she didn't show up. I knew that you two had been friends . . ."

"She came here several times," Sahrman agreed. "Often at my suggestion, as often on her own, and she slept with me."

Tom would not be shocked. "I figured that things were that way. She's only eighteen, Sahrman, and now, or so she tells me, she has been told that she has syphilis."

"Do you think I told her that?" Sahrman got to his feet. He leaned over Tom. "Do you think I gave her syphilis?"

Tom shrugged. "I don't know, in either case. I want her to have treatment, and I was hunting her."

"And you came first to me. That is the way with a refugee in your country."

Tom set his wine glass on the maple coffee table. "Now, what has your being a refugee got to do with it?" he asked.

"My friend, I will tell you."

"We let you come to our country, you want to come, as being a better place than your own country."

"That is true, but do you know the life we lead here in your country?"

"Because you can't practice medicine until your citizenship is established."

"Because we cannot practice what we have learned in good medical schools, in good hospitals."

"Steven, I—"

"I know what you have tried to do for me, Dr. Kelsey. And I will say that, though you are a naive man, you have come closest to being a friend to me."

"Why naive?" asked Tom.

"Because you do not know that people are trying very hard to manipulate you, that they call you—it is a term I cannot understand as applied to you—but I have heard it said: 'He is the white-haired boy. And he will come around.'"

"What does that mean?" Tom asked, his eyes blank. "Will come around to what?"

"Do you know why they call you a white-haired boy?"

Tom tugged at a lock of his black hair. "I understand the expression," he said. "It means someone in favor. But I'm not even that . . ."

"Dr. Lewis likes you. Dr. Scott does, and Dr. Bass."

"Well, they'd like you, too, if you'd give them half a chance."

"No, they do not like me. They would try to help me—even you try to help me."

"Well, why not?"

Sahrman sat down again. "Have you ever been in a position where, though you are capable of taking care of yourself, everyone must try to help you?"

Tom considered this. "Patronage," he decided. "Yes, for me—and probably for you—that would be hard to take—in daily doses."

"It is hard. Just as daily doses of suspicion are hard."

"Suspicion?"

"Oh, yes, Dr. Kelsey. Why else do you come to me when your pencils are stolen and returned?"

Tom made a gruff sound of disclaimer.

"Perhaps you do not take that seriously. But you do take seriously that your young protégée should acquire syphilis, and the first one you suspect is Steven Sahrman, not?"

"Now look here, Sahrman. I knew you'd been seeing that girl. . . . Incidentally, she is in no sense my protégée. But she is missing, and I thought you might know her well enough—better than I do—and could tell me where to start looking for her. She needs medical treatment, and that is my chief and only interest in her."

"I will see what I can do to help you," Dr. Sahrman answered Tom—still grudgingly. "She may even come here."

"I hope she does. She has not been at her mother's home."

Sahrman regarded his visitor thoughtfully. "I have not seen her recently, and I did not give her the syphilis," he said.

"She told me that she had picked up a bum . . ."

"Aggh! These girls. They think they know so much, and they know so little. She talks about reading books—Thomas Mann and so on—but actually she has cut herself off from acquiring the knowledge and the background which would make her intellectual."

"Her mother," Tom said, "believes that Elene is going to start to college this fall."

"Her mother," Steven repeated. "Will you have more wine, Doctor?"

Tom shook his head. "Thank you, no. I came here only to see if you would help Elene."

"I am glad you did come. We refugee doctors lead a life of great boredom."

Tom looked up in surprise. "You do?"

"Of course. We have few friends. We have no prestige as a professional man. We have to live in this sort of place."

"You're not paid too poorly, Sahrman," Tom reminded the man.

"No, I am not. In my country, I would be a fairly rich man with such an income. Here I must save a great part of what I am paid in order to establish myself in practice once I get a license, and eventually to marry, have a home, and start a family."

"You had no family . . . ?"

"I left behind my mother, who is very old, and a brother who does have a family. But—" Sahrman's shoulders lifted in a shrug—"here I have nothing. Here I am bored. And I make tramp girls like your Elene serve for the woman I really would like to have. It is not an exciting life."

Tom could only regard his knees and be sorry. "I'm helpless," he said. "I should come to see you—"

"Not out of that patronage, Doctor."

"No. Of course not." Tom stood up.

"It is not good," said Sahrman, following his guest to the door, "to sit alone in a dreary room like this and contemplate the waste of my abilities. I contemplate them, too, at the hospital where I spend my days taking case histories, examining sick people, but never staying with them long enough to cure them or even know of their progress."

"You did much more than take histories over at Research," said Tom.

"Yes. Because that was a public-funds organization. But I was moved."

"I had nothing to do with your move. In fact, I protested it."

"I knew that you did. But—" Sahrman shrugged—"thank you for letting me talk to you, Dr. Kelsey."

"You'll work out your time," Tom told him. "I suspect during these hard years you have often wondered if you were at all wise to make the move."

"Yes, but it was a final move. Except for homesickness and my thoughts, I cannot consider any return."

"Knowing what you know now," Tom asked, "would you still have left your country?"

"Yes," said Sahrman readily. "I would have come here, and I would have tried to change things. I still plan to try to change them."

"I'll help you!" Tom held out his hand. "I—frankly, Steven, what you've told me tonight—I suppose a little thoughtfulness on my part would have let me figure out your situation. But I didn't put myself into your place . . ."

"Some of the things I have had to endure you could not have changed."

"No," agreed Tom. "Especially the homesickness."

"And the suspicion, Doctor?"

"I have not been suspicious of you, except in your relationship to Elene, whatever you may think."

"But others . . ."

Tom nodded. "We'll sweat that out together," he said engagingly. "We white-haired boys have an expression, Steven. It's 'Hang in there, Doctor.'"

Sahrman laughed. "I am long familiar with what that expression means, sir. Good night."

"Good night."

As it happened, neither Dr. Sahrman nor Dr. Kelsey found Elene. She managed to get into the hospital on her own. Before that week was out, one very early morning, she was brought by ambulance to the emergency room. She had wrecked her mother's car and was found to be in a precarious condition due to drugs. Amphetamine, probably.

In any case, Tom Kelsey was sent for—through Evalyn, Karen told him, though Elene, having worked for Clausen, might still have carried an identification card.

Tom called emergency admissions, found out where she was and what had happened. Elene was hurt, but her broken leg and her cuts and bruises could be cared for. The drug would wear off. "Come when you can, Doctor," said the resident. "She seems convinced that you should. Though there is no urgency."

"I'll be there," Tom promised. "I have a few things to attend to first."

It was afternoon before Tom made it, which didn't bother him because he preferred to have Elene somewhat settled down before he showed up. And when he did come into her room, he found the lad whom, in his mind, he had always called "Elene's nice boy"— Jimmie Ellsgood—standing beside her bed and talking pretty roughly to the girl, who looked miserable, and looked more miserable by the minute because Jimmie was telling her how disgusted he was with her.

After a bit of this, Tom stepped forward. He put his hand on the boy's shoulder. "Lay off, son," he said. "This is no time to tell her she has lost the love of her life."

Jimmie stood like one shot, stunned, unbelieving, then ready to crumple before the impact. "M-m-me?" he stammered.

Tom unhooked the chart from the foot of the bed. "Possibly," he said indifferently. "Though we do have a refugee doctor around here whom Elene has thought exciting. Or—" his eyes traveled down the work-up sheet; he was reading the test reports. Yes, the syphilis had been detected. "Or—" he glanced at Elene—"or some bum she picked up off the street. Maybe even me." He hung the chart back into place. "But let's assume it is you, Jimmie." He stepped up along the side of the bed. "How're you doing, kid?" He held out his hand.

Elene did not see it. She was looking the other way, at Jimmie. Anyway, Jimmie was holding both of her hands. Tom watched them for a minute, then he melted out of the room. There were some things beyond the care and cure of a mere doctor.

And then the gremlins got busy again—really busy. Tom saw them and their work, Dick Scott did, and Carter. They watched the things happen, and wondered.

"Somebody's trying to tell you something," Dick assured Tom.

"All right. But what?"

"I don't know. But they expect a nice guy like you to get the message."

"I'd gladly accommodate them, even to the point of becoming a nice guy."

There had been the ambulance call. An ambulance service called Tom's office; they were bringing in a patient. O.B. should be alerted.

"Look," said Tom. "You've called the wrong clinic. This isn't the place to . . ." He broke off and looked at the phone in his hand. The dial tone hummed. Slowly he put the instrument back on its stand. There had been another case, he reminded Dick Scott when he told about the call. That woman had walked in and had died. But she did come to Research and was cared for. . . .

"Wasn't a lawsuit filed?"

"Yes, the lawyers for the insurance company settled it."

"Did anything happen this time?"

"Just the call. Nobody showed up. But it did give me a bad case of the shivers."

"Which is what you were supposed to get."

"I can't figure it out, Dick."

"If you can't get the message, they'll make it plainer."

"Who are they?"

Dick shook his head. "I keep turning up suspects. They don't qualify."

"Me, too," Tom admitted.

When two more calls came, directly to Tom's office, announcing that an ambulance was on its way to Research, Tom decided that kids were doing this thing. Teen-agers. Pranksters.

But that didn't hold up, either. In each of these calls, names were given—names of recent patients who were known, who had been in the clinic, in the hospital.

The calls had sounded legitimate. One named patient was a sickle-cell child; the Clinic had to be ready. Tom explained this to Scott, and to Carter.

"Do these calls always come when you are in the office?" Carter asked. "Are you asked for?"

"Yes, but I deliberately establish a personal relationship with the patients I am investigating. Like the sickle cell. When they leave us, patients of that nature, in our research program, are told to return if anything crops up."

"Of course."

"So we have to be ready."

"But nothing shows up."

"Not in these recent happenings. No. It's about to drive me out of my skull, too. I feel as if I live perpetually on a trampoline."

"Is that what they are after? Such a feeling? Or maybe even a breakdown?"

That could be the explanation, but Tom wanted to know who "they" were, what was wanted of him. "I've run out every stroke in this game," he told Dick—"if it is a game. Seriously, I'll take tennis."

Then a call came that sounded phony. Karen and Tom agreed that it did, but that time the ambulance arrived, and it brought a child to them in such a condition as to require full staff consideration. Tom asked to have Dr. Bass come down for a consultation. This seemed to be a case for a hematology expert.

Dr. Scott learned that something had happened, and he came down late that afternoon to ask Tom the particulars. Carter was there.

"Tom looks as grave as a judge," Dick pointed out to her.

"Why not?" Tom asked. "This could have been the call I decided to ignore."

"What happened?"

"Well, I was down the hall when the call came in; Karen sent for me. And it sounded like a child on the phone. Actually it was a child—one of our outpatients, an anemic child. His mamma . . ." Tom flushed and brushed his hand back through his hair. "I get to talking like these people," he confessed.

"His mamma . . ." Carter prompted, glancing at Dick. Both were concerned.

"Yes. She had told him to call me. Because—they live

in a project house, and there was this neighbor child—oh, he's about ten, and nothing but long, nobbly bones. This woman decided that he, too, had what she calls sickly anemia."

"It's a good name for it," said Carter, shielding her eyes from the late afternoon sun.

"This mother thinks we've helped her boy."

"Have you?" asked Dick alertly.

"Not really, I'm afraid. Though we are hopeful for the urea technique. Anyway, this woman tried to get the boy's parents to take him to the clinic, or to bring him here. They did not, and this morning he collapsed completely. She told her boy to call me; the number had been given to them. And—" He wiped his face.

"There's anemia, all right," Carter agreed.

"The kid was more dead than alive when he arrived," Tom said. "We really made things fly around here. One of the interns claims *he* got a glucose i.v."

"What are you doing for him? The boy, I mean."

"He's in intensive care up on Carter's floor. Tests will determine just what is his basic trouble."

"It isn't sickle cell," she said. She was frowning at the curtain. Some sort of shadow was crossing it.

"At least," concluded Dick, "this wasn't a gremlin call."

"No," said Tom. "But I came within a thread of deciding that it was and obeying the impulse I've been building up to. To yell at the caller."

"Wheee!" said Dick. "That would have been—something." Now his eyes, too, followed the shadow in the curtain and across the wall. He got up and turned off Tom's desk lamp.

Tom looked up at him. Dick pointed to the shadow. It was again on the curtain and jiggling up and down.

"It's Karen in the outer office," Tom explained.

"Karen left ten minutes ago," Carter reminded the men. "She called good night, and we answered her."

Tom drew a deep breath. "Then—" On soundless feet, he was around his desk and out to Karen's anteroom. No one was there.

When he returned . . . "It's gone," said Dick Scott, pointing to the curtain.

Carter was hugging her arms across her breast; she was white. "You and your ghosts!" she accused Tom. Her voice trembled.

"I'm sorry," said poor Tom.

"Somebody had to be in the outer office," declared Dick, roaming about the room.

"Or outside," suggested Tom.

"No. From outside, he couldn't have got a shadow on the wall beyond the curtain."

"He," said Tom thoughtfully.

"One of your *they*'s" Dick explained. He was experimenting with Karen's desk lamp and a sheet of paper, and he managed a shadow similar to the one that had visited them.

"Let's go someplace for a drink," Tom suggested. "I've stopped speculating who is behind all these things."

Dick came back into the room. "I've a theory," he told his friends.

Tom began putting papers into his desk drawers. "Let's have it," he said.

"Your enthusiasm inspires me."

"It's only," Carter explained, "that poor Tom has theorized himself into near coma."

"I don't wonder," Dick agreed. "This sort of thing . . ."

"What was your idea?" Tom asked. "If you turn your

backs, I'll change my coat."

Dick chuckled. "I'd better tell my theory quickly," he said. "It's getting a bit anemic, too. But—well—it struck me a day or two ago that Tom has been here for about a year. He came in here, and things happened to make it seem that he was the original white-haired boy. He did some spectacular diagnoses. He was made Chief. Then . . ."

"The gremlins began," said Tom.

"Yes, they did. And, since I know there is such a movement afoot, I think 'they' are trying to get you to tell someone to let the Hospital Staff run Research. You'd be listened to."

"Do they think they can drive me far enough up the wall that I'd do that?" Tom demanded.

"Well," Dick said, "maybe they don't know you as well as some of us do. Anyway, it's only a theory."

"It's better than a lot of mine," Tom conceded. "Let's go get that drink."

They went to the hotel bar and, after his drink and some more talk, Dick departed for home. Judy, he explained, preferred that he not prolong these pleasant interludes with other women. Tom and Carter lingered, then decided to eat dinner there at the hotel. They could relax after their strenuous day. Tom located them to the Institute switchboard.

They ate crab Imperial, a huge salad, and listened to soothing music. And Carter, primarily to turn Tom's thoughts away from gremlins and all such manifestations, asked him to tell her what had happened when he left the medical group with which he had been affiliated. As he answered her, she watched him, waiting patiently on his long pauses.

"I told you," he said, "that I felt I was not performing well in group practice."

"Not with that group, at any rate."

"So I found a place where I could share an office—that is, I shared the waiting room, the receptionist, the lab and its technicians—even the X-ray setup. But I was my own man, an internist. The other men were respectively an allergist, an eye surgeon, and a pediatrician."

"Did you like it?"

"It was all right. The place was pretty plush, and the procedures were all set up for me before I moved in. The man before me had died rather suddenly, and I inherited some of his patients."

"Did your mother like it?"

"She kept hoping I would settle down."

Carter smiled. "What about Dorothy?"

"Oh. Well—my mother, in that connection, admired Dorothy for pushing me out of the group. And since my mother's admiration was a rare thing, we basked in it."

"And you did well." Carter filled his coffee cup from the small silver pot.

"It was a little bit slow at first," Tom said reflectively, "but success was steady. I learned to dress conservatively but well; patients began to refer their friends to me. I rescued a man with a kidney stone from a gall bladder operation. I diagnosed mononucleosis for a boy supposed to be suffering from one of those vague virus diseases."

Carter smiled.

Tom nodded. "Yes. I did the usual things. Hodgkin's disease detected in a youngish man, but of course not cured. However, the family seemed to like my methods."

"Why not?"

"I'm not really bragging, Carter. But I did get more patients right along, and the future began to seem rosy for me."

"Then you decided to come to Research."

"Oh, no. Not then. I didn't live here. What happened was that my mother died."

"Oh, dear."

"Yes. Our relationship—I owed so much to her, Carter. She had worked so hard for me, to maintain our home, to keep me at my education and then my profession. I think she too thought, before she died, that my future was assured, and she was proud of that."

"But something happened."

"Yes." Tom sat silent for a time. "I still don't fully understand it, and I surely didn't at the time. Dorothy, my girl, turned away from me. She broke our engagement, gave me my ring—the works."

"But Tom—that was a terrible thing to do!" Carter spoke angrily, her blue eyes flashed.

Tom put his hand over hers. "Calm down," he said.

"She never loved you!"

"Well, maybe she did, Carter. In her way. She told me, you see, that she would never marry a son."

"What on earth did she mean by that?"

"It took me a time to realize what she meant. But after a year of being hurt and thinking about it, I realized what she meant, and then I could see that she was right. With her, at least, I had been turning first to my mother—to her precepts, at any rate. My first consideration of any problem had been to decide what would please my mother. No girl, no wife, should come second with a man. So, after that bruising year of self-examination, I knew that that phase of my life was over. I had begun to work extra hours in a public health clinic, and when I decided to make a complete change in my life—town, office, everything—I learned of an opening here at Research. I applied, and because of my work with public health, I was interviewed and I got the position. I came here. . . ."

"And you will stay here, won't you?" Carter spoke anxiously.

"Probably," said Tom. "Possibly." He smiled at her. "I hope."

CHAPTER **12**

A DAY OR TWO LATER, Carter came down to Tom's office. Karen said she could go right in. "He's busy, but he needs a break."

Carter smiled at the girl. "I'm glad you take such good care of him, Karen."

"I'm crazy about the guy."

"Me, too," Carter told her silently, but framing the words with her lips. She went on through to Tom's big and pleasant office, her first glance for the curtains at the wide window.

Tom looked up, a frown between his eyes, then he smiled, took off his glasses, and stood up. "Is it lunchtime?" he asked.

"Haven't you eaten? It's eleven forty-five." Carter sat down in his desk chair.

"Are you inviting me to lunch?" he asked, pushing his stack of papers out of the way so that he could see Carter, always a pleasure.

"That wasn't my first thought, but I'll do it if you insist." She rummaged in the pocket of her lab coat. "I brought this to show you." She drew out an envelope and held it toward Tom.

"What is it?" he asked.

"Look at it."

He spanned the envelope in his hand. It was a regular postage paid envelope, eight cents postage stamped in the corner of it. The address was typed—Dr. Carter Bass, and so on. Addressed to her apartment.

"I found it with other personal mail in my box last night," Carter told him. "It had been there all day."

Tom glanced up at her.

"Look inside," she suggested.

"It came from Chicago," he announced.

"Yes, I noticed."

Tom cupped the envelope in his hand so that it spread open a little. Inside was what loked like Kleenex, many layers of it, yet he could feel . . . He pushed his papers still farther away, clearing his desk blotter. He pulled the Kleenex out of the envelope, several sheets of it, then he fished with his forefinger and drew out a small package, something folded into more Kleenex. Again he looked up at Carter.

"Open it," she said, watching him closely.

He did, unfolding the packet, and then he sat staring at what lay before him. A ring. A diamond ring. A beautiful, expensive diamond ring.

He reached again for the envelope. "Eight cents postage," he said, almost prayerfully.

"Yes," Carter agreed. "From Chicago."

"But who sent it?" Tom asked.

Carter nodded, her eyes on his face. "That's a good question," she agreed. "Who? Who took it? Who sent it?"

Tom sat shaking his head. Slowly, he folded the ring back

into its papers, slowly he put it back between the layers of Kleenex in the envelope and handed the whole thing to Carter. "I wonder if we'll ever know," he said. He leaned back in his chair and put his fingertips to his eyelids. "I wonder if we'll ever know who did the burglaries. To do those—to take that ring—those were real crimes, Carter." He dropped his chair forward and gazed at her. "The police and the insurance companies have traced some of the loot from the burglaries, but—"

"I'm sure the insurance company tried to find my ring."

"Have you told them . . . ?"

"That it's been returned? Not yet. I shall this afternoon. I wanted to show it to you first."

"Hmmmn. Because it could be my gremlins who took it to Chicago."

"I don't really think so, Tom."

"Why not?"

"Because I think this, and maybe the burglaries, too, would lead us to some person who had been taking advantage of your gremlins, of the crazy things that have been going on down here. They saw a game being played . . ."

"Who saw?" asked Tom, his eyes steady, his mouth almost hard.

"We did," said Carter. "Various ones. Karen must know about the happenings. Dick Scott did. Dr. Lewis."

"Yes," Tom agreed. "For a time I was afraid it might be Sahrman."

"He wouldn't risk all it would mean should he be caught."

"He risked quite a lot with Elene Trice."

"Oh, but she was to blame there."

Tom shook his head. "You women . . ."

"We know what we know. But this—I've suspected everybody. For a time, I suspected Dr. Hubbell."

"You couldn't!"

"No, that idea didn't hold up very long. But I did suspect him. He needed the money. He was around . . ."

Tom held his head in both hands. "That would be terrible," he moaned.

"The whole thing is terrifying," she reminded him.

Tom read about the development in his morning newspaper, and was angry that he had not received some sort of notice about it on his desk previously. He would then have been able to tell Sahrman himself—

Still, it was a pleasure to know that the State Board of Registration of the Healing Arts had voted to permit the three hundred foreign doctors now working in the state to take the examinations and, having passed, to work freely as physicians.

From now on, men like Sahrman need not serve only in public institutions, and the doctor shortage, especially in rural areas, could be relieved. Certainly this was exciting news! Tom crushed the newspaper in his hand and planned to go to Sahrman as soon as he possibly could.

He finished his breakfast, tidied the kitchen, finished dressing, all the while in a whirl of thinking—about his busy day—the usual routines, of course—a class—a consultation with some city officials. That evening, a sort of part-picnic, part-parade celebration at Clausen. Somebody would say how fine Clausen was, and somebody else would ask why there wasn't another Clausen—or several. Tom could tell them about Vernon. Only he wanted to talk to Sahrman first, to be sure he understood about the Attorney General's ruling on foreign-trained physicians.

He drew some deep breaths and went out to his car. And when he reached his office, he found that Karen had made an appointment for Dr. Sahrman to see him at eleven o'clock.

Fine! "What does he want?" Tom asked Karen.

"I don't know, Dr. Kelsey. He seemed excited."

"Then he's heard about the ruling which will let him take the examinations to practice. Have you heard about that, Karen?"

She had not, so Tom could tell her.

"You're excited, too, aren't you?" the girl asked him.

"Yes. I really am. Though I did have a job lined up for Sahrman."

"At Vernon?"

"At Vernon. He'd be fine there. And I want to work with that center—get patients from there, I mean. Especially for my sickle-cell project."

"Dr. Sahrman started you on that, didn't he?"

"Oh, yes. He detected a case; then he said that such an hereditary disease, one that cripples and blinds, should be investigated, the family lines traced, and a cure sought. He got so interested in that investigation that I thought he'd take off for Africa any day."

Karen laughed. "But you have begun the research into why only Negroes have that anemia."

"A blind alley, so far. But yes, I am working on it. There has to be some difference which accounts for it."

Karen smiled at him. "You do throw yourself into a thing, Dr. Kelsey," she said admiringly.

Tom smiled at her and told her to send Dr. Sahrman right in when he came.

"Oh, I will!" she promised.

Sahrman was prompt and Tom, rising to greet him, commented on it. Had it been difficult for him to get away?

"No, sir. I am no longer assigned to Diagnostic."

"Oh?" said Dr. Kelsey. "Did something happen?"

Sahrman sat down in the chair beside the desk. He was wearing a yellow shirt and tan trousers, very slim. He looked quietly self-assured; no trace of his usual anger burned in his eyes.

"You've heard about the Attorney General's ruling?" Tom suggested.

"Yes, sir, and of course I plan to take the examinations."

"Any help I can give . . ."

"I shan't need help, sir. For three years I have been preparing."

"Of course. And you'll pass them. Which may not be good for me, because I was about to offer you, or suggest to you, another job, Dr. Sahrman."

"You have always before called me Steven."

"I know. But you don't call me Tom, and if that continues when we hold down similar positions . . ."

Steven leaned across the desk toward Dr. Kelsey. "Were you about to offer me the directorship of Vernon?" he asked intently.

"It is not mine to offer, Steven, but I think my word would go far in selecting the Director for the new health center." He smiled at Sahrman, who also smiled.

"This is not Clausen, you understand," Tom explained. "For a year or more, the thing will operate out of three trailers. It will offer services in internal medicine, pediatrics, and obstetrics-gynecology. Also dentistry. It will serve about seventy-five thousand people living in the northwest part of the city. I've worked on the plans for it. Like Clausen, it will be open from nine to nine; we will operate a small bus for the transportation of those patients who positively cannot get to the place. The service will be free; there is a Federal grant—for about twenty thousand people. Others will be charged according to their ability to pay. A permanent center will be built next year, and I have already started to train thirty neighborhood residents at Clausen. In a month they will be ready to help the staff at Vernon."

"Eighteen doctors, ten dentists, thirty medical aides," said Sahrman softly.

Tom looked alertly across at him. "You know about Vernon, then?"

"Yes, sir. I came here this morning to tell you that I am going to be the Director of it."

Tom was delighted. He said he was, he looked as if he was. "Will this lifting of the ban on your licensure make any difference?" he asked anxiously.

"No, sir. This is the work I want to do. My one proviso is that I may continue my work for the Center at Rock Forest. You know about that?"

"Yes," said Tom. "It is a health center started out in that black community."

"Started by a church and a church hospital. Yes, sir, it is."

"Have you been working there?"

"I have. Last night I treated a strep throat, sewed up a facial laceration, referred a boy with an eye problem to a hospital, gave a college girl a physical examination, diagnosed a case of heart failure, prescribed diets for two overweight girls, and detected diabetes."

"Whew!" said Tom, shaking his head. "You don't need another job."

"All the doctors at Rock Forest have other jobs. We each work one night a month. We are trying to give some health care to those who otherwise could not afford it. We bring that care to them, because that's where those people live. We have acquired some sponsors, and now we operate one night a week for adults, two for children. We have twelve doctors on register, nineteen nurses, two nutritionists, and eleven students from a Catholic nursing school. We don't give the ultimate in medical care, of course, but we do fulfill a need in that community. I should like to continue, and wanted to ask you if it would be possible . . . ?"

"After you take over Vernon? I don't see why it shouldn't be. I'd like to serve a turn there myself."

"The Board would be glad to have you," Sahrman told him.

"You do know," said Tom, "that once you pass your exams, you won't be limited to public health or institutional work?"

"Yes, sir, I know. But you do it, and I admire you for doing it. You have been a real friend to me."

Tom sat thoughtful. "For a time there," he said slowly, "I thought you were trying to get my job."

"I did try," said Sahrman. "Back then, I resented you and your promotion. I had been working for the Institute, I knew the work. You came in and stepped ahead of me . . ."

"I pulled no strings. I really did nothing."

"But you understood what it took to be the Director. When I figured that out, I began to study and prepare myself."

"And you applied for Vernon."

"Yes, sir."

"I could have helped you."

"And I was ready to ask for that help—except that I knew you disliked what I had done to that silly girl."

"Elene?"

"Yes, Elene. I used her."

"A woman told me that Elene herself was to blame there."

"Partly, that is true. The American phrase is: 'She asked for it.'"

Tom nodded. "I'll have to agree."

Sahrman looked unhappy. "I am sorry . . ." he began, hesitated, then blurted the words. "I am sorry that I resented you. I did not, really. Not you as you are."

"I believe I always knew that," said Tom earnestly. "Your resentment was for me, an American-trained physician, and my past, as contrasted to your past, not only as a physician but as a man, a boy even. You thought everything had come easily to me."

"Did it not?" asked Sahrman with honest curiosity.

"No," said Tom. "It did not. I can recall your telling me on various occasions that I knew nothing about your past. I knew that I didn't, but, on the other hand, you . . ."

"I thought you did not have a past," said the refugee with simple honesty.

"That's nonsense. Everyone has a past—the richest man, the most successful. Men like Lonnie, men like you. And me, too. Certainly you should have learned that from your work here at Research."

Sahrman smiled ruefully. "It would seem that I have much to learn."

Tom took Sahrman to lunch, and from there he decided to go see Elene. She was still in the hospital, her leg in traction. Tom had kept a check on her treatment and on her progress. Today he would go to see her. Perhaps she would talk to him.

She did. It was as if a new girl lay there on that bed among all the pulleys and apparatus. Her accident, the hospital experience, something seemed to have cleansed her mind. She was aware of what she had been doing, of the mess she could have made of her entire future.

"You've changed," Tom told her.

"I just woke up," she agreed. "When I smashed that car, it woke me up."

Tom said something about her having been a heavy sleeper, but she looked at him solemnly. "I've been thinking about everything," she told him. "About me, and life—what I did, what I had, what I have, and can still have."

"That's a lot of thinking."

"I'm being realistic," she said. "I've decided that dreams are just the refuge of cowards."

"Oh, no," said Tom quickly. "They are a part of youth. So long as you have them, you have youth."

"Do you still have them?"

"Oh, yes. And you will, too."

"I thought . . ."

"Maybe you did wake up," said Tom. "But maybe you're still not fully grown."

"When I am . . . ?"

"Probably you will also be fully awake."

She considered this; her fingers played with the wrappings of her cast. "Will I hate it?" she asked in a troubled way. "Being grown up and fully awake?"

"Sometimes you will," he conceded. "Generally, you won't. Because, you see, Elene, there is so much work to do in the daylight." He took her hand in his, ready to leave.

"I wish you could have loved me," she said softly, clinging to his hand.

"I do love you."

She laid his hand firmly down upon the blanket, and she laughed. "You love your hippies, too," she reminded him.

Much later that same day, he decided to talk to Carter, and he went up to the second floor, only half expecting to find her still in the Institute. Because of the children, he liked that floor. He always looked in through the windows at them, and even those in bed would wave back to him. He found Carter finishing her day, already changed from her white garments, which were becoming, and wearing a slim, sleeveless dress of black and white linen, which was even more so. She had just combed her hair and tied it back with a bright scarf.

"You don't look like the end of a hard day," Tom told her.

She smiled at him; then the smile faded. "I'm afraid you do," she said, "Are you finished?"

"Except for a celebration over at Clausen later on tonight. About eight or eight-thirty."

She nodded and looked at her watch. "Two hours at least," she decided. "I'll take you home and refresh you."

"Sounds fine."

It was fine. Carter's apartment was a pretty place. Flooded by evening light, the yellow walls of her living room were brocaded with a white tracery; the chairs and couch were white, with yellow cushions tucked invitingly into corners. About the room, silver gleamed richly—a candelabra, a coffee service on a side table, a silver bowl of white flowers. Carter told Tom to find a soft chair, she would bring him something cool. "Remember the celebration," he called after her.

"Lemonade?" she called back. He could hear the rattle of ice.

"No need to go overboard."

She brought the Collinses in tall, frosted glasses, and she was laughing. "Now tell me about your day," she said, sitting down in one of the low armchairs.

So he did tell her—about Sahrman, about Elene's growing up.

"What about the boy friend you always call nice?"

"Jimmie," Tom agreed. "And he is a nice lad. But, for some reason, Carter, I rather hope Elene finds herself another boy. A new man."

"If she's grown up . . ."

"A man is what she needs." Tom drank from his glass. "It was a long day," he said. "But a good one."

"Do you think you solved some of your problems today? Are you feeling that the gremlins won't bother you again?"

"Will they? Tom asked. "Shouldn't I feel that way?"

"You've found some clues," Carter said slowly. "Dick and I were talking about that earlier this afternoon." Her face brightened. "I wish we had brought him with us. He thinks . . ." She stood up. "I'm going to call him," she said. "If he's still at the hospital, we could go back there."

"Have him come here," Tom amended. "He loves a Tom Collins."

Carter laughed. She picked up the telephone.

"If Evalyn Trice is around," said Tom, "ask Dick to bring her along. She's known about my gremlins."

"I'll bet she has," said Carter, dialing.

"Oh, come on now, Carter," he protested. "She's been interested . . ."

"I do not think Evalyn should be in on this conference," she said flatly and firmly.

Tom stared at her while she talked. She nodded to him. Dick was still at the hospital . . . Then Dick came on, and she talked to him. Tom was there, she said. If Dick could come over . . . "He thinks he has his gremlins on the run. It shouldn't take long; no more than the time for one long, cold drink." She paused. "I could call Judy and tell her it's in a good cause."

She was smiling when she put the phone down.

"He's coming?"

"Right away. He was just starting home. While we're waiting, I'll mix his Collins and get you some crackers and cheese. You may miss dinner."

Tom followed her to the kitchen, and he was still perched on a stool there when Dick arrived. He and Carter sat down at the small table in the alcove.

Tom watched his friends, the balding man with the immaculate, clever hands . . . Dick appreciated his drink, and ate some of Tom's crackers while Carter told him about Sahrman.

"I heard of his appointment," Dick said. "I thought you surely must know, Tom."

"I didn't. I've been too busy, evidently."

"Hubbell told me. When he did, he said he was sure you'd be pleased. He felt certain you didn't think it was Sahrman who had been deviling you." Dr. Hubbell, lately, had been working in the lab on Dick's floor, experimenting with mice and various diets which might cause or invite cancer.

Tom brushed crumbs into his hand. "What else did he tell you?" he asked. "Does he know who the gremlins are?"

"Oh, yes. He told me, and I told Carter earlier this afternoon."

Tom stood down from the stool; his face was white. "And now you will tell me," he said tightly. "Hubbell couldn't—"

"Hubbell was sure you wouldn't believe him. So he told me, as your friend. I think he hoped I could have stopped the process without your having to know. As a matter of fact, I have started to do just that."

"But I'm still not to know?"

"Oh, sit down, Kelsey! I'll tell you if you don't make it take too long."

Tom glanced at Carter, who smiled at him. "All right," he conceded. "Make it as short and painless as you can. Who's been making a fool out of me?"

"Only trying, son," said Dick. "Only trying. And Hubbell was right. You wouldn't have believed him. The men behind this didn't think he mattered, either."

"Oh, now see here, Scott!" Tom protested hotly.

"I know what you think about Hubbell, and what you are doing for him. But as things stand and have stood, the man, by his own will and wish, has been able to fade into the hospital background. He can go along the corridors, eat in the cafeteria, even take a break in the lounge, and people don't see him. They talk in his hearing . . . When he found out what was happening to you . . ." Dick put up his hand to prevent interruption. "I told him, for one thing," he explained. "Then he saw for himself, and when he was sure, he came and told me."

"Told you what?" Tom stood against the work counter. His face was stony; his eyes were very blue.

"He told me that there was a group—mainly doctors—who wanted to discredit the Institute's work. They had nothing against you individually, but when you came in they decided that they could use you. You were new at the job, young—inexperienced in the Complex . . ."

"I was green all right," Tom conceded. "But how did they use me? What did they want?"

"They employed various methods to accomplish various things. Their prime purpose, of course, was to get the Institute back under the Medical Center's jurisdiction. Its direction. They didn't want me to be Chief of the surgical cancer research unit. They didn't believe you—or Bonley at the first—should have your own unit. That could all come under their social service department. And so on. Especially they didn't want Dr. Lewis to be Director of Research."

"Did he know that?" Tom came to the table and sat

down, now completely interested.

"Oh, yes, Lewis knows it. He's watched these people; he's watched you."

"Did he name me Chief as a come-on for them—these disrupters?"

"Oh, Tom!" Carter protested.

"He knows Lewis better than that," Dick calmed her. "He knows he was appointed as one able to do the job. But Lewis did watch these people and their methods."

"Childish, some of them," Tom agreed. "And dangerous. To play games in a hospital! I talked to Lewis about what was going on."

"They aren't to blame for all the things that seemed to happen to you, Tom," said Dick. "But they did do various things. At parties they propagandized. They played games to make you uneasy, uncertain; they brought in outside developments, used outside people."

"They spent a little money . . ." said Carter.

"Bribes?"

"Inducements," said Dick, warming to his account.

"Like starting lawsuits?" Tom leaned forward.

"They thought of everything."

"Mhmmmn," said Tom. "They didn't like my hippies."

Dick laughed. "Well, after all, Kelsey. Some of those people—when they paint their toenails purple . . ."

"I know, and they can smell like boiled urine."

Carter gasped.

"They do," Dick assured her. "But remember these plotters were eminent scientists."

"Rosenthal," said Tom. "Dr. Daives? Yes, Dr. Daives. Was Jack Lenox in on this infantile scheme? I remember talking to him, walking along a corridor or someplace beside him the day I found half of that sick birthday card in my jacket pocket."

"You are catching on," Dick told him.

"But what did they want of me?" Tom asked. "To leave?"

Both Dick and Carter answered at once. "Oh, my, no!" they cried, then looked up, one to the other, and smiled.

Tom got to his feet and went back to the counter. He stacked crackers on a plate, sliced some cheese. "What is all this?" he asked, not turning around.

"You tell him, Doctor," said Carter.

"They wanted you to decide that things were not being managed right," said Dick.

"At Research." Tom brought his plate to the table.

"Yes, of course."

"But I like things the way we do them. From the first, I have liked the setup."

"Even with your ghosties and gremlins?"

"Yes! I did." Tom again looked stubborn.

"They tried," said Carter, "to show you that you didn't like it."

"There's that *they* again," said Tom. He ate two crackers sandwiched with cheese. "What good would it have done me, and Research, if I had decided I didn't like the way things were managed?"

"They judged your character well enough to decide that you would speak up if you didn't approve."

"Tell someone? Who?" Tom flushed. "Whom," he corrected himself.

Dick and Carter laughed aloud.

"They thought you would tell Lewis," said Dick, "or a Staff administrator."

"But," cried Tom, "I would never do that! If I didn't like the situation, I would have left."

"Yes. They thought you might. But they also thought you would say why."

"I see. And what would have happened then?"

"They thought things would change. They would have insisted on a full Staff consideration."

"Just because I didn't . . . ?"

"They knew that the Board and Staff wanted you to stay. You were doing great work. You were their white-haired boy. I think I've called you that before, Tom."

"Yes," said Tom. So had Sahrman. "All right, tell me more."

"Well, as I say, they talked to you, at you, and about you. They said things should be different. They asked you if you liked the way things were being run. Or they asked about what you didn't like. Didn't they?"

"Well, yes," Tom conceded. "Some did. Lenox, Rosenthal . . ."

"Ah-hum," said Dick Scott.

Tom began to grin. "I remember their doing that, and all I said was that I didn't like the restrictions on interoffice romance." He got up and moved about the small kitchen. "Oh, brother!" he cried. "Oh, *brother!*" He turned around. "I still can't see why they were so elaborate."

"They didn't want you to be involved, with the Staff, that is, in your dissatisfaction."

"But if it was their main purpose . . . Of course, I've always thought someone was taking advantage of the gremlin thing and playing along. But these people, Lenox and the others—why didn't they just argue the matter with me?"

"Because," said Carter, "they are devious people, using devious ways."

"But I'm not devious," said Tom.

She laughed, Dick with her. "No, you are not," he agreed.

"And that is where they failed. They didn't bother to get to know you."

Tom nodded. "They saw nothing but my white hair," he mused. Then he looked up. "It needs cutting, doesn't it?"

"I never saw it when it didn't," said Dick. He stood up.

Tom still was thinking hard. "You persuaded me," he said, "that the accidents—in your o.r., in our lab—were simply accidents. Though I remember that something was said at that time about the management. Then—did all this begin with the lights blackout?" he asked.

"I don't think they managed that, but when you were concerned about it, perhaps they seized upon that to start their campaign."

"And the lawsuits . . . ?"

"They brought in a lawyer, Sax . . ."

Tom groaned. "They really did!"

"They tried to persuade Evalyn Trice to sue you, but she wouldn't."

"Well, good for her."

"By then, both she and Elene had fallen in love with you."

Tom made a face of extreme distaste.

"She knew what was being done, Tom, the build-up of the talk about Trice's death and all. And she didn't tell you. Then there was a baby born, wasn't there?"

"Oh, yes."

"And these characters were the ones to start and continue the bad publicity on that."

"How would they dare do these things? They had their own jobs to consider."

"Yes, but there were ways. By word of mouth—within the personnel ranks, a word getting outside, a discreet hint to the press."

Tom nodded. "I suppose. What about Sahrman? Did they try to use him?"

"Oh, yes. And their efforts were successful enough that they got him moved away from your service."

"Do they still have plans?"

"Maybe not the original one. That when they get you in the proper frame of mind, they could take over and get things changed."

"All this time, have you and Carter known what was going on?"

"Oh, no. Don't get that idea. We worked along our own lines of investigation, trying to figure out what was happening. It's been only lately—remember the shadows on the curtains?—that we consolidated our ideas. Then it didn't take a lot to confirm what we'd been suspecting."

"Suspecting what they wanted to accomplish?" asked Tom. "I only wish I knew what that was."

Dick and Carter both laughed again. "Tom," said Carter, "you really are wonderful."

"I know," he agreed. "And dumb. So, to save time, would you please line out . . . ?"

"Look," said Dick, going to him, putting his hand on Tom's arm. "This group—your three choices were only the instruments. In the Complex, that Byzantine complexity of contending forces—our Medical Center—there is a sizable group who want to put the Research Institute under Staff men. They would hire us to do the work, you for socio-medicine, me for cancer research surgery, Carter here for hematology research. And on down the line, or up it. The point is, the Staff men—the Chief of Surgery, the Chief of Pediatric Medicine, and so on—would get the name and the credit for what we do. Your department's sickle-cell investigation, for example. Their status would increase, and their tenure. But, and most important, they would gain control. For instance, I'd not do much surgery on what they call experimental bases."

"And the gremlins, the ghosts, were all a part of this. It seems too ridiculous—graffiti, phone calls—what about the burglaries?"

"Oh, that was something else and apart. If it disturbed you . . ."

"It did," said Tom grimly.

"They knew that and accepted their luck. But the burglaries . . . someone, maybe some two—hospital people are most certainly guilty. For a time, one of your hippies was closely watched."

"Scooter," said Tom. "But he didn't have the brains or the background."

"No. The police have decided that. But it has to be someone—orderly, nurse—" Dick broke off. "Did I hit a nerve?"

Tom flushed. "There was a nurse," he said. "I had her transferred, for stealing. Later, she was fired, for the same reason. She would have known how to turn back a bed. She knew the Institute people. I should tell the police, I suppose?"

"You probably should. For now, the burglaries surely did add to the confusion around you."

"Yes, they did. I believe our plotters were even ready to use Hubbell. But you thwarted that."

"I find it ironic," said Carter, "that you, Tom, should have been the one to hold him to his work here in the hospital; then he turned around and discovered this silly plot."

"Silly to you, perhaps," Tom told her. "I've become permanently goose-pimpled. And I'm still short one tweed jacket."

Dick and Carter laughed at him. "I've got to go," said Dick.

"First tell me . . ." Tom followed him to the foyer. "What happens now?"

"Nothing."

Tom gaped at him.

"It won't," Carter agreed. "You've made the struggle for the continuance of Research's work, and for its control. The Institute will continue as it is."

"Don't give me credit. I did all my fighting in the dark."

"It served. And this faction knows it. They—"

"But who are *they?* Beyond Lenox and Rosenthal, I mean."

"Do you need to know the others?" Dick asked.

"No," said Tom. "I guess I don't."

"I think it's better if you don't, Tom, if you can go on as you have been doing. You have a great gift for friendliness . . ."

"Well, thank you very much. I hope you read me right. They didn't. I'm a man to follow the administrator, the boss, especially when I see him doing good work. If I hadn't thought Dr. Lewis was that kind, I'd have left. I would have known I was the wrong man for the place I held."

Dick put his hand on Tom's shoulder. "I think they can read you now."

Tom held out his hand. "Of course you know I thank you, Dick? And Carter. My mother would have admired you both."

"From what I know of your mother, that's great praise."

"It is a great relief to hear you say that, Tom," said Carter. "Because, you see, I am going to marry her son, and—"

Tom turned sharply to look at her—at her pretty hair, at her clear and lovely eyes.

Behind him, Dick opened the front door and went out, closing the door behind him.

"Tactful guy," said Tom, stepping toward Carter. He drew her to him, her hands went up behind his head. They kissed and held each other close. And kissed again.

"Your picnic-parade," murmured Carter against his cheek.

"Oh, yes," Tom agreed. "You'll have to come with me. From now on, you'll do everything with me."

"I'm no good at tennis."

"I'll show off before you there. Now—" He smiled down at her.

"Say!" he cried. "I forgot the ring. Your ring. Who stole that? Someone who thought you would blame me?"

"No," she said readily. "I believe it was someone here the day I moved. Someone who needed the money, and then chickened out of selling it."

Tom put his arm around her shoulder and led her into the living room. The sun was low in the west, and the lovely gold and silver and white room glowed in its light. "I was here." He began to list the ones—"Dick, Judy, and their kids. Tim is developing a fine net game, did you know that?"

She laughed. "I am delighted to hear it."

Tom kissed her. "Who gave you that ring?" he asked her.

She peered up at him. "Who . . . ? Oh! It belonged to my aunt. She died two years ago and left it to me. I've put it in the safe deposit box. It had become a nuisance."

Tom nodded. "Good. I'll give you one that won't be."

"It will please Mr. Franzel, too."

Tom laughed happily. "So will the plain round one that goes with it," he promised.